FORGOTTEN
COUNTRY

FORGOTTEN
COUNTRY

Catherine Chung

RIVERHEAD BOOKS

a member of Penguin Group (USA) Inc.

New York

2012

RIVERHEAD BOOKS
Published by the Penguin Group
Penguin Group (USA) Inc., 375 Hudson Street, New York, New York 10014, USA •
Penguin Group (Canada), 90 Eglinton Avenue East, Suite 700, Toronto, Ontario M4P 2Y3,
Canada (a division of Pearson Penguin Canada Inc.) • Penguin Books Ltd, 80 Strand, London WC2R 0RL,
England • Penguin Ireland, 25 St Stephen's Green, Dublin 2, Ireland (a division of Penguin Books Ltd) •
Penguin Group (Australia), 250 Camberwell Road, Camberwell, Victoria 3124, Australia (a division of
Pearson Australia Group Pty Ltd) • Penguin Books India Pvt Ltd, 11 Community Centre, Panchsheel
Park, New Delhi–110 017, India • Penguin Group (NZ), 67 Apollo Drive, Rosedale, North Shore 0632,
New Zealand (a division of Pearson New Zealand Ltd) • Penguin Books (South Africa) (Pty) Ltd,
24 Sturdee Avenue, Rosebank, Johannesburg 2196, South Africa

Penguin Books Ltd, Registered Offices: 80 Strand, London WC2R 0RL, England

The author gratefully acknowledges permission to quote an excerpt from Li-Young Lee, "The City in Which
I Love You," from The City in Which I Love You. Copyright © 1990 by Li-Young Lee. Reprinted with the
permission of The Permissions Company, Inc., on behalf of BOA Editions Ltd., www.boaeditions.org.

Library of Congress Cataloging-in-Publication Data

Chung, Catherine.
Forgotten country / Catherine Chung.
p.   cm.
ISBN 978-1-59448-808-5
1. Korean American women—Fiction.   2. Sisters—Fiction.
3. Family secrets—Fiction.   I. Title.
PS3603.H853F67   2012   2011047577
813'.6—dc23

Printed in the United States of America
1   3   5   7   9   10   8   6   4   2

Book design by Michelle McMillian

FOR MY

MOTHER AND FATHER

But this is the only world.

—Pilar Gómez-Ibáñez

my birthplace vanished, my citizenship earned,
in league with stones of the earth, I
enter, without retreat or help from history,
the days of no day, my earth
of no earth, I re-enter

the city in which I love you.
And I never believed that the multitude
of dreams and many words were vain.

—Li-Young Lee

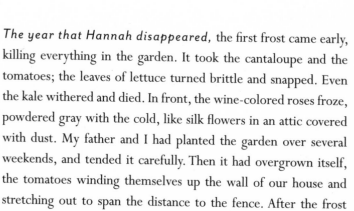

1.

The year that Hannah disappeared, the first frost came early, killing everything in the garden. It took the cantaloupe and the tomatoes; the leaves of lettuce turned brittle and snapped. Even the kale withered and died. In front, the wine-colored roses froze, powdered gray with the cold, like silk flowers in an attic covered with dust. My father and I had planted the garden over several weekends, and tended it carefully. Then it had overgrown itself, the tomatoes winding themselves up the wall of our house and stretching out to span the distance to the fence. After the frost we'd left it all winter without trimming anything back. Now we stood on the lawn, surveying the ruin, tracking damp patches of ground wherever we stepped.

"We're selling the house," my father said, blowing warm air on his hands.

"That makes sense," I said, but it felt suddenly difficult to breathe. My parents had told me they were going back to Korea, so I'd known selling our house was a possibility, but I hadn't expected it.

"We're going to have to clean this up," my father said, gesturing at the garden.

"It's cold," I said. "Let's go inside."

He nodded. The tendons in his neck were taut. His breath steamed slowly around his face. Everything was inside out, or at least the cold had turned the insides of things visible. The green tomatoes were now gray and translucent, their skins puckered at the stems, still hanging from their frozen vines. "We want you to find Hannah," he said.

"When are you leaving?" I asked.

"As soon as possible," my father said.

"I want to go with you."

My father shook his head. "Find your sister," he said. He had blamed me after the initial panic, when we discovered that Hannah hadn't been abducted or killed, but had simply left without telling us, without leaving us a way to contact her. I was her older sister, living in the same city. He thought I should have seen it coming.

When I moved back home for the summer, my father grilled me about her. He wanted to know everything about the months prior to her departure: what she had looked like, what she had said. What I had noticed: why I hadn't noticed more. He was already sick then, but didn't know it yet. I wonder if Hannah would have been able to pick up and leave like that if she had known.

Inside, we made tea and sat at our kitchen table, waiting for my mother to come down. My father's hands relaxed on the table, his fingers eased into a slight curl around his mug. They looked fragile against the smooth blue ceramic, his veins raised thick and soft. For a moment I wanted to cover his hands with mine, even though they had always looked like that.

Growing up, Hannah and I worried we'd inherit those veins, huge and tinged blue. It was true that my father's body had pulled into itself in the last couple of years so that his bones protruded, but his eyes were still sharp and discerning, and his hands were the same hands that had built this table, the same hands that refused to let anything go.

"I want to go with you when you go to Korea," I said.

My father grimaced. "It's more important that you find Hannah. You need to bring her home."

"I can't do that."

"She's your only sister."

"She's a brat."

My mother's footsteps sounded down the stairs, and together we looked toward the hallway. My father tilted his head and called out, "We're in the kitchen!" He leaned forward and took my hand in his. It was warm. He whispered, "Don't upset her."

One word about Hannah was enough to make my mother dissolve into tears for at least an hour. "Dissolve" was not too strong a word. When my mother wept, the whole world vanished. My father and I ceased to exist, and even Hannah's shadowy figure was obscured. This could happen anywhere, at any time—even in public. At first I wondered how my mother could sustain such anxiety, how one body could hold it all. Then I realized it was a question of density.

There's a theorem in mathematics that says if you take something the size of an onion and cut it into small enough pieces, you can take those pieces and construct something larger than the sun. In those first months after Hannah went missing, we learned to be careful around my mother. We had no past. Everything was off limits. Coming home was entering oblivion—my father was obsessed with my last conversations with Hannah, and my mother resolutely surrounded herself with silence. So when she came padding into the kitchen, I slapped a smile onto my face, same as my father.

To be honest, I never really understood what Hannah had against my parents. Sure they'd made mistakes, but nothing we shouldn't be able to get over. They had tried their best. When Hannah left for college in Chicago, I was already in my junior year at the University of Michigan. My dorm was a forty-five-minute drive from our house, and I came home every other weekend to visit. The summer before Hannah left for school, she broke curfew nearly every night. At first my parents waited up for her. As the summer wore on, they waited until morning to pound on her door. How she slept through all that pounding, I'll never know. I woke up after two seconds of it. I'd jump into the shower to drown out the noise. Besides, I knew what came next. After several minutes my father would call, "I'm coming in!" and pick her lock open with a toothpick. Then my parents would stand over Hannah's defiantly sleeping body, prodding her shoulders to wake her up. And Hannah would turn, scowling, hugging her pillow over her head.

"Let me sleep," she murmured. "Go away."

In the end it was her unwillingness to engage that defeated my parents. Even when she was awake she didn't argue, a polite little smile frozen to her face. "I got into college, what more do you want from me?" she asked at breakfast one morning after a late night out.

My mother unleashed a tirade about gratitude, filial duty, and decency.

"I guess I just don't agree," Hannah said, as if there was nothing more to say.

When she left for college she wouldn't even let my parents drive her. She took her own beat-up Corolla packed full of clothes and books and music. "I don't need anything else," she said when my parents insisted on going with her. "I'll be fine."

My mother cried the day Hannah left, but Hannah pulled away. "I'll call you when I get there," she mumbled, shaking my father's hand. Then she got into her car and pulled the door shut. My parents and I stood on the driveway, watching her. She started the car and didn't look back, but opened the window and waved once. Then her arm relaxed as though all the good-byes she had to make were taken care of, and she let her arm hang limply out the window as she drove away.

You'll never understand," she said the last time we came home together for Thanksgiving. "They were useless as parents—when did they give us what we needed?" The sleeves of her red shirt were pulled over her hands; her thumbs beginning to wear familiar holes along the seams.

"They gave us food," I said. "They gave us water, shelter, life."

"Whatever." Hannah waved those things away. "Big deal."

I'm not sure when things changed for her, but until Hannah forgot how to speak Korean, we had spent hours pretending to be our parents in their youth: it had been the best and deepest of mysteries to us. Long ago, my father used to jump trains as they passed. He was very poor and lived in the mountains: walking to school took over an hour. If there was a train going by he jumped on and took it as far as he could and jumped off. He had shown us the scar on his hand from a particularly bad fall.

Hannah and I pretended that our swing set, which our father had built for us, was a train. We ran at the swings, yelling, "We have to catch this one if we're going to make it on time!"

Sometimes Hannah missed the swing on purpose. "Give me your hand!" I yelled, pulling her along until she leaped up. "That was a close call," we said to each other, wiping our brows. We didn't know then that wiping your brow meant that you'd been sweating. We had just seen movie actors do it after tense situations, and it felt grown-up and dramatic. Then we'd swing, standing up, until I cried, "It's time to jump! Clear the track!" and off we leaped, rolling into the grass.

Sometimes we reenacted our father's injury by smearing berry juice on Hannah's hand. "It hurts!" she said.

I peered at it worriedly. "I think it's going to leave a scar."

Other days, we played the Dead Auntie game. My mother's sister had died when my mother was still a child. When we still lived in Korea, we followed our parents up the mountains to the graves of our ancestors to offer them food and wine on the day of the harvest moon, and I wondered why we left my aunt's burial mound unattended. In front of the other graves we shouted out our names.

"Grandfather, we are here! Haejini and Jeehyuni! We are saying hello!"

We bowed to our grandparents, then to their parents, then to the seven generations of ancestors buried on that mountain.

The path to my aunt's burial mound was overgrown, full of snakes and biting insects. We did not bow in front of her grave, or call out our names. My mother quietly trimmed the grass that grew over the mound with her long curved blade, chanting the Buddha's name.

Once Hannah cried out exuberantly, "Auntie, we've come to visit you!" and my mother knelt and slapped her in the face. After that we were not allowed to visit that grave, but waited for my parents at the edge of the path and played among the trees that shaded the mountain, tapping long sticks on the ground to keep the snakes away. Hannah swore she saw a woman following them once, picking her way through the overgrown path, her long white dress catching on the brush underneath and snagging on the trees around her. Hannah swore she heard her singing as she braided her long black hair.

The adults would never tell us how our auntie had died. But alone, we pretended I was Auntie, and Hannah was our mother. Sometimes we switched roles so I could play the bad guys who killed her, or the doctor who diagnosed her with a fatal disease. We would actually weep as we played this game, imagining my mother's family at the news that our auntie was dead. I always played our auntie brave, never giving up hope to the very last, never betraying national secrets to the North Korean spies, always standing up for what she believed in and protecting those she loved.

The year I became a math major, Hannah and I started growing apart. She never understood my chosen field, and considered it a defection to my father's fortress of reason and logic.

"You can't even divide up a bill," she said. "You're horrible with numbers."

I tried to tell her about complex and imaginary numbers, primes and transcendentals, numbers with families and personalities, but she rolled her eyes.

"I don't know how you can think any of that is important," she said. She was studying to become a biologist, deep in the gunk of life and committed to saving the earth, and could see no beauty in what I did.

But math had come with me from Korea to America, and its familiarity had pulled me through those first bewildering years. I liked its solidity, the possibility of discovering a truth around which no further argument need swirl. And Hannah was right to feel left behind, maybe even betrayed. Because something changed between my father and me when I started talking shop with him.

My father had always wanted a son. We women were unreliable creatures, prone to fits of emotion and flights from logic that generally ended with him at the receiving end of a pointed finger. "Yes!" he'd said, when I told him I'd decided to study math. He reached out his hand and said, "Shake!" While he pumped my hand up and down, he said, "Math lasts."

One day in the summer after my sophomore year of college, my father and I tried to construct the seventeen-gon with a straightedge and compass. As we talked, something in him eased up and fell away. He laughed, made jokes about our family in mathematical terminology. When we talked math, the words flowed, pure and easy. Here were rules we could both abide by, here was a language that was eloquent, and spoke to us about the world.

Later, we sat in our backyard going over what I thought at the time was a particularly complex proof. My mother's roses were in bloom at the edge of our lawn, and we could smell them faintly, their perfume drifting over on the occasional breeze. A beetle flew onto the picnic table and landed on our paper.

"Do you see this beetle?" my father said, pointing at its shiny back with his pencil. "Just think—it's mathematical fact! Even the tiniest insect has as many points on its back as the entire universe."

He tapped his pencil by the beetle several times. "Life is like that," he mused. "Think about it! The tiniest insect contains infinity on its back: each life contains as much meaning as all of history." Then he leaned forward and blew a quick, sharp breath on the beetle, which unfolded tiny translucent wings, lifted into the wind, and flew away.

I called Hannah that night. She was spending the summer in Chicago. I said, "Who knew? Dad's getting mushy." I felt like a traitor as soon as I said it, but I had to put the sarcastic note in to get her to listen.

"Not interested," she said.

Hannah had called me a couple days before she disappeared, crying because the baby of a woman she worked with had died the night before. I'd suddenly hit a wall in my dissertation, and when Hannah called I hadn't slept for days, and had spent the morning pacing, swiping at a blackboard I had put up in my living room.

"He's dead," Hannah wept as soon as I answered the phone.
"Who's dead?"
"The baby," Hannah sobbed.
"What baby?"

"Marjorie's, a woman from work."

A wave of relief passed over me. "Jesus Christ," I said. "Are you trying to scare me to death?"

"Her neighbor's children *threw* her baby out the window while she was at work."

"Holy shit," I said. "Who was watching it?"

"His brother."

"How's your friend?"

There was a sharp intake of breath. "How do you think?" And then a pause. "I'm not really close to her. I tried to find her phone number, but it's not listed."

"Oh, Hannah, that's awful," I said, and wrote *What the fuck?* on my blackboard, quietly so she couldn't hear the chalk.

On cue, Hannah started to cry again.

"Stop," I said. She didn't even know these people.

"They were only twelve years old," she said. "I don't know how to deal with this."

I didn't respond, outraged somehow that she could take this woman's tragedy and try to make it personal. As though the world hurt her in particular and no one else. Some people have real problems, I wanted to say. That woman whose baby died, *she* has problems.

"Hannah, please don't cry," I said, but that only made her cry harder. I waited for her to stop. I could think of nothing to say that would help.

A couple months after Hannah disappeared, the kids who had thrown the baby out the window went on trial. I followed the case out of some perverse loyalty. It turned out Marjorie wasn't a colleague of Hannah's, but a cleaning lady who worked in her building. She lived not in Hannah's trendy North Side neighborhood but in one of the South Side housing projects.

Her surviving son's name was Kevin. He was ten years old. The neighbor's kids had been giving him trouble for some time. The lock on his door had been broken for weeks, and they had come to rifle through the things in his house, to eat his mother's food. When they came he was sitting on the sofa watching cartoons; his baby brother was in his lap.

Roadrunner was outwitting Wile E. Coyote, whose Acme mail-order products never quite got the job done. Boulders, buildings, pianos hung suspended in air a beat too long. Roadrunner zoomed fearlessly beneath impending doom, but Wile E. Coyote, always too slow, was flattened on the desert landscape.

That day his neighbors asked Kevin for candy. They pulled his baby brother out of his lap and pushed him. He began to cry, but he had no candy. So they held his brother, dangling him by his legs out the window. His brother loved it, gurgled with laughter, held seventeen stories above the ground.

Kevin's eyes met the boys' who held his little brother. There was no sound when the boys let go. Through the open window they saw an empty sky.

Kevin turned and ran out the door of his apartment. His feet pounded one hundred separate steps. He didn't know about the laws of gravity or physics. He imagined his brother hung suspended in the air. He thought if he could just make it down in time, he could catch his little brother before he hit. He ran down the stairs and out the door: his gaze aimed at the sky, his arms outstretched.

. . .

After the trial, I couldn't sleep at night. I stopped working on my dissertation and stopped answering phone calls from my friends. I stayed up thinking how I should have done things differently. When Hannah called, I should have taken a movie over to her place, and some tea, and told her our old jokes until she laughed. At night I should have lain in bed next to her and stuck my feet between her legs and asked if she remembered how mad she used to get when I did that. I should have wrapped my arms around her and talked about places we'd lived and games we had played until she was wrapped up in the comfort of who we used to be. Where was she? I wondered. In those days I lost weight and watched my parents suffer. I should have spent that night with her, I thought. If I could have done it differently, I wouldn't, no matter what, have said nothing and let her go.

2.

In the first anxious days after I realized something was wrong, I drove to Hannah's apartment and knocked on her door. I asked her neighbors if they'd seen her. I searched desperately for my extra key to her place, which she had given me months earlier to hold on to in case she lost hers, and which I had promptly misplaced. I called the police and the hospital; I called her school and her friends whose names I knew. There were no leads. Meanwhile, I missed classes and canceled meetings. I told no one I knew what had happened.

Hannah had never cut me out of her life before. With a growing sense of dread, I called my parents. I had to explain to my mother three times before she understood, and then she moaned in a low voice and said, "Not again."

After that, I went to the police station where I formally reported my sister missing. While my parents drove down to Chicago, I met a policeman in front of Hannah's apartment, and with the key I had finally found buried in a bowl of loose change, we entered her place together.

When we entered the apartment, the place was clean and already bare. The rugs on her hardwood floor had been rolled up and propped against a corner. I slipped off my shoes and looked around. Wherever she was now, she had left this place intentionally.

"Huh," Officer Morris said, looking around and folding his arms. "Was she moving?"

"No," I said. "Not that I know of."

While he took a cursory look around the place, I ransacked Hannah's bedroom for clues of where she'd gone, for any note. I looked behind her bare desk and under her swept-out bed. In the kitchen, there was a note on the refrigerator, written in her loopy, crooked handwriting. *Anything left in the apartment is free to take.*

The refrigerator itself was empty. I'm not sure what I expected when I opened the door. A pizza, a half-eaten can of peas, a carton of milk, maybe. It was when I saw the blank insides gleaming out at me that I knew she wasn't planning on coming back. She had even polished the trays.

Before we left, I went to the kitchen and took Hannah's note. I wondered who she'd expected would find it. She'd been so deliberate, so thorough in leaving that I stopped worrying she'd had a breakdown, or that something terrible had happened to her. Instead, I began to be afraid of all the ways in which she would hurt us when we found her.

My parents met Officer Morris that evening in my living room, and he told them not to worry. He said the case seemed straightforward and that he was confident that no foul play was involved. Still, he took everything my parents had brought: her dental records, her medical history, and a list of physical identifiers, including a description of a constellation of four moles on her cheek that exactly matched the diamond pattern of moles on my shoulder.

"Why haven't you started a search party?" my mother asked. "She's in trouble. Someone might have kidnapped her."

"Most missing person cases are solved within seventy-two hours without police intervention," Officer Morris said. "The person in question almost always returns or makes contact of his own volition."

"It has been over seventy-two hours," my mother said. "According to her professors, she's missed classes for over two weeks."

"Ma'am, I'm a parent, too. And I feel for your situation, but I'm afraid there's nothing more I can do. A daughter skipping class is not a job for the police department, and frankly, it's no crime to drop out of college."

"We're paying the tuition. We're her parents. We have a right to know what is going on in her life."

"Well, legally, that's not exactly true."

"There are killers out there," my mother said. "They're in the news all the time. Someone might be hurting her right now." Her voice broke.

"Ma'am, do you have any evidence that she was being threatened by anyone?"

"You don't understand," my mother said. "She's sensitive. You have to help her." She turned then to my father. She hissed, "Tell him."

I wasn't sure what she was talking about. While it was true that Hannah was sensitive, I'd begun to think her disappearance was more an act of selfishness than a cry for help.

"Are there any medical records proving that she might be a danger to herself?" Officer Morris asked.

My mother took my father's arm. "Tell him," she insisted.

This, more than anything, confused me. What was there to tell? My father seemed equally lost: he took a step back and lifted his hands up in the air. I don't know why he did that, why his first reaction was to show her his empty hands.

"Listen," Officer Morris interrupted. "All evidence shows she left without coercion or violence, and of her own volition. This is about as straightforward as these things get."

"It's your job to make sure she's safe," my mother said. "Isn't that what you do?"

"Mom," I said. I was worried if she alienated him, he'd drop Hannah's case altogether. She turned to me and flashed what Hannah had always called The Look of Death. I was quiet.

"This is your job," she repeated firmly, stepping toward Officer Morris. "Bring my daughter home."

He shrugged. "I'll see what we can do," was all he said.

As soon as he'd left, my mother turned to my father and me. "How could you not tell him about her problems?" she asked. "How could you just stand there like that?"

I didn't know exactly what my mother was referring to, but Hannah had always been sensitive and had often succumbed to fits of hysteria as a child. As a baby, Hannah had had this trick. Right before she started to cry, she made a spit bubble with her mouth. If my parents or I could get to her before the bubble burst, she would be comforted and remain quiet. But if the bubble burst, there was no way to quiet her down.

I had been the first one to notice this. Every time the bubble burst, Hannah would descend into a fit of crying that didn't stop for hours. Her fits lasted so long that her doctor kept her in the hospital for observation once, convinced no healthy baby would cry that much. It turned out she was perfectly fine, and we took her home, but it took two straight days after that to quiet her down. At some point in my childhood, it became my responsibility to watch for the spit bubble.

"She's a very good baby," my parents often said back then. "She is always so happy as long as we catch her in time."

I was the one who had to catch her in time. And Hannah could reach a point beyond comfort, a point beyond which we could do nothing to bring her back. I was the official spit-bubble monitor until she was about eight years old. It was at that age that it first occurred to me that Hannah knew exactly what she was doing, and was in complete control of the reaction she created in the rest of us.

It became clear in the following days that Officer Morris was not going to do much to look for Hannah. So at my parents' request, I assembled a list of Hannah's classmates and closest friends, and sent out mass e-mails. When there was little response, I began systematically calling them. No one seemed to know where she was: for the most part, they sounded truly shocked to hear that she'd vanished. It made me wonder. Hannah had always had more friends than I did: I'd always been more of a loner. There was no one, for instance, with whom I felt I could talk about Hannah's disappearance. I told my thesis advisor what had happened only when it began to affect my work, and while he was sympathetic and encouraging, we only talked about it in terms of how it would impact my productivity.

I would have expected Hannah's friends to either be worried or in the loop: at least to have noticed when she went missing. I'd always been a little jealous of how easily she seemed to surround herself with people who liked her. This made me wonder if I'd been wrong all this time: if she'd been lonely as well.

In those first months, my parents expected to hear from Hannah at any moment. At dinner in the living room in front of the television, they would look up at the slightest noise outside. They sat with their bodies tensed, as if she might be at the doorstep already and all they needed to do was rise and let her in.

After a couple months of this, a friend of Hannah's admitted that she'd heard from her recently, but didn't know where she was or how to reach her.

I drove home to tell my parents the news in person. "She's okay," I said. "I don't know any more than that, but her friend has heard from her, and she's all right."

My mother burst into tears.

"Where is she now?" my father asked. "Is she in Chicago? Michigan?"

"I don't know."

"What's her phone number? What is her address?"

"Her friend didn't know."

He stepped toward me. "That's the crucial information. Next time, get the facts!" He turned away and started to walk up and down the length of the room.

"This is progress," I said. "I drove all the way over to tell you— and I got as much information as I could."

"Bring me that girl's number," he said. "The one who talked to Hannah."

"What do you think she's going to tell you?"

"Just get it."

When I brought it to him, he punched the numbers into the phone. Until now, he had not done much in the process of searching for Hannah, content to grill me instead on what progress I had made. Now he gripped the phone impatiently, waiting for the girl to answer.

"This is Hannah's father," he said. "Where is she? What do you mean you don't know?"

His voice was too loud. "Doesn't her number show up on your caller ID? Can't you get it from the phone company's records?" The knuckles stood out in his hand. I wondered when he'd gotten so gaunt. He paced back and forth, jerking the phone with each word. "I can call the police," he said. "You're refusing to cooperate and withholding information." His voice rose louder and louder.

"Dad," I said, but he waved at me to be quiet, one quick, furious dismissal. "Do something," I hissed at my mother. She rose from the sofa and pulled the phone from his hand.

"Hello," she began, but her voice broke. She wept into the mouthpiece. My father moved forward and took the phone back. He held it to his ear. "Hello?" he said. "Are you there?"

"She hung up," he said, turning to me.

I nodded. "Yeah." I felt embarrassed for him.

"I wasn't finished."

"Well, you were kind of rough on her."

"I'm calling her back."

"Maybe that's not such a good idea."

My mother raised her head. "Whose side are you on?" she asked.

"I'm not on a side," I said. "But that girl isn't our enemy."

My mother's voice was like cracked glass. "Since we're so clearly an embarrassment to you," she said, "and this stranger's feelings are so much more important than ours, why don't you call her yourself and handle it however you think is more proper. You can do it the elegant way."

I flinched. "That's not fair," I said.

"Give her the phone," my mother said, and my father handed me the handset.

"You can at least ask me nicely," I said. I made the call.

When the girl answered the phone, she was angry and impatient. "I don't want your family to harass me anymore," she said. I tried to apologize, but she insisted, voice rising, that she had no information about Hannah's whereabouts. "Stop calling me," she said, and I did not push her. I hung up, and shrugged at my parents. I'd tried.

A month later, someone else who'd gone to high school with Hannah told me she'd moved to California. This time, I was able to get my sister's number. It was my mother who made that call, my father clutching the other phone to his ear while she spoke. "Haejini?" she said. "Is this Hannah?"

There was silence.

"Is it her?" I asked. My mother waved at me to be quiet, nodding her head.

"How have you been living?" she asked. "Do you need money?"

"Are you okay?" my father jumped in, unable to wait. "Where are you?"

And then Hannah hung up on them. I knew it from the way

both my parents pulled their phones away from their ears and stared at them.

My father recovered first. "You call her," he said, turning to me. "She'll talk to you."

I shook my head. "No."

"She will," he repeated. "She always does."

"I don't want to," I said. I looked at my parents: they looked so old. My mother was clutching her phone to her chest.

"I'll call, but not in front of you," I said.

I went to my room to do it. The phone rang and rang. "Hannah," I said into her voice mail, "I don't know what's wrong. Tell me what I can do. If you're in trouble, I'll help you. If you tell me to leave you alone, I will. Just call. I'll give you whatever you need."

I hung up and waited. I was sure she would call me back. I kept checking my phone every ten minutes to see if I'd missed her call, to make sure the ringer was on its loudest ring: I checked my voice mail, my e-mail. I waited a day. Two. A week. She never called back.

Meanwhile, I went back to school, and the days kept passing. My parents kept calling Hannah, keeping vigil, leaving messages she always ignored.

One day, my father called me and said, "Come home. I have something to tell you."

"I have plans this weekend," I said. This was the first free weekend I had planned for myself, and I needed to catch up on work. I'd missed several recent appointments with my advisor, and needed to get back on track. "I have work to do."

"I'd really like you to come," he said.

"I've been home every weekend for the last two months," I

said. "This is an important time for me." I'd lost momentum on my dissertation, and I'd begun to feel a sense of growing panic in the last few weeks, worried that if I didn't get a grip on this now, my whole life would spiral away from me. "This is taking over everything. I need some time for myself," I said. "I have to get back into my work."

My father didn't argue. He was just very quiet.

His quiet angered me. "You're the one who wanted me to do all this," I said, meaning math, and a Ph.D. When I'd briefly considered switching majors to history in college, he had pressured me to continue with math. He made it clear he wanted me to get my doctorate in it: that anything else would be a disappointment. My mother had actually been much more supportive, telling me I should do what I wanted, explore, that this was why she'd come to America in the first place. But I stuck with it in the end, gratified that my father cared so much, that I could do something he found worthwhile.

"I can't just stop now," I said. "I'm already committed to this." And I was. I'd sacrificed too much and worked too hard to let it go now.

When he was still silent, I was hit by a wave of fear. "Is this about Hannah?" I was flooded with guilt: I imagined her in a hospital, unconscious. "Tell me."

"No," he said. "It's something else. But I don't want to tell you over the phone."

"Daddy," I said.

There was a pause. "I'm sick."

"Sick how?"

When he answered, his voice was light. "What's the worst thing you can imagine?" he asked.

"AIDS," I said, but I knew what it was, and my stomach was sinking.

He laughed. "Not quite," he said.

I swallowed. "What is it?"

"Cancer."

I sat down. "Is it bad?"

"We'll talk when you're here. It's fine."

For a moment I couldn't say anything. "How long have you known?"

"Not too long. I wanted to wait to tell you until we knew the prognosis."

"Daddy," I said, and then couldn't continue.

"I'm worried about your mother."

I nodded. My whole body felt weightless. "I'll come home."

drove home that same day, numb and dazed, until a police car pulled me over, lights swirling. I handed the policeman my information with trembling hands, and then startled him by bursting into sobs as soon as he handed me my ticket.

"I usually drive better than this," I gasped.

"Everyone gets a ticket eventually," he said, standing awkwardly at my window.

I nodded and turned my head away. "I don't normally cry," I managed to say, but then I couldn't stop. My hands were shaking on the wheel, and I pulled them onto my lap. I said, "I'll be all right."

He stood there for a minute longer, and I was relieved when I finally heard his footsteps on the gravel as he walked away. After he was gone, I sat there and cried. When I was finally exhausted and looked up, I wiped my eyes and glanced at myself in the rearview mirror. In the reflection I saw the police car still behind me. Its blue and red lights were still silently swirling. When I finally pulled back onto the highway, I looked back, and the policeman gave me a little wave out his window.

It was strange, but I was encouraged by that wave. I thought all of a sudden, waving back, that things would be all right, that at least I'd make it home okay.

At our house, my parents were anxiously waiting.

"What took you so long?" my mother asked. Looking at my face, she said, "Never mind." She picked up an envelope from the kitchen table and said, "This came today." The envelope contained their first communication from Hannah: she'd sent back a copy of the flyer they'd made when she first disappeared with her photograph, the words "Have You Seen Me?" in block letters underneath. Her handwritten scrawl, unsigned, *I am not a child.*

I stared at it. I thought, *My father has cancer, and this is what my sister has sent us.* I was seized by fear in that moment, for Hannah and whatever she might have called down upon herself from the universe for having done such a thing.

But if anything, my parents seemed reassured. They told me what my father had: stage IV metastatic stomach cancer, but in their weekly phone call to her, they did not mention it. They left the standard message pleading with her to call back. They told her they missed her. Meanwhile, I researched my father's disease and read all the data, which was grim. I called hospitals. I called doctors. During this time, my parents walked around with drawn, frightened faces, and they waited hopefully, stupidly, for a phone call from my sister, a postcard, a visit, anything at all.

They tried to get me to call her, too, but this infuriated me. "Enough," I said, and meant it. Things were serious now, my father was sick, and Hannah didn't deserve any more from us. Part of me wanted to punish her, wanted her to return after my father's illness had played out to its end. It was a cruel impulse, I knew, cruel to my parents as well as to her. But I wanted her to suffer. I wanted her to miss all of it, and know when she returned that her absence was unforgivable.

3.

I'd grown up always worrying about Hannah in one way or another. My mother's favorite story to tell about me was how at five years old I'd insist on holding my baby sister, and would drag her around so carelessly that my mother was terrified I'd accidentally kill her. She had to keep constant guard over us because whenever she looked away I'd be back at it, picking Haejin up like a doll.

I don't remember that, but I do remember how after we moved to America my sister would cling to me in front of the school each day when we got off the bus, and how I had to walk her to class or she'd sit down and cry in the middle of the sidewalk. I was late every day because of her. Back then I used to wonder what my life would have been like without a sister. It was impossible to imagine. It was like trying to answer the questions Hannah used to ask. Like what I thought it was like to grow up blind, or a boy, or a penguin. She'd get mad when I refused to answer. Once she asked me what I thought it was like to be her. I looked at her and blinked.

"Don't *you* know the answer to that?" I asked.

"Just tell me," Hannah scowled. She always took her games so seriously.

"It's too horrible to contemplate," I responded. "There must be no worse fate on earth."

"I'm *serious*," Hannah said, that pout in her voice always needling me to give in.

One of the only memories I have of my life before Hannah was born is of my mother, from when we lived in Korea. It's strange to me that I have memories of my mother in which she is younger than I am now; it makes me feel an unexpected tenderness toward her.

In my memory I'm maybe two or two and a half years old, and my mother is holding my hand as we're walking up a hill. I'm laughing because my mother is taking exaggerated steps and stomping loudly. The ground is bright with snow; it hurts to look at the light flying off it.

"Huy, huy, huy," she says to the beat of her steps. I look up, and her hair is waving in streamers around her face. I want to grab hold of it, but it is too far away. This is my only memory of my mother with long hair. She is laughing. I try to match her steps, which are too wide for me, and she holds me up when I stumble.

Two days before Hannah was born, my mother doubled over moaning. I rode down with my parents in the elevator, pressed up against my mother's legs, listening to her breathe. In the taxi I listened to her moan, and when we got to the hospital, I sat in the waiting room with my father, who stood and paced. I could tell that something was wrong. My uncle came to take me to my grandmother's house, and when I left my father barely looked at me. "Be good," he said, distracted, running his hand over my head as he looked down the hall to the delivery room where my mother was.

I followed my uncle, dragging my feet and crying, sure I would never see either of my parents again. But when we reached the sliding doors to exit the hospital, there was a perfect square of sunshine that fell in a neat block onto the hospital floor. My uncle stopped there, and when I looked up at him, he swung me up into his arms.

He lifted me onto his shoulders and took me into the park. He let me pick the flowers there, even though it was forbidden. When a passing nurse scolded us, he tossed me effortlessly back upon his shoulders and took me away. That afternoon in my grandmother's apartment, he led me through martial arts forms in the living room. Ever since I could walk, he'd been teaching me the basic forms. I practiced with him, barefoot, following for as long as I could until he was done. Then he watched me, his hands correcting my posture or the tilt of my hands and head. I loved the attention, the sense that he knew the proper way to do things and that if I let him, he would show me how. We practiced until my grandmother returned, and between those hours, lost in the rush of my uncle's unfaltering attention, I was happy.

When he left me alone with my grandmother that night to go back to his college dorm, I felt abandoned all over again. It was my first night away from home without my mother, and the room my grandmother put me in felt large and frightening. When she came in, she found me crying. I had cried so hard I had given myself a fever. She wiped my face with a wet towel and chanted the Buddha's name.

When I still wouldn't stop, she shook me. "Jungshin chalyuh," she said, by which she meant pull yourself together; discipline your mind. Both the command and the impatience in her voice surprised me into silence.

"You are too old to be crying like this," my grandmother said. "You will be an elder sister now, and you have new responsibilities."

I nodded, struck by the gravity of this.

"There are things you need to know about your family," she said. "Let me tell you how I became an older sister, many years ago." And, with that, she told me the story of her own sister's birth.

When my grandmother was five years old, her father was taken away by Japanese soldiers. She did not know what her father had done, but she knew it had to do with the day everyone yelled, "Mansei." She had wanted to go outside, too, but her mother had said, "What if the baby comes," and my grandmother had stayed indoors. Her mother would not even let her swing in the courtyard or climb a tree to look out over the gates into the streets.

"Can I say mansei?" my grandmother asked. "Can I say it from here?"

"Quiet!" her mother said. "Do you want someone to hear you?"

Everyone was shouting out in the street. My grandmother could hear the voices of the other children, rising tinny above the men's.

"No one would hear me," my grandmother said. "It's noisy outside."

"If you make another sound, I will send you out tonight for the tigers."

My grandmother sulked. Then she asked, "What does mansei mean?"

Her mother stopped sewing, the needle arrested in midair, the string stretched taut. Her mother repeated the word very quietly. "Mansei," she said. "It means ten thousand years." The needle resumed. "It means, long live Korea, ten thousand years."

That night when my grandmother's father came home, he was haggard and exultant. He reached under her mother's sleeping mat and pulled out a handful of papers. He unrolled a beautiful silk sheet. My grandmother had never seen a Korean flag before, and he let her touch the red and blue circle swirling in the center, the stark slanted strokes at the edges. He knelt beside her and touched the center of it, the deep red above and the brilliant blue below.

"Remember this," her father said. "Hold it in your mind."

Then he and her mother folded the sheet together, and he went outside. Through the window, she watched him bury the flag and papers in their garden. She did not ask why.

The next day soldiers came into their house; they overturned everything. They took her father away. When she asked what her father had done, her mother would not answer. The streets, which had been raucous with shouts for several days, were filled with screams. My grandmother thought of the dirt her father had washed from underneath his nails, and of the beautiful flag under the ground. She wept in a corner, but her mother sat steadfastly in the center of the room, sewing. When the air turned dark and gritty, and the strange smoke seared their eyes and throats, she closed the windows and covered them with blankets. She ordered the servants to bring all their meals, quietly, into their room.

It grew ominously quiet. My grandmother strained her ears: she could hear nothing but the steady marching of soldiers up and down their street.

When her mother went into labor that evening she ordered my grandmother to stuff her mouth with rags so that no one would hear her scream. She told my grandmother not to remove them until the baby was born. For one day and one night she writhed on the sheets, grabbing at the air and the rags in her mouth. She became slick with sweat, and the sleeping mat where she lay grew heavy and wet. Her hair stuck in clumps to her face. Her skin began to cool and grow clammy. She looked like a ghost.

My grandmother was sure her mother was dying. In the morning my grandmother disobeyed her mother's command and removed the rags to pour in some water.

Her mother gagged and grabbed my grandmother's wrist with cold, slippery hands. My grandmother poured more water into her mouth. Her mother swallowed and moaned. Her body shook with a long contraction, and she cried out sharply. My grandmother hurriedly stuffed her mother's mouth back with rags, but it was too late.

The soldiers, always marching outside, rushed in. My grandmother crouched protectively over her mother. The men spoke to her, but she could not respond. To speak Korean to these men was forbidden, and she did not know Japanese.

The men pushed my grandmother aside and pulled the rags out of her mother's mouth. Her mother gagged, then screamed, and the soldiers hoisted her up and took her away. My grandmother would never forget the sight of her mother's exposed thigh, a man's fingers digging into the flesh.

When her father returned the next day, my grandmother ran and clung to his leg. He sat down on the floor and handed her a bundle.

The soldiers had brought his wife's breasts to him on the tip of a bayonet, and then released him from jail. He had brought the child, my grandmother's sister, who had been cut out by the same blade, and had somehow survived. He had been released, but was not allowed to leave their house.

Together they sat indoors, and he did not speak again for a long time. My grandmother and one of their servants tended her little sister for days, feeding her rice water bit by bit until she died.

I shouldn't remember the things my grandmother told me; I was too young to understand. But after my grandmother told me this story, I crawled into her lap and held on to her loose night-clothes. I was dry and stiff with fear. My grandmother taught me the words to chant to the Buddha then, and together we chanted and prayed: all night we prayed for a brother.

My sister was not born that night or the following morning, but the next morning after. My mother had been in labor for nearly two days. By that time we were gathered in the hospital; my father, grandmother, uncles and aunts and I in the waiting room, wondering what was wrong.

When they hooked my mother up to new machines to see what the problem was, they saw Hannah pushing down into the birth canal and at the same point every time, bouncing back off. The baby would not come out. When her heartbeat began to slow, they cut her out.

My grandmother sat in a chair and prayed, murmuring words I

couldn't distinguish, her breath one low, articulated groan. When the doctor announced that Hannah had finally been born, my grandmother started to cry in relief.

My father rushed into my mother's room then, and all my relatives started talking at once. The burst of noise after all that silence was jarring. Everyone else was relieved, but my first emotion was dread.

"In our family," my grandmother had told me, "a sister always dies."

A few hours later, they finally let me see my mother. My sister had already been taken away to be cared for in the nursery, but my father had promised me, smiling, that he would not let her out of his sight while I visited my mother.

I climbed into her bed even though my relatives warned me not to. My grandmother tried to pull me off, but my mother said, "Let her come." She wrapped her arms around me. She was limp and sweaty, but I snuggled into the comfortable softness of her warmth. They had cut her open, but she was whole. She looked very tired and sick; on her gown, blood bloomed like a slow flower.

"You have a younger sister now," my mother said. "Her name is Haejin. I hope you will always take care of her."

I nodded so gravely my aunts and uncles laughed.

"So serious!" they said, patting my head.

I shook my head: I didn't want them to touch me. I only wanted my mother.

But then she said it again. "Haejin," my mother said, cupping my face in her hand. She smelled like sweat and sickness, and when she said my sister's name, it was as if she was calling my own.

4.

Hannah had always been the one who cried to see a wounded animal, the one who was inconsolable when someone else was hurt. I learned to control myself in front of her. Once, when we were little, a bluebird flew into one of the windows of our house. We heard it thud against the glass, and ran out to find it flapping on the ground, its bright head stuck to the ground, its one eye staring. We shrieked at my mother to come out. She came running, wiping her hands, and when she saw what we were pointing at, she knelt beside the bird. She put her hand over the bird's head until it stopped flapping.

She began to sing to it in a low humming voice. "Oh my darling, oh my darling," she crooned. It quieted, calm and trusting under her soft, bare hands. My mother had healing hands, I thought, watching her. She would take her hand away and the bird would fly. She picked it up carefully, gently. Her fingers closed around it. Then she twisted it between her hands: a quick, sure motion. The bird's neck popped, a quiet sound, and it was dead.

Hannah screamed. She jumped up and backed away from us. I almost screamed, too. But then I looked at the bluebird, which looked so soft against my mother's skin, its beautiful feathers ruffling, its bright eye open.

Then my mother sent me to fetch a cloth and a garden trowel, and I followed her to the backyard: the movement of her walk jostled the small body just enough to make it look like it was breathing. It was so blue. I wanted to touch it. We dug a hole beneath our largest tree. I scoured the lawn for the prettiest leaves, and picked a few flowers to keep it company. My mother lined the hole with leaves, and placed our bird inside it. She covered the bird with leaves and flowers, and covered the mound with soil. As my mother sang, Hannah kept far from us and stared.

Afterward, I drew pictures of the bluebird. I wanted to dig it up and look at it again, but my mother told me that would be wrong. I wrote poems, and left them on its grave. I didn't know then that dead things decay, and I thought the bird would remain in the ground intact and blue, beautiful and still.

By the time I went with my parents for my father's endoscopy, I had started keeping track of the things Hannah had missed. This was a big one. After the procedure my father lay on his bed in shorts and a paper gown. I didn't like seeing him that way. He looked so vulnerable, and the paper gown so flimsy. He was still woozy, but his gastroenterologist sat beside the bed and drew a picture of my father's stomach and the tumor inside it. The lines of the tumor overlapped the lines of the stomach.

"I don't understand," my father said. "What does it mean?"

Dr. Abraham shrugged. "It's been there a while," he said. He spoke with a thick accent I couldn't identify. "It has spread already. Everywhere."

"How long has it been there?" I asked.

"Years," he said.

"How many?" I wanted to be able to pinpoint the time it started growing.

"At least five," he said. "Maybe more."

When my mother burst into muffled sobs, I caught my father's eye. He gave an incongruous smile. I wondered if I was in a dream. The scene seemed so familiar, and I had dreamed my father's death all my life. When I was very young, I woke from those dreams weeping. Sometimes my mother would see the salt crust around my eyes and ask, "What was it? What did you dream?" I liked to tell her about my bad dreams then if I remembered them—as if the telling erased them. But the dreams about my father's death, I never spoke out loud.

My father cleared his throat. "What do you mean, everywhere?" He sounded frightened.

Dr. Abraham snapped the folder in his hands shut, and stood up.

"Doctor?" my father said.

Dr. Abraham didn't even look at my father. He seemed angry, and with a shrug of his shoulders, he walked out of the room.

My father called after him. "Doctor?" he said, and then again louder, hopefully, as if it might bring him back. But Dr. Abraham didn't turn around. He kept on walking.

After that, my father was quiet. My mother stopped crying. We sat there, the three of us, not speaking, staring at the chair the doctor had sat in. I wanted to ask if that had really just happened, but I bit my lip.

"I have to go to the bathroom," I said finally. Both my parents nodded.

"Go," my father said. "We'll be here."

I walked through the hallway, past the nurses, following the signs and grateful I didn't have to ask anyone for directions. In the bathroom, which was empty, I went to the farthest stall and sat on the toilet. I opened my purse and found my cell phone. I called Hannah. I sat and listened to the phone ring.

She doesn't deserve this, I thought. But my hands were shaking, and I wanted to tell her how this doctor had treated our father, how he had walked away from him as if he was no one.

But she didn't pick up. I got her voice mail, and I have never been as lonely as when I heard the recording of her voice come over the line, breaking up a little as I sat in the bathroom stall. I clicked my phone shut and leaned my forehead against the door. In the last two years my father had grown thin, and I had attributed it to stress. A year ago his hairline had begun to recede. He had started to smell different. Embarrassed, I had attributed it to age. After we found out my father was sick, I felt as if I had failed him by dismissing these signs, that this was my punishment for worrying about the wrong person, the wrong thing, the whole time.

On our way home, I tried not to think of the picture the doctor had drawn on his notepad. I waited for Hannah to call back. I don't know why I thought she might this time, why I thought she would have sensed that this was a call she had to return. When she didn't, I told myself it was over, that the moment had passed. And it had: when I'd called her from the hospital I had wanted to tell her that this doctor had treated our father as if he was nothing, and that we needed her now to come back, to let him know that he mattered. But I could not imagine saying any of this now. I could no longer imagine saying any of it out loud.

In the following days, I filled the time I had formerly spent calling Hannah's friends by researching cancer treatments, putting my father's name on waiting lists at cancer centers with reputations for coming up with miracles. I ignored my work during this time. My parents asked a few times if this was all right, and each time I assured them it was, even as my anxiety about it grew. I felt I had to make up for Hannah: if she gave nothing, I would have to give everything to even it out.

So I spent my time calling facility after facility, and noted where they offered things like yoga classes, massages, and acupuncture. I liked the places that sounded like spas. None of these places would see my father if he'd already started treatment, so my father held off on doing anything until he could get a second opinion.

Eventually we got an appointment with a world-famous stomach cancer specialist at a cancer center in Texas called MD Anderson, and we traveled there to see him. We carried my father's scans and files with us from Michigan, and after the doctor had looked them over, he leaned toward us and asked my father where he was from.

"Michigan," my father said.

"No, I mean originally. What country did you come from?"

"Korea," my father said.

The doctor nodded. "Korea is conducting the cutting-edge research on your kind of cancer," he said. "If I were you, I'd consider going there for treatment."

"To Korea?" my father asked in surprise.

"It's the best shot," the doctor said. "They're testing a new drug regimen using S-1 and cisplatin. It's a new chemotherapy combination that's seen some success. It's been shown to increase survival by up to three months. It starts in Seoul in about a month."

"It might increase survival by three months?" my father said. "Three months over what?"

The doctor was matter-of-fact. "Five to six months, usually. This could give you eight to nine."

My father asked the doctor to repeat himself. I sat, digging my fingers into my leg. My father asked about other possible treatments, and the doctor said there were none that would cure him. My father asked again, was disappointed again. That was the problem: my father wanted answers the doctor could not give. He asked for numbers and percentages. He asked the same questions one after another, as if the answers might change with repetition.

"Hopeless?" he asked.

"Terminal," the doctor said.

My father shook his head. He held up his hand, all his fingers splayed. "What are the statistics, though?" he asked. "Isn't it possible to survive longer?"

"Anything could happen," the doctor said, and then: "But I have never known a man in this stage of your disease to survive five years. In fact, I have never known someone to survive for even two."

It was irrational, but the shock of that word "never" made the doctor's statement easier to dismiss. It was too large to comprehend: it was absurd. And it seemed that if this impossible thing was true, the opposite could also happen. It seemed as if this was my father's chance to be someone extraordinary, to be a miracle. He could survive and be the first. He could be the miracle to give hope to others.

"What would you do in my situation?" my father asked.

"I'd go to Korea," the doctor said.

And that was it. The next day, we flew home to Michigan.

Afterward, I told my father—always a numbers man—that the numbers meant nothing. "You will survive," I said. "Just decide to beat it."

"Listen to Jeehyun," my mother said. "What do the doctors really know?"

My father raised his shoulders, not entirely convinced. "But if we go to Korea," he said after a moment, "what will Haejin do?"

"That's not a reason not to go," I said.

My father sighed. "It's not only that," he said. "I just never planned to return. I don't know if it's the best idea."

I nodded. My mother had wanted to go back in the early years, I knew, but my father had never considered it. We had left Korea suddenly and without explanation; my parents had never discussed it with me. My father looked down at his hands, and I wondered if now my parents would finally tell me the whole story.

But after a moment my mother sighed. She said, "I'll make some calls," and my father followed her out of the room. They left me at the table alone.

decided to go back to Seoul after I spoke with your Komo," my father said, the day he announced he'd be selling our house. "She said everyone knows Korea is the best at treating my kind of cancer."

"Oh," I said. Komo was my father's older sister. She'd lived in

Indiana when we first moved to America, but she and her family had returned to Korea shortly after their first and only visit to our new house in Michigan.

"She must be glad you're coming," I said. My Komo did not like my mother or the rest of our family.

My father nodded. "I'll take a medical leave from work," he said. "It will be a chance to relax and take a break." His voice was overly bright.

I smiled. "That sounds good."

"I'll finally be able to go golfing," he continued. "I'll be in better shape than ever at the end of this."

That day, my parents went to see an herbalist who gave my father a special tea. He came home that evening exuberant and hopeful. He poured the concoction carefully into its measuring cup. He said with glee, "The herbalist said that this cures ninety percent of all cancer patients!"

He knew better. "If that's true," I said, "why are people still dying of cancer?"

My father smiled and shrugged. Then he said, "I guess you're right." He made a face as he swallowed the liquid. His shoulders slouched a little.

Before I could take back what I'd said, my mother took me by the arm and said, "Come with me." She pulled me out of the kitchen and down the hall, all the way into the study, her fingers painful on my arm. She closed the door behind her with one hand.

"How dare you say that," she said. "He was laughing today. He felt hope."

"I didn't say it couldn't work." I tried to pull out of her grasp. I felt terrible. "I just said it couldn't work ninety percent of the time."

"Be quiet," my mother said, digging her fingers deeper. "If you want to help, if you want to do something, find Haejin. He's waiting for her. That's why he's taking this medicine instead of starting treatment here or moving to Korea." She shook me a little. "And don't you dare say such a thing to him again." She glared at me, and left the room.

I stayed put. I felt queasy. I had done damage with my doubt. It wasn't a question of science, it was a question of loyalty. It was a question of faith.

We drove the next day to a Buddhist temple in Detroit. It had been built after I went to college, and my parents had gotten in the habit of going every weekend. When we arrived, the monk met us at the door, and took us straight to the altar with three sitting gold statues of the Buddha and his bodhisattvas, and we lit three sticks of incense in the cold, unheated room, and bowed three and a half times to each.

The scent of incense was familiar and heady, and reminded me of daily trips in my childhood to the temple in Seoul to pray with my grandmother. This memory made it seem more real that my parents were returning there, and I wondered if my parents had ever spoken to the monk here about Hannah: if he knew she had run away.

When the monk withdrew to his private office with my father, my mother and I remained in the room with the statues of the Buddha. They gleamed gold on their altars. I closed my eyes, pretending to meditate. My mother was breathing funny, and I sneaked a look at her, afraid that she was crying and that I would have to comfort her. But she wasn't crying. She was just sitting very still and calm.

"I'm afraid," I said after a while, and even though I spoke quietly, my voice sounded loud, echoing in the room.

My mother didn't answer for a moment, and then her voice was rough. "You're grown up now; you have your own life. What do you have to fear?"

I didn't respond. I knew this was a reprimand: she did not want me to burden her with my anxiety. I was old enough to bear it myself.

"What?" she asked.

I bowed my head, resentful of her question and ashamed to name all the things that frightened me.

"Speak up," my mother said. "What are you afraid of?"

I shook my head. "Never mind."

We sat there for a long time in silence, until the monk returned. He called us into his private sitting room where my father was already waiting. There, the monk poured tea into tiny cups, and while we held the cups on our laps and took small sips, he began to tell us a story about a woman who had lost her child.

This woman had gone to the Buddha, distraught, and asked him to perform a miracle. She told him she'd lost her only child, and she asked him to bring her dead child back to life. The Buddha listened carefully, and then he said he would restore her child to life when she was able to bring him a blanket from a house that had not known a sorrow. And so this woman went from door to door begging for such a blanket, but each house had its own story, recent or long ago, of tragedy. So the woman returned to the Buddha resigned, having accepted what he meant her to learn: that no one can be spared loss, that this is the cost of life.

I sat and listened to the monk tell this story. My grandmother had told it to me once, and I hadn't liked it then, either. I'd wondered then what good that knowledge of other people's tragedies was. I listened to the monk utter the familiar words: emptiness, grief, sorrow. "I have known people to survive such a prognosis before," the monk said. "But regardless of whether we die today or fifty years from now, life is always transient, and true enlightenment is letting go."

I thought of everything my parents had already let go of, how much they had lost. All the homes they had ever lived in, Hannah, my aunt, my grandfather, my father's entire dead family. That everyone dead in their lives had died before I was born was always a secret source of selfish relief to me: I was glad I had not had to suffer, or witness my parents' grief. Sometimes I was grateful that there were fewer people to keep track of, that there was less to lose.

I watched my father's face as the monk spoke, and I could tell he didn't want to hear this lecture either. I wanted to get up and tell the monk to stop talking, to stop telling us how everything passes away, to stop telling us to let go when all we'd come for, all we wanted from him, was a way to hold on.

5.

There was something familiar about packing up our house and getting ready to move: nearly twenty years ago we had dismantled everything and come to America, and now my parents were leaving everything again to rush back. I had been eight years old that first time, and though no one would explain the circumstances, I knew we were running away. While my parents never used the words "blacklist," or "exile," or "enemy of the state," these were words I learned in the months before our move, though I never spoke them aloud.

I knew they were linked, however, to our leaving, and to the night my uncle came to our apartment and stood in our living room in tears. That year, President Choi had been assassinated and General Han had taken power through a military coup. Ever since, there had been pro-democracy demonstrations, and crowds in the streets, with soldiers and policemen and roadblocks and air horns. General Han tried to shut down criticism by closing all the universities and arresting all his opponents, but the demonstrations continued all over the country: so many citizens demanding democracy.

During all this, my uncle was deployed to Kwangju to put down an uprising there. He was doing his year of mandatory military service, and when he left Seoul, none of us knew much about what was happening out there. Several student demonstrations had been staged throughout the country on the same day urging democracy. In Kwangju, when some students were fired upon and killed, the city rose up and armed itself. Many of the protesting students had themselves just served their mandatory military service, so they were able to fight. When the military was sent in to contain them, they were told that it wasn't a student demonstration at all, but a communist uprising.

There were rumors of another civil war. There was talk of a massacre. My parents and I sat in my grandmother's living room, watching the news. No one believed the official number of two hundred casualties. Everyone knew more people had died. In front of the television, my grandmother prayed. We sat all evening, and then Hannah was packed off to sleep, but my grandmother insisted I stay up and watch.

"This isn't for children," my parents said. "She'll have nightmares."

But my grandmother ignored them. "She is old enough," she said. "This is not the first time such a thing has happened." All her life in Korea, people had been killed for their ideas. Students had died asking for change.

Long ago, when she was a child, families of dissidents had been driven to churches and town halls and burned into piles of ash. You breathed in that ash, my grandmother told me. It covered your skin. You held that ash inside you: it coated your lungs. It clung to your eyelashes and settled on your hair.

"Mother," my mother interrupted. "Things are different now." She covered my ears with her hands, even though I had already heard it, and could hear through her fingers anyway. When I shook my head, she stroked my hair. "Don't listen," she said. "All that was a long time ago."

"It was not so long ago," my grandmother said. To my father she said, "Your parents died in the war." He looked startled. I saw his jaw clench, but he did not respond.

"Mother," my mother said again, a warning in her voice, but my grandmother ignored it. Water in her village, she told me, had run red. It had tasted like iron. For years, she said, skulls would rise out of the ground during heavy rain, so that human bones were discovered along the fields and then reburied, as if they were seeds. "And now it is happening again," she said.

My father shook his head. "Things have changed. But be careful what you say," he said. "You still never know who is listening."

My parents were in the habit of cutting off conversation when it became most interesting.

Even though the massacre in Kwangju was important, outside of that night we spent watching the news in the living room, we never talked of it openly again. I stayed quiet, too, but without understanding. I did not know that the massacre had become a censored topic, and even bringing up the town's name could be considered a suspicious act. At the time I thought my parents were the source of the silence around the event. I had not yet learned that any powers beyond them existed.

Weeks later, my uncle returned, and I knew then that he'd been diminished somehow. Injured, perhaps. Grieved. But my parents seemed not to notice. When he finally came home they ushered him into our living room, and punished him. They pushed him for information. How many innocent victims had been killed? He did not know. Hundreds? Thousands? He could not say. The dead were mostly college students. They were young men, barely grown out of boyhood, his age. Had he killed anyone? my mother asked. Had he fired into the crowd of students? Had he any blood on his hands? He stood in the center of the room, facing my parents, our summer fans whirring around them and blurring all their voices. He was not supposed to tell. He was not supposed to talk about these things, but my parents would not relent.

My grandmother should have stepped in and stopped them then, out of love or pity, but I think they were punishing him for their own relief at his safety. They had worried about him ever since the first reports of the conflict. In any case, my grandmother left: she left my uncle in my parents' hands.

He responded haltingly to their questions. He'd been told the students were communist sympathizers. He'd been told the students had declared war on their current government. He'd been given direct orders to do what he did. "I had no choice," he said.

"Everyone has a choice," my father said. "Even if the choice is between honor or death, you can still choose not to kill innocent victims." This comment terrified and exhilarated me. He sounded so heroic, so willing to bear anything.

Then I looked at my uncle's bent head, and I wanted to run into the room and take his hand. But I stayed put. It probably wouldn't have made a difference if I had gone to him. I probably would have been sent back to my room and put to bed. Still, I have always wished I had gone and stood by his side.

He stood with his head down, and his shoulders shaking. My parents did not touch him, but stood, watching him. It wasn't until much later that they would come to regret the work they did that night.

When I woke up the next day, my uncle was gone, and my parents were grim and tense, and would say nothing about it. Something happened in the following weeks: one day they just turned against each other. My father had written a pamphlet about the details they had been able to glean from my uncle, and published it under the pen name of Eun Po. This man had been a famous poet and scholar and advisor to the king in the fourteenth century, and had been murdered for refusing to betray his king. Only my mother and two of his close friends knew my father had written this pamphlet, but my mother was furious at the danger she believed he'd put us all in.

For the next several days, they fought. They argued over the dishes, on the way to the grocery store, everywhere they went that we were alone. In public they were silent, but they stopped taking us to the playground, they didn't go to the store. They stayed at home and fought. They shouted at the table between bites of food.

"You're a mathematician," my mother said. "This isn't for you to do."

"I'm a citizen and a patriot. I did the right thing, the honorable thing."

"You did nothing but put us at risk. And no one will notice if something happens to you, or us."

"I thought you would support me," my father said. "When we met, you felt differently."

"That was before we had children."

"Someone has to protest. We can't always yield."

"You're risking the lives of our children."

"You used to believe in things."

"I believe in new things now. We have a family."

"You used to be brave."

"You call yourself brave?" My mother drew in her breath. "I should never have married you," she said. "I should never have given you children."

Then my father was silent. Perhaps my mother's words had lodged in his heart, as they had in mine. She was wishing her marriage to my father undone, Hannah and myself unmade.

Several days later, my parents called us into the living room. At first neither spoke. Then, "We are leaving," my father said. "We are moving away."

He didn't say more. After a moment I asked, "When are we going?" and Hannah let out a whimper, and puckered herself up to cry.

My father turned to her. "Come here," he said, opening his arms. She crawled over me to get to him and leaned her head against his shoulder. She was comforted so easily.

"We've been thinking of moving for a long time." His sister, my Komo, who had lived in America since before I was born, had found him a job. Both he and my mother thought it'd be best if he took it. He said this with a sideways look at my mother. He sat up a little straighter and shifted Hannah in his arms. He held out his hand to me. "Shake," he said.

I reached out and shook his hand. In school we had learned that this was how they greeted each other in the West. This was how they made a deal.

When my father let go of my hand, I turned to my mother. She had fixed her eyes on the building across from us, her whole body angled away. "Umma?" I asked. "Will you come, too?"

She tapped her foot against the ground, but she didn't answer. She didn't even turn to look at me.

"Umma?" I asked.

She stopped tapping her foot and touched her forehead as if to clear away a stray hair.

"Are you coming?" I repeated.

Her laugh was brittle. "I have no choice, since your Komo says to do it. Your father listens to his sister when she tells him he's in danger, but not to his wife."

I looked from her to my father and back. "So you're coming?" I repeated in a small voice.

My mother looked back at me, her face hard to read. Then she shook her head and said, "Oh, you little fool," and her voice was unexpectedly warm. She stood up and reached down for me, picking me up off the ground and hugging me hard. The relief of her touch was miraculous. I let it wash over me and was silent, as if I had asked the only question that mattered.

Our last months in Korea were spent packing up our things, visiting relatives, and taking leave of ancestors who lay buried on mountains an hour's drive and then an hour's walk away.

There were so many people, dead and alive, to say good-bye to: we walked from bus stop to bus stop, apartment to apartment, up mountain after mountain, bowing on wood floors and in the dirt, calling out in heat that did not subside even after the storms came.

It rained for days, but afterward it was no cooler. We couldn't tell whether the dampness on our skin came from ourselves, or the humid air. It felt as if we were being steamed alive like oysters, and one day my mother discovered a colony of tiny red bumps growing under my armpits and behind my knees. Once I knew they were there I couldn't stop contorting myself to get a better look at them. They hurt when I scratched and itched when I didn't.

Haejin got the same rash a couple days later. It spread all over her body. She clawed at herself until she bled. My mother held our hands down and poured baby powder all over us to dry out the sweat. My bumps got smaller, but Haejin wouldn't stop scratching. Whenever we weren't looking, she turned away and went to work, shrieking as she carved furious red lines into the white powder crusting her neck.

To stop her, my mother bandaged Haejin's hands until they were two white stumps. For a whole week she couldn't use her hands. I had to open doors for her, take her to the bathroom, and feed her, but she couldn't scratch anymore. Strangers stared at her, whispering about what might have happened to her hands. Haejin loved the attention. When she caught them looking, she would sing and dance, wiggling her body. This made my parents laugh helplessly. My mother said she had no shame. But Haejin loved it. I stood apart from the scenes she commanded, my own body crusted over with a layer of powder, aware of my own awkward invisibility.

At home, my mother and relatives packed things into boxes. There were so many things to account for, and so many things we could not take. The desk and bookshelves my grandfather had built when my mother was a young girl had to be left behind. We could not take my mother's lacquered cabinets with their inlaid mother-of-pearl villages. My father said heavy things were too expensive to ship. When he left the room, my mother touched the cabinet that had been a wedding present from my grandmother. It had passed from daughter to daughter for five generations.

My mother did not want to go to America: this much I knew. I knew it by the way she became distracted and impatient with my sister, by the way she stopped tucking us into bed at night. I knew it from watching her feet, which began to shuffle after my father announced the move, as though they threw down invisible roots that needed to be pulled out with each step.

Four days before we were supposed to board our flight to America, my mother went grocery shopping, and did not come back in time for dinner. That evening my father waited until long after the usual time, and then laid out the rice and the side dishes on paper plates.

His mouth was a grim line as he chewed his food.

Hannah made a soft whimpering sound in her throat, and he turned to her, his voice harsh. "Not tonight," he said. "Enough."

None of us ate much, and afterward I helped clean up, throwing everything into the garbage.

After a couple more hours of waiting, my father called the police. Two officers came over, in uniform, and they crowded into the living room. They looked at our boxes, and asked questions about our move in loud voices. My father stood very straight with his hands behind him. He said nothing about America, only that we were moving to another apartment soon. He asked them to call him if there was any news about my mother.

After the policemen left, none of us slept. Haejin whimpered from the bed next to me, and I could hear my father pacing in the other room.

My mother finally returned late the next morning, close to lunchtime, her face swollen and ugly from weeping, her words garbled, her explanations lost. She pulled Haejin and me to her, breaking away from my father and clutching at us.

"Where were you?" I asked, crying.

"I don't know," she sobbed. "I don't know, I don't know."

After a while, my father pulled us away from her, his hands pushing us firmly off. He led her to the bedroom. I thought he would yell at her, and followed them, ready to beg my father to be gentle. But when I got to their door, he was whispering to her in a soft voice, and lowering her into their bed. "Rest," he said, one hand on her waist, the other already pulling back the sheets. She was still crying, but he drew the blanket over her, and passed one hand over her hair. He covered her eyes with his hand, and for a second she reached up and held it there with hers.

She slept all day. My father left the door cracked open, and all day long Haejin and I peeked in at her, to reassure ourselves that she was still there. I don't know if she ever told my father what had happened. I never asked. Instead, I watched her carefully after that for a long while, as if at any moment she could shatter.

My uncle did not come again to our apartment during that whole time. I waited for him. Even at the airport, when we were leaving, I looked for him in the group of relatives who'd gathered to see us off. I couldn't believe he wouldn't come. No one had said we were leaving forever, but I felt it was true. Still, he was not there. I was so disappointed that I worked up the courage to ask my father where he was.

My father fiddled with his luggage. I asked again. He looked up. "Ask your mother," he said.

My mother's hands were full of last-minute gifts from their relatives, and when she saw me approach, she turned away to put them in our suitcase. Both she and my grandmother were crying, and she wiped at her face with my grandmother's handkerchief, and pushed me away.

"Go away, Jeehyun," my mother said, when I asked about my uncle. Her hands were full and her face was wet. "I don't know."

I threw up twice in the toilet before getting on the plane. Strapped into my seat, I was grateful to the beautiful stewardess who brought me and Haejin each a little toy plane and a pin with wings. For me, that was the promise of America: I'd been told I'd have my own room, my own raised bed, that there would be things that would be mine alone.

We finally arrived in Detroit, relieved and exhausted after a layover and Haejin's unfortunate bout of airsickness. We collected our luggage and went through customs. The glass doors to the rest of the airport slid open, revealing a crowd of strangers. I had never seen so many foreign faces all at once before, and was dazzled by the fair hair, the different-colored eyes, all those tongues navigating a language I could not follow. I realized with a shock that I would live among these people now.

. . .

Our new house did not look like the block apartment buildings in Seoul, or like the old houses in the countryside with their sloping roofs and broad gates. This new house was white and brick with a pointed roof and bump-out windows. I stood in the driveway blinking at it, trying to reconcile myself to the idea that this was our house. I was impressed by the size of our lawn, that vast expanse of mowed grass. Other children were playing in front of their houses on their own lawns, and there was something reassuring about this, and surprising. It was so different from Seoul.

One thing that was familiar was that it was as hot in Michigan as it had been in Korea. The first thing my mother did was turn on the air-conditioning. It was one good thing about America, she said: central air. That first day, while we began to get settled in, the realtor who had sold us the house long-distance came over. He took us from room to room, speaking slowly, so that I was able to catch words here and there from the English class I'd taken in school the previous year.

Out back, he pointed at some bushes, one by one, counting them. "Those are some awful weeds," he said. "I'd get rid of them if I were you. They spread like crazy and leak a poison that kills other plants."

My father nodded, looking at the overgrown weeds that bordered our house, considering.

That day the dark came quite suddenly. It was bright and sunny, and then it was abruptly night. We set up our sleeping arrangements downstairs in the family room, rolled up in blankets on the carpet. None of our furniture had arrived, and all the rooms were large and empty. The carpet was thick and white, and so plush we didn't need mats.

I kicked Haejin under the covers we were sharing, and she kicked back. I poked her, and she yelped and giggled. When my mother told us to stop in a soft voice meant not to wake my father, Hannah sneaked her hand into mine. We squeezed back and forth. One squeeze meant: *are you sleeping?* One squeeze back meant *yes,* and two meant *no.* Three meant: *do you see a ghost?* We squeezed until she fell asleep, and then I turned and looked out the large curtainless windows. I didn't want to sleep. If I turned my head just right, I could imagine there were no walls around me, no windows, just America, this place where we had come to live.

A couple who knew my Komo through a church association came by the next morning and took my father to take his driving test, and after that to rent a car. They were an older American couple who drove a blue van and smiled at us, but after they dropped my father off that first morning, we never saw them again. The first thing my parents did with that rental car was go grocery shopping. They returned with bags of food in unfamiliar packaging, and while Haejin and I looked at it all, my father put on a pair of thick brown gloves twice as big as his hands, and went into the backyard.

One by one, he attacked the tall weed-bushes the realtor had pointed to along the perimeter of our yard. By the end of the afternoon, there were eleven weed-bushes spread against the green lawn, their naked roots still clinging to the dirt, sprawled in the light. My father left the twelfth standing where it was. He didn't have the energy left to pull up that last one, he said when he came in for water. His hands shook as he held his cup.

The next day we all went together to a nursery to pick out trees: evergreens, maples, and cherry. We planted them around the edge of our lawn, some of them in the soft pits of brown earth that the weed-bushes had left behind. The trees scarcely reached my father's waist, but he said, "They will protect us one day." He scanned our yard as if he could already see how tall they would grow.

Later, the lone weed-bush my father had left untouched would turn out to be a raspberry bush that bore dozens of berries. Eventually the trees we'd planted would grow twice as tall, until our entire yard was enclosed, protected, a space that belonged only to us.

6.

As abrupt as the move to America had been, the move my parents were planning to make back to Korea seemed somehow worse. They'd built a life in Michigan, and it seemed a shame that they would have to leave it now that they were finally comfortable. It had been over twenty years, and we had not returned once, not even to visit, not even after my father's friends had written him and told him they were sure it was safe for him to come home.

Still, as my parents packed up our house, they did not talk about that first move. Instead, we talked about practical details: four suitcases would go to Korea. Movers would come and pack up our things. Almost all of it would be put in storage.

Over dinner, my parents and I argued about whether or not I could join them.

"Come over vacation," my father said. "After your classes next quarter."

"I don't have to teach classes next quarter."

"What do you mean?"

"I'm taking a break, too."

"No." My father shook his head. "That doesn't make sense. I won't allow it."

"Yubbo," my mother interrupted, her voice calm. "Chew your food."

My father waved her off impatiently. He said to me, "You need to get back into your work."

"I want to come to Korea. I want to be with you."

"Jeehyun," my father said. "You have to finish your studies."

"It's not a big deal," I said. "It's just teaching. I'll still be able to work on my research. And, Daddy," I said in the sudden grip of an idea, "I was thinking that we could work on my dissertation together. I can tell you more about my work, now that you'll have more time."

My mother looked at me sharply, but my father seemed struck by the idea. He nodded slowly, mulling it over.

"I could use your perspective," I said, "and this way you can see what I've been working on."

Then he shook his head, and I thought he was going to argue with me.

"My advisor doesn't mind," I said. This was a bit of a lie. My advisor had warned me that I'd already taken too much time off, and had stressed how difficult it would be to get back into my work once I left it. "Really," I said now. "He said the break might do me good, and it'd be great to be able to show it to you."

My father smiled then, and reached his hand out to me. "Shake," he said, pumping my hand up and down.

. . .

When the movers arrived, what horrified me most was when they infiltrated Hannah's room. They packed everything in there, even the unused paper that had been left in a pile on her desk. I couldn't help looking in every time I walked by. The sight of strangers in her room finally made me realize that our house would no longer be ours. And more than that: as I looked in and saw it barren, stripped of its stuffed animals and twin-size bed, emptied of her books and posters, it seemed as if it was the end of our childhood.

"Enough," my mother said one day as we sat on the floor, surrounded by meticulously labeled boxes. "Your father and I are leaving in a week. You must call your sister."

By then I was ready to be bullied, and I didn't protest.

"I never had the chance to find my sister," my mother continued. She reached over and took my hand. She squeezed hard. "You're lucky."

I tried to pull my hand out of my mother's grasp, but she held on. She had lost her sister; she had lived in the aftermath of war. This was always what it came down to, in the end. My grandmother had told me once that my mother had never gotten over the death of my aunt. "Never talk of it," my grandmother had said. "Never bring it up."

When I asked her what had happened, she told me my aunt had died after disobeying her.

"How?" I asked, fascinated. "What did she do?"

But my grandmother would not tell me, and there was only one story my mother ever told about her sister. When Hannah and I were children, this story had the power to make us forgive each other instantly. I memorized it and repeated it to myself as if it contained some clue about my mother, or the curse my grandmother said haunted our family.

My mother's family had lost its estate when my grandfather passed away. He had died right when a law was passed that cut the family land in pieces to be distributed to the peasants. There were no men in our family old enough to formally claim their portion, and when he died the land was lost and belonged to no one. They had lost everything: even the mountain my grandfather and all our ancestors were buried on.

In their old house, they'd had their own rooms, but in this new house, my mother and auntie had to share a room that was very small: my mother could cross the room in six long steps, and my auntie could cross it in five. My mother was secretly glad. She and my auntie even had to share a bed. This made my auntie angry, but my mother pretended not to notice.

Their new house was near a heavy wood that was still green with many old trees. Back then, my mother said, the mountains were not the deep rapturous green that my sister and I remembered, but a barren mixture of brown and black just beginning to speckle with growth. During the occupation and the war, the mountains had lost nearly all of their trees to fire and bombing. When my parents were growing up, the whole country, especially students, would go out to the mountains regularly to plant trees. Those were the trees that covered most of the mountains in Korea now. So that forest was rare at that time, my mother said.

Also, they had more freedom out there, where there were no

servants to watch over them. My mother and auntie went into the forest to fetch water from the well every day, and when they went out they explored the different paths around their new house. There was one path that had been roped off by scarlet cords, and the word "danger" had been carved onto one of the smaller trees.

One day my auntie jumped over the barrier, and following her lead, my mother ducked beneath it. She asked her sister what she thought they would find. "A duckbill brown bear," her sister said. "A rooster with three tails."

They went on laughing, and when they came to the end of the path they were astonished to find a second well they had never known existed. My auntie grabbed my mother's arm and pointed to something blocking the path. It was a large metal ball, large enough to sit on. It was as tall as my mother's waist. She didn't know what it was, but my auntie said it was a bomb.

My mother clutched my auntie's hand, but my auntie shook her off and told her to wait where she was. My auntie walked closer to the bomb and knelt in front of it. "They must have built a new well to keep us away from this," she said. She reached out her hand.

My mother ran forward, on tiptoe, and stood by my auntie's side. "It can't go off now, can it?" she asked.

"Of course it can," my auntie said. "It happens all the time, don't you know anything?" She stood and stepped closer. She laughed. "I'm going to sit on it," she said. She flashed my mother a look that my mother didn't understand, a look of defiance my mother would always remember.

"Don't," she cried. She took my auntie's sleeve.

My auntie shook her off. "I can't take you anywhere, you little brat," she said good-naturedly. Then they were both quiet. The bomb faced them smugly. It was nestled deep in a bed of heather, and covered in moss. Slender white flowers grew along the cracks.

My auntie leaned forward until her face was very close. She was almost touching it: my mother could see her breath swaying the tips of the heather. Then my auntie reached out a hand and plucked a flower from the moss. My mother stepped forward, in wonder, but a branch broke beneath her foot, startling her. She turned and ran, screaming at the noise, her pail banging against her legs. Through her scream she heard my auntie running behind her, laughing. When they finally stopped running my auntie was still laughing, the flower dangling weakly in her hand.

Embarrassed, my mother said, "I'm telling Umma what you did."

"Do what you want." My auntie scowled. "No one's stopping you." And she turned and ran toward home, leaving my mother alone to fetch the water from the other well and to carry the heavy bucket home by herself.

When my mother got home, my auntie was alone in their room. The flower lay discarded on the floor.

"I wasn't really going to tell on you," my mother said. She was angry and embarrassed, but she was also sorry.

My auntie was unmoved. "I can't share this room with you anymore," she said. She pointed to the flower that lay in the doorway. "That flower marks half the room." She had placed it there before my mother returned on purpose, to let it mark what had come between them. "This side is mine," my auntie said, stomping. "Take care not to cross over."

"The bed's on your side!" my mother cried.

"Too bad for you."

The rest of that day they glared at each other across the room, their hostility unbroken by the onset of darkness. My mother grew angrier and angrier, but when my grandmother asked at dinner-time why they were fighting, she said nothing.

That night, she lay down on the hard wooden floor without blankets, expecting my auntie to relent. When she didn't, my mother kicked the bed.

"My side," my auntie said. My mother kicked the bed again, and pounded her hands on the ground. My auntie was quiet.

My mother forced herself to be quiet as well. She closed her eyes. She would not beg. But she was on the brink of tears. She counted to twenty. To thirty. One hundred. It was a trick her father had taught her before he died. And then, just like that, she felt cool hands grab her ankles, fingers tickling the bottoms of her feet. She kicked at her sister's hands, unwilling to make peace. But they returned until she relented and began to giggle. And then they reached out and grasped her hands, and pulled her into bed.

This was the story my mother had always told to make peace between my sister and me, and now when my mother said, "I want to tell you a story about your auntie," I thought she would tell it again. But instead she told me another story I had never heard before.

When the time came for my aunt to go to college, my grandmother was in the middle of a long illness, and my mother begged her not to leave. To go would be selfish. My mother was too young to keep house herself. "How can you leave this all behind?" She swept her arm around to include their house, the trees behind it, their mother, their brother, herself. "You will be sorry," she said. She did not understand then the dread with which her sister faced the threat of being bound forever to this house, with all its reminders of what had been lost. Of course my auntie left.

Afterward, my mother went to fetch water by herself. She played with her wide-eyed younger brother, whom they had always treated like a baby. He became her new playmate, and my mother learned how to be an older sister, too, for once. She nursed jealousies of whomever her sister might be friends with now, at school. Those girls who got to be near her. At night she stretched out, covering their mattress alone.

Then one night my mother woke to the dim form of my grandmother hovering at her doorway, her feet falling out of her slippers. She stood there with a startled look on her face, her hand opening and closing, rubbing her throat.

Frightened, my mother said, "Is it morning, Umma?"

"Your sister is missing," my grandmother said in a strange and trembling voice. Then she shook herself, seeming to wake, and whispered, "Go back to sleep." She shuffled away.

At breakfast the next morning, my mother's uncle was there. He sat across from her at the table. He had come from Seoul sometime in the night, to bring the news to the family himself. "What happened?" my mother asked. "Where is she?"

"She's dead," her uncle said simply. My mother looked at her brother. They were having rice and soup for breakfast, like always. My mother had set eight side dishes in neat little bowls; my auntie had disappeared, and my great-uncle said quite calmly that she was dead. He reached across the table and put his heavy hand on my mother's shoulder. "We are reporting her dead."

She did not know how to make sense of it. My auntie had been living in a girl's dorm. It was her second year of college. The North Koreans had been kidnapping people for years, especially girls, and this had intensified in the last several months. And then the North Koreans had raided my auntie's dorm and carried her off.

Three days later, my mother's family made a burial mound for my auntie in the mountains near where our ancestors lay. They piled great heaps of dirt on top of an empty coffin. My mother shivered, and thought of the silent bomb she and her sister had discovered next to the abandoned well.

"What if she comes back," my mother asked, "and finds out what we've done?"

Her uncle turned and gripped her arm. He wanted her to understand the situation, he said. His words were terse. She would never be able to marry, to leave Korea, to get a job, if anyone found out what had happened to her sister. Even worse, if they knew she had a sister in the North, her entire family could fall under suspicion themselves, and be taken away to disappear.

My mother understood then that her uncle was afraid for himself and his own children. She imagined the rest of her family vanishing, one by one, leaving four empty mounds beside each other on a hill. Did she understand? my uncle asked. Did she understand what had to be done?

My mother nodded yes, but she thought to herself, *We are killing her.*

They never spoke of my auntie after that, but each night my mother dreamed of men invading her room. They entered with bugles and shouting. With guns, and long machetes meant to cut stalks of rice. Sweet music like a parade, girls filing out in their nightgowns, her own heart fluttering birdlike as her mother's hand. No one ever spoke of what happened to those girls, except in whispers when she wasn't supposed to be listening: *raped*, she heard a neighbor say once, another time, *brainwashed*.

My mother helped my grandmother make the food and clean the house. She served her younger brother his food and sat silently. No one talked at meals any longer, though her brother tried. In those days, he started going out to sit on the roof. All my mother ever knew for certain was that her sister disappeared that night. My auntie left no clues, no trace. It was better not to wonder.

When my auntie disappeared, there was no search, no photographs sent out. My mother's family never asked, what if, and where? This was a sin and a betrayal my mother could never comprehend: how easy it was for my auntie to be forgotten.

"We are lucky to have what we have," her family said, and she learned to banish my auntie's name from her speech. My mother left it there to linger: a weight on her tongue.

She fetched the water alone. One day she walked the path to the abandoned well. This was her first time back, but she had heard at some point that other children played carelessly around it now, as though the bomb that blocked the path couldn't still, unexpectedly, explode. She tiptoed around it.

She touched it then, and thought, *This is real.* The bomb, the world, didn't seem possible. The world changed too quickly: the sky opened without warning. Her sister had disappeared, and once long ago, this bomb had come quietly like a beggar in the night to block the path to the well. She ran her hand over it, made the green weeds that grew out of its cracks bend under her hand, and thought, *This is real. I am real.*

. . .

Later, when my mother went to college herself, she walked past her sister's dorm each day. She walked in once, her palm flat against the old wood as she pushed the door open. She walked up and down the hallways, looking for the room that had once been her sister's.

"Are you looking for someone?" a girl asked.

My mother spoke her sister's name.

The girl shook her head and said, "Wrong building. No one by that name lives here."

My mother thanked the girl, but lingered, looking for clues smudged into the walls, for something dropped in the hall. There was nothing but the lilting voices of the girls who lived there now.

My mother told this story, and then she said, "I couldn't go after my sister, but you can still search for Haejin. You are lucky to have the chance to find and bring her home."

"It's not the same," I said. "Hannah left us. It was her choice." But I understood what my mother was telling me. My suffering had been so small compared to hers. I was ashamed. "I'll go," I said.

My mother nodded then, and finally released the arm she'd been holding on to the whole time. "Tell your father," she said.

I went to him then, and told him I'd decided to go to Hannah and talk to her. He smiled with such relief and happiness that I felt jealous and guilty at the same time. He stuck out his hand. "Shake," he said. He shook my hand vigorously.

"I can't make any promises," I said, pulling away, already wanting to back out.

But he said, "Bring her home," holding on to my hand. He looked right at me, and nodded. Then he turned to the window and pointed at the setting sun. "What do you think?" he said.

"Three minutes," I said. We'd played this game for as long as I could remember, trying to predict how much time was left in a sunset before the sun would disappear beneath the horizon.

"Forty-five seconds," my father said, looking at his watch.

I always thought it would take longer than it did for the sun to set. My father, somehow, could predict it nearly to the second.

We watched it sink behind the trees. I said, "I'm joining you in Korea. After I've found Hannah, I'm coming." I talked fast. "It's all clear with my advisor. We'll check in by e-mail and by phone. That's part of the deal. I'm going to find Hannah so that then I can come to you."

My father smiled. "I'm glad you're coming," he said.

That last morning before my parents' flight, my father sat on the kitchen floor, the light filtering in through the sliding glass door onto his face and shoulders. It reflected off the linoleum back up at his face. The bones of his face looked sharper, his skin more translucent. His cancer markers had shot up in the last several weeks. His local doctor had urged him to start treatment as soon as he could.

"I wish I could stay," he said, squinting. "This is my home." He was surrounded by light so bright that everything seemed to move slowly inside it. "I don't want to go." He rose, and slid open the door. He stepped outside.

It was a beautiful day. I thought our backyard had never looked so gorgeous, the bare branches of the trees swaying slowly in the cold bright air, all of it so familiar. My mother and I watched my father pace the length of our backyard, touching the trees. Some of them had grown ten times as tall in twenty years, and standing next to them, my father looked suddenly more fragile than I had noticed in the last few weeks.

My father bowed then to his trees, his hands clasped together in front of his chest. I couldn't tell if he was praying, or if he was saying good-bye. When he turned back toward the house, my mother and I busied ourselves in the kitchen, as if we had not been watching.

In the end, we left our house bravely: we did not go from room to room talking about old memories. We did not stand and stare, or turn back for one last glance. We locked the door behind us and piled into the car with our luggage, smiling at each other, as if we were going on vacation. We did not speak of how the house would be emptied and gutted and sold. We did not say to each other, We will never come back. But at the airport, when we separated, and I stood watching my parents ride up the escalator to their gates, when I saw them walking away from me, I thought of our house, and of Hannah's empty room. I thought of our toys, packed away, our entire childhood sorted through and boxed. And she would never have to see it; she would never really have to know.

7.

The first summer after we'd moved to America, my father's sister had called and said she and her family were driving up from Indianapolis to stay for a month in August. To help us get settled in, she said.

My mother said that we had already settled in just fine, and if she'd really wanted to help she should have come earlier, before we'd bought our car and found the grocery store and unpacked all our boxes.

"It's still kind of her," my father had replied.

I'd never met my Komo: she'd moved to America long ago, and had two American-born sons. She was ten years older than my father, and the two of them were the sole surviving members of a family of eight. My father had been the baby of the family, the third and last son in a brood of five girls and three boys.

He was six years old when the rest of his family was killed by American soldiers, gunned down in front of their house while he hid with his sister indoors. His sister had sneaked him out of the house in the dead of night, and lifted him past the bundles near the door that he only realized years later were the bodies of his family. He never knew if they were buried.

My mother said my Komo carried my father over the mountains, singing to him the whole time. There was a cousin on the other side who might take them in. The cousin's own father had already died. That's how it was in those days, everyone gone, their lives so short.

So began the first of my father's many exoduses: it was his first loss, his first death, the first house he left behind. Everything I knew about his family I knew from my mother and the stories my father's cousins had told me when I was growing up in Korea. Once I asked him about it—six people gone in one day, whole lives over in an instant—and my father shrugged and said he was too young to remember. When I said I still remembered being six years old, and the day Haejin was born, he said he was so old that his new memories had crowded out his old memories. "That's what happens when you grow up," he said. For a long time after that I tried to go over certain memories in my mind every night before I went to bed, afraid that if I didn't guard them this way, they would disappear.

The stories I knew of my father all began after he and my Komo had crossed over into what would become South Korea, after their ancestral home had been lost, and everyone was already dead.

"We had only each other," my father said of my aunt, and sometimes when he said it an odd, hard expression would flicker across my mother's face.

As children, my Komo and my father had walked to the library through a foot of snow, the two of them pretending to be martial arts masters who could skim over ground so fast they left no trace. After a blizzard once, he had shown me how they did it, and I had copied him, lifting my feet as little as possible, sweeping forward as fast as I could, "like the wind," my father said. "Try to be as subtle and swift as the wind."

The nearest library had only let fifty people in at a time, he said, and during my father's two-month winter vacations, he and my aunt woke at daybreak to walk to the library and wait in line so that he could stay warm inside all day, studying while my aunt trudged home alone, returning all the way back to fetch him when the library closed.

I loved these stories of my Komo, this determined and willful guardian of my father, but when I found out I was finally going to meet her, I felt uneasy and a little jealous—just for the power she wielded over him. For the debt she held over his head.

My father had told me many times that I looked like his sister, and I knew the thought gave him pleasure. Secretly, I imagined her beautiful and gracious. I believed she would prefer me over Hae-jin. I imagined her still as the teenage girl she'd been in my father's stories, the girl I hoped to one day resemble.

Of course she disappointed me. When she finally arrived, I was the one to answer the door. She stood on our porch laden with luggage and two boys and a husband. Her face was lined and her smile was hard, and it held no warmth for me. Her hair was short and permed tightly against her head in a style that all Korean ajumahs seemed to adopt once they reached a certain age, and she did not seem special at all. For a moment I did not register that this was my aunt, my father's sister. When I did, I put my hand to my face, hoping whatever likeness existed between us was very faint.

She saw me touch my face as I looked at her, but just as she was about to speak, my parents arrived at the threshold, bowing and exclaiming in welcome, reaching to help with the suitcases. At the same time, my cousins pushed past my aunt and through my parents into our house. They came in as if they owned it, barely pausing to greet my parents. Kicking off their shoes, they ran up the stairs to explore the rooms. My parents would never have permitted us to behave that way, but my mother said, laughing, "They're so vigorous." As if it was something to be proud of. We could hear them stomping upstairs.

"Let me show you your rooms," my mother said to my aunt and uncle, leading them up after Hannah and I had made our bows and been properly introduced. She'd made up the guest bedroom for my aunt and uncle, and Haejin's room would go to her sons Gabe and Keith. We would share a room for the time that they were visiting.

But the boys had already commandeered both of our bedrooms and were throwing our stuffed animals at each other across the hall. My mother paused at the top of the stairs, watching them.

When she told the boys they'd be sharing Haejin's room, they flat-out refused. My mother turned to my aunt smiling, expecting support, but my aunt said only, "They are used to having their own rooms at home."

"Yes of course," my father said quickly, stepping in before my mother could respond. "Jeehyun and Haejin can sleep in our room with us."

My mother pressed her lips together but did not disagree, and watching my cousins whoop and pelt each other with our pillows, I felt a little relieved that we would be sleeping with our parents.

In the following days, my cousins paid no attention to us, but I observed them covertly. Gabe was the eldest, at twelve. His face was chubby and cheerful, he had one of those laughing faces that would have led me to believe he was good-natured. Keith was ten, and nearly the same height. He was not overweight like his brother, and looked totally normal by himself, but somehow disappeared when he was next to Gabe, and became an extension of him.

My cousins spent their days throwing water balloons in the backyard and playing on their identical Game Boys. But when we crossed their paths, they yelled, "Scram," and chased us away. At meals, they kicked us under the table until our legs were covered in bruises. "Girls," they sneered, punching us on the arms when we walked by, or digging their hands into the soft spot between our shoulder blades. "What can you do with two girls?"

At mealtimes, my uncle snatched food off Gabe's plate and instructed my mother not to offer him seconds. Watching him eat so little, I wondered how he stayed so fat. One morning, I walked by Gabe's room and through the half-open door I saw my aunt fitting a girdle around his waist. As she fastened the snaps, the folds of fat on his body came together and held. My obnoxious, cocky cousin stood absolutely still, the way he held his body clearly protesting this indignity. I walked quickly by, feeling as if I had witnessed something I should not have seen.

I felt sorry for Gabe then, and resolved to be kind. But he despised my attempts at friendship, and made fun of both my Korean and my English. He told me my family was going to hell, and he called my mother a heathen. He pinched me and hit my arm, and I let him, frozen by the thought that underneath his clothes, he wore a girdle. Keith stood by and laughed, his gaping mouth showing all his teeth.

When I complained to my mother, displaying the bruises on my legs that my cousin had left, my aunt overheard. She knelt down to look at my leg, smiling what my mother called her Christian smile. "Jeehyun," she said, "that's just how boys are." She gripped my calf and turned it to get a better look, her fingers clasping a particularly tender bruise. I cried out.

"Perhaps if you had brothers, you would know how to play with them better," she said, talking to me but looking at my mother.

That was the first time I heard her mention a topic that would grow to become a central issue in my family after she departed. My mother had never given my father a son, and my aunt blamed her for this, as well as for not stopping my father from writing his pamphlet on Kwangju. My aunt had sacrificed so much for my father, her education and her youth, and she resented my mother, who she thought had come in and carelessly thrown everything away. "You are the last of your line," she said to my father. "You are responsible for more than yourself."

Nevertheless, I felt some of my aunt's inexorable will pulling me in during her visit. She was hard to resist. When we ate, she asked us to join her family in bowing our heads at our table. Even if we weren't Christian, my aunt said, we should join hands and respect God. Gabe sat to my left, and when we prayed he squeezed my fingers until they ached. We closed our eyes and listened to my uncle pray with somber slowness, first in Korean and then in English, and the whole time Gabe would twist my hand and try to make me cry out.

It was my uncle's voice that got me through it: he had a deep and confident voice, and even through my discomfort it occurred to me that my aunt had married my uncle for his voice, so suited to command a small gathering, solemn and thrilling. Sometimes when no one was around, I repeated my uncle's prayers out loud to myself, trying to capture the feeling I had when I heard my uncle say certain words. I liked hearing them come off my own tongue: The Father, the Son, and the Holy Ghost.

I had never liked the idea of heaven—it sounded too much like one more country where everyone spoke a different language. Still, sometimes I wondered what it would be like to go somewhere that everyone my parents mourned so intensely would be, and if they were just watching us, and waiting.

Even though I didn't like the idea of heaven, I did fall a little bit in love with Jesus that summer. I couldn't bear the thought of his suffering. In my daydreams I imagined speaking on his behalf and rescuing him from the cross. I kept it a secret, I kept all my crushes secret, but when I was alone I imagined how if I had been there, I would have saved Jesus so he never had to get nailed on the cross, how I would have protected him and kept him company. I felt sorry for him—having to love everyone so much, having to forgive everyone's deepest sins. I thought he must have been lonely, having to be the Son of God.

That July, Haejin carried around a large doll everywhere she went. It was the size of a real baby, and heavier than most dolls. It warmed to your body like a real child. We'd spent weeks going to toy stores: my parents said the doll would help Haejin get used to sleeping alone. To my disappointment, it had not occurred to them to also buy something for me. Worse, when the doll was finally found and admired and purchased, I was dismayed to discover I wanted it for myself. I had never owned such a toy. The doll had plump arms that you could squeeze just so, curly brown hair, and glittering green glass eyes. My mother dressed her in a frilly red baby dress, the only one she'd brought from Korea as a souvenir of our infancies. The dress had been mine before it was ever Hannah's, and though I had no recollection of having worn it, I still felt a proprietary indignation. Then Haejin named her doll Baby. This was the final straw. If the doll had been mine, I would have given her a beautiful, romantic name, like Guinevere. I would have sung to her, taught her things, comforted her when she was tired or sad.

Haejin had always wanted everything I owned. She'd tried to steal or beg my toys away. Once she acquired Baby, however, she lost interest in all other toys. She carried that doll around and fed it, sang to it, and talked to it. She even took it to the bathroom several times a day to let it pee.

One day I hid Baby in the laundry hamper while Haejin was having her bath. She emerged dripping and howling, and would not be still until hours later when my mother finally pulled the doll out from beneath the dirty laundry, scolding Haejin for not being more careful. I should have been ashamed of myself, but what I felt during those few hours of Haejin's desperate search for her doll was a sharp pleasure in being the only one who knew where Baby was.

Baby was captivating, and eventually even Gabe and Keith took notice. The first time they asked to see her, Haejin offered her up proudly, holding her out with both hands.

When Gabe turned Baby upside down and lobbed her over to Keith, Haejin screamed. Keith laughed, and pulled Baby's dress over her face before throwing her back to Gabe.

"Stop it," I said, but I knew that I would have joined their game if they had let me. When my mother came in to see why Haejin was crying, they threw Baby on the floor and ran into another room. Haejin guarded Baby obsessively after that, and wouldn't let her out of her sight. She took her into the bathroom with her, and slept with her clutched against her chest. My parents were embarrassed at her obsessive behavior, but my aunt nodded approvingly and said Haejin would make a proper mother one day.

In the third week of their monthlong visit, my parents took my aunt and uncle to the local golf course as a special treat, leaving us with my cousins in the house. My Komo said they were old enough to watch us, but I was relieved when they left the house after our parents did, with the intent of going to the neighborhood pond to try to catch some fish.

I knew I should play with Haejin, but it had been so long since I'd had any time to myself. It was like being set free, and I was wild to do something on my own. But I couldn't leave Haejin alone in the house, so I left her in the living room playing with Baby, and went up to my parents' room and locked the door behind me.

I was filled with energy and didn't know how to spend it. I thought about climbing out their bathroom window onto the roof, or taking a bath in the fancy tub with the jets. Instead, I went to my mother's dresser and opened a drawer. It was filled with her underwear, and I pulled each piece out, the old cotton briefs with the sagging elastic, the soft silky ones with the lace trim. I touched all her bras, unclipping and reclipping the backs.

For as long as I could remember, I had been a snoop. When my parents weren't home, when Hannah was sleeping or otherwise

occupied, I ransacked their drawers. I found medicines and con-
doms, trinkets and jewelry, my mother's engagement ring, old
photographs of people I didn't recognize. It seemed to me that
everything important in our lives was hidden. That was why my
mother hid our money in wallets she stashed in drawers. That was
why she hid jewelry between her neatly folded scarves. After I
found the first little box, lined in velvet and containing a brilliant
ruby ring, I hunted for more. I spread all the little boxes in front
of me on the carpet, opening them up one by one, trying on every
pearl and emerald, fastening the necklaces around my neck and
looping them over around my wrists.

I listened for Haejin—if she had come up, I would have thrown
everything back into the drawer and closed it, and pretended I'd
been reading a book. I wanted this to be mine alone, my secret.
After I was done with my mother's underwear drawer, I searched
the sweaters, the T-shirts, the pants. There was money hidden in
envelopes, letters, black-and-white photographs of my mother at
different ages: her parents, her sister, my uncle as a baby flashing
a toothless grin.

Then I went to my parents' closet, pulling out all our suitcases,
checking all the pockets for coins, letters, stray papers, anything
at all. There was a small roll of Korean candies in my mother's
carry-on bag. Perhaps she'd been saving them for later, or forgotten them unpacking. I opened the roll and peeled off one round
candy and put the rest away.

Finally, I lay down on my parents' bed and rolled around in
their blankets, sniffing their sheets, which smelled like them. When
I finally shook myself out, I was hungry. I headed downstairs to
make myself a snack. On my way to the kitchen, I noticed my cousins' shoes scattered in the hallway in front of the door. I had not

heard them return. Their shoes were damp and smelled sharp and slightly rotten when I picked them up to stack them against the wall, but I dropped them when I heard my sister cry out.

"Haejin?" I called, walking through the hallway to our kitchen, which led into the living room. I stood for a moment on the threshold to the kitchen—there was no one there. Then there came another moan, and I saw the bump behind the curtains and Haejin's legs kicking out beneath them.

I ran to the windows and yanked the curtains aside. Keith was holding Haejin still by the back of her neck. Gabe knelt over Baby, whose dress was pulled over her face, poking holes in her stomach with a dinner fork. Her skin puckered and gave way. A thick clear gel oozed from the holes and clung to the fork in a long strand when he pulled it out.

Haejin squirmed away from my cousins and shook herself, a strange, quick reflexive movement like a fit. Half-crawling, half-rolling, she scrambled up to her feet and jumped away from them, wailing. Gabe burst out laughing. A moment later, Keith joined him. I went to her and tried to pull her toward me, but she wrenched herself away and stumbled from the room. She thumped up the stairs, crying loudly. I couldn't stand the boys' grinning up at me, or Baby splayed against Gabe's legs. I bent and snatched her up. As I stomped away, they continued to laugh.

I took Baby upstairs. Before I went to find Haejin, I went to the bathroom and took out the first-aid kit. I applied Band-Aids to Baby's oozing wounds. The gel, I realized, was what made Baby feel so human, what gave her weight and give. The raised gooey bumps on Baby's skin reminded me of the pimples on Gabe's neck.

Haejin had gone to her room, which was temporarily Gabe's room, and had thrown herself down on her bed. She whimpered when I held Baby out to her, and turned away. That's when I saw the marks on her neck where they had held her down. I ran my hand over them, then bent down and kissed them.

"My darling," I said. My mother's tenderest word. I went to the door and put a chair against it. I lay down next to her in her bed and stroked her back, running my fingers up and down her skin.

Her sheets smelled like Gabe. A pair of his socks had been kicked off at the foot of her bed, and his suitcase lay open on the floor beside us. His dirty clothes were rumpled on top of his clean ones, some underwear spilled over the edge.

I sat up after a moment. "Let's go," I said. I wanted to take her to my parents' room, but she wouldn't budge. I tried to pick her up, but she could make herself a dead weight when she wanted to, letting her head droop and making every limb go completely limp.

I tugged on her arm and she turned her head and wailed. "Haejin," I said, but she looked so wild I was getting scared. I covered her eyes with my hand. Instead of struggling, she quieted immediately, like a caged bird. She even fell asleep. I carried her sleeping to my parents' room. While she slept, I opened and closed all my mother's drawers, making sure the clothes were folded and that everything was in order. I went into my parents' closet and put all their suitcases back. I worried what I would have to tell my parents if they found out what had happened while they were gone. I didn't know what I would say I had been doing when I should have been watching my sister.

When Haejin finally woke in their bed an hour later, I held her in my lap and tickled her. She giggled. She seemed all right. I thought maybe we wouldn't have to tell my parents anything, and I asked her to promise not to tell our parents about what Gabe and Keith had done to Baby. She leaned into my arms and agreed. I was filled with relief. Sometimes things could pass like this, I thought, as if nothing at all had happened. There would be no lasting harm. I was so glad she was all right, and equally relieved that my parents wouldn't have to know how I'd neglected her in their absence.

A few days later Gabe and Keith and my aunt and uncle finally drove off to return to their home in Indiana. My family stood at the door and waved, watching their car pull away. We smiled and smiled at their departing car—waving as if we had enjoyed the visit, as if we wished they would come again. We'd all gotten along a little better in the relief of the last remaining days, knowing it would soon be at an end.

Right after they left, our house fell into a sort of bliss; it was good to be alone together again. My mother washed all the sheets and vacuumed the house. Haejin and I played in our backyard while my father dragged large bags of mulch from tree to tree. We discovered that the lone weed-bush my father had left in our yard had borne dozens of raspberries.

"I should be happy about this, I know," my father said when we showed him, "but I can't forgive myself for the ones I pulled up."

It seemed to me that the remaining bush bore berries to make up for the loss. There were so many that first season that every evening Hannah and I picked berries until our clothes were stained. My parents sat on lawn chairs, side by side, watching us. Those days they looked tired, and sometimes I'd look back at them and remember how hard my father had worked that first day, pulling up all those bushes alone.

ater that week my father found Baby stuck headfirst in the trash, her bare, dimpled feet pointing up at him. He pulled her out and noticed the Band-Aids plastered all over her oozing abdomen. He showed this to my mother, and then sat me and Haejin down at our kitchen table, Baby lying on her back, stripped of my baby dress, her body exposed. Hannah flinched each time my father waved the doll in front of us.

My father reminded us how expensive the doll had been. He listed all the stores we'd visited to find it. "It's your special doll," he said to Haejin.

She started to cry. "They cut her up," she said.

My father looked grim. "Who?"

Haejin wept.

My father looked at me. "Who?" he said.

"Gabe," I said. "And Keith."

My father sighed. He patted Haejin on the head. "Stop crying," he said. "It's not your fault."

"It was a cruel, vicious thing to do," my mother said. "But we can fix her."

She got up and cleaned Baby off with a towel, wiping her down very gently. She sent me to the medicine cabinet for the first-aid kit, and then she put pieces of surgical tape over the wounds, which showed less than the Band-Aids had. "See? She's all better," she said, smoothing Haejin's hair.

Haejin shook her head and pushed the doll away from her. "No," she said.

"But she's your little baby," my mother said, stroking the doll. "She's better now."

"I don't want her," Haejin wept.

"Behave," I leaned over and whispered in her ear. My parents were trying, and I could see how much she was upsetting them. She was upsetting me, too: I'd thought she'd gotten over this, and if my parents found out now how I'd told her to keep quiet, I'd really be in trouble. "It's not that big of a deal."

My mother sighed and looked at my father. He shrugged his shoulders. A few days later, Hannah put the doll back in the trash, and they let it be taken away. I was relieved when it was finally gone.

8.

In Korea, couples dress alike to show the world that they're together. Families, sisters, teams, groups—delight in wearing a uniform. Grandmothers wearing the same shirt, same pants, same hat, same sunglasses, go hiking in the mountains together, singing the same song. Here is the lesson: nothing is more important than belonging. Nothing is as satisfying.

On our first day of school in America, my mother dressed Haejin and me in the same outfit. She put both of us in little blue-and-white sailor dresses embroidered with anchors. Haejin sat on the sidewalk in front of our bus stop crying, her legs splayed beneath her white skirt. My mother, kneeling beside her, whispered, "Haejin, keep your legs closed, please—everyone can see you." She patted my sister's back, crooning, and with her other hand tried to push one errant knee closer to the other.

The other kids and mothers stood at the same corner, and gave us a wide berth. I noticed that none of the other girls were wearing a dress. They were all in shorts. I started counting by twos to calm myself down, a trick my mother had taught me in Korea for when I was afraid.

As the bus pulled up, Haejin threw her head back and screamed. "Oh my," said a woman. The older kids snickered. Even the other little kids, sniffling into their hands, stopped to stare. I started counting by threes.

We waited for everyone else, and then my mother stood resolutely and picked Haejin up, hoisting her onto the bus. Haejin whimpered. My mother turned to me. "Take care of Haejin," she said, and shoved me on behind her. Before I could turn back, the bus driver shut the door.

I pushed Haejin into a seat near the front and settled us in. "Look, Haejin." I tried to distract my sister. "Let's wave at Umma." But it was just as well she didn't stop crying to look. My mother was running away. She had already made it half a block toward our house. The sight of it frightened me: it stayed with me all day.

A few days later, my mother was called in, and both Haejin and I were escorted to the principal's office. I thought we were in trouble, but it was my mother he wanted to address. "Just call me Mr. B.," he said, winking at the three of us. I warmed to his friendliness.

He said to my mother, "Your girls need names."

"They already have names," my mother said.

"Proper names," Mr. B. clarified. "American names." He spoke loudly. In those days, everyone spoke more loudly at my parents than they seemed to speak to anyone else.

"But they're Korean," my mother said. "They've grown up with these names."

"Try Janie," suggested Mr. B. He leaned forward, tapping his fingers together. "And Hannah for her," he said, pointing at Haejin. "It won't take long for everyone to adjust."

My mother looked away from him, but was silent. She did not resist. And so we left his office that day with new names. "Janie," my sister and I repeated over and over. "Hannah."

We were excited by the novelty of it: it seemed like a game, like make-believe. It was surprising at first to be addressed by a different and unfamiliar name at school, but it soon felt somehow reassuring as well. Being called by a name everyone was able to say was less disorienting than having everyone say my real name wrong, and anyway, I liked it. It made me feel as if I belonged. It was only my parents who minded.

Soon after this, my father took us out to our backyard to watch the shooting stars. This was something we did every year in Korea with my grandmother and uncle, and my father's cousins— my father tracked the peak of the yearly meteor shower, and we all went out to the countryside and wandered out to look at the sky on the night the stars fell. Some years there was nothing, and some years so many lights streaked across the sky that our necks grew sore from watching. One of my earliest memories was of a streak of light across darkness and the quiet afterward, and the feeling of wonder.

In America, my mother told us now, you could wish on these falling stars. She said the wishes would come true as long as you didn't tell anyone what they were. I thought it was a strange sort of magic, but it made sense: a wish that gained strength by the silence around it.

We stayed up way past our bedtime, out in our backyard, lying on our backs on a blanket on the lawn, pointing at the sky. Haejin kept falling asleep in my mother's arms, but whenever my mother got up to take her in, Haejin would wake up and refuse, and say she was going to stay out as late as me.

The showing that year was slight, but it was warm enough outside to be pleasant, and we were surrounded by fireflies. I had made a list of wishes, and didn't want to give up until I'd exhausted my list. I don't remember how far I made it down my list, only that I woke up the next morning in my own bed with no memory of being put there. That first year in Michigan was also the last year my family watched the falling stars together: I don't know why.

Around this time, my parents decided they wanted to have another child. They wanted to try for a boy. I hadn't been particularly impressed by our cousins, so I hoped they wouldn't succeed. I don't know what Hannah thought of the whole affair, but I saw the force of my parents' desire for a son as a failure on my part, a yearning I could never fulfill.

For as long as I could remember my grandmother had pressured my parents to keep trying until they had their boy, but my parents had said they were happy with Hannah and me. I didn't know what had changed.

"It's necessary," my grandmother had told my mother. "You are nothing without a son."

She had recruited me as well. "Don't you want a brother?" she'd asked, drawing me aside. "Tell your mother you'd take care of him," she said. "Tell her you'll help." She smiled. "Do this for me." But I didn't want a brother. I would look down silent, unwilling to ask my mother for this, remembering the night Hae-jin had been born.

My grandmother wasn't the only one pressuring my parents. During her visit, my Komo had pushed them, too. She'd said to my father in low, urgent tones, "You're the last one now. It's up to you to make sure our line continues."

As happy as a son was supposed to make everyone, trying to have one did not make my parents happier. They fought worse than they ever had. Their anger flared up without warning and singed everything. In those days, my parents' moods were like the weather: inexplicable, changing.

There were other problems, too, of course. My parents knew no one in Michigan. Our neighbors encouraged my parents to make an effort to befriend the owners of a Chinese restaurant in the next town over. Every time we met someone, they asked, "Have you met the Chongs who own Double Fortune?" Each time, my mother recoiled. In this new place, she felt marked everywhere she went, simultaneously visible and overlooked. Maybe this was why my parents needed a son so badly: a male heir might root them in this country; a boy might have the power to connect the present to the past.

At work, my father had to be careful all the time. At night they tried and tried again to conceive a child who would not come.

"I spend all day with strangers," my father yelled one night during a fight with my mother. "All I want when I come home is someone I can talk to comfortably. Someone I can communicate with." He pointed his finger at my mother. "I don't come home for this," he said. "Not for this!"

"So don't come home then," my mother shouted back. "Or let me go back to Seoul. I never wanted to come in the first place."

When she said this, Hannah and I ran forward and clung to her legs. We wept and begged her to stay, and she cried, too, until my father, unrelenting, ungentle, slammed his hand on the table and yelled at all of us to shut up.

That first year in America my parents became unfamiliar to me. They became unsafe. Hannah and I could enrage them with the slightest wrong tone, the most trivial task done incorrectly. Sometimes, in the morning, we would wake up and the mailbox would be knocked off its post and lying battered in the street. I always thought it had to do with my parents' fights. My father would put the mailbox in the garage and go to work. He'd spend the evening pounding the mailbox back into shape, nailing it back onto its post. The next morning we'd wake up and there it would be, crushed on the sidewalk. My father would shake his head grimly, sigh, and bring the decapitated box back in to fix again.

One night, my father parked his car outside in the driveway and not only was the mailbox off its post the next morning, but all the windows in our car had been shattered. There were so many pieces of glass inside the car that my father couldn't get in to drive it to the mechanic. We had to get it towed. He missed work that day, and spent it nailing the mailbox back on. He called the police.

It was probably some neighborhood prank, the policeman said on arrival, and my parents nodded and said yes, these things happen. But even then, I knew that these things only happened to our mailbox, our car. Secretly, I thought it was my parents' anger, too explosive to contain. I thought their fights broke the windows in our car, knocked the mailbox off its hinge. There were silences at dinner that lasted for days, then the fights resumed without warning, ignited as suddenly as flame. I worried about how tired my father was each night, and the way my mother got sadder and sadder, and how the meanness between them wore away at their love.

One morning the mailbox had been knocked so far off the post it was in our neighbor's yard. I watched from the window as my father crossed the lawn to retrieve it from where it lay. Our neighbor wiped his hand on his pants before shaking hands with my father, and then they stood talking for a while, our dented mailbox swinging in my father's hand. The neighbor's boy, who was Hannah's age, laughed while my father talked to his father. I watched our neighbor reach over and touch his son's hair. I watched the boy prance around him, laughing, and I wondered if what we were really missing in my family was a boy.

My parents loved us. I never doubted that. But sometimes I still wonder if they would have traded me in for the son they wanted. I never asked. I did know that my mother aborted two girls before she refused to keep trying, and that her refusal sparked a coldness between my parents that lasted for years. One night, after a fight that continued downstairs long after I had gone to bed, my mother sneaked into my room. She was crying.

"Jeehyun," she said, lying down next to me on my twin-size bed. "You must not be like me. When you are a wife, do not fight. Obey your husband. Fulfill his wishes. Bear him a son. Jeehyun? Are you listening? Earn his love."

I crawled into her arms and felt her tremble against me. I did not cry. I told her instead that I would practice. I would obey. I would be everything a husband could want, everything my parents might wish.

If I had to mark a moment, I would say it was then, in the dark, that I first learned that love is a kind of disappearing.

9.

I had never been to Los Angeles before, and I wondered why Hannah had chosen to move there. I couldn't remember her ever mentioning it in the lists she'd occasionally draw up of potential places to live. I arrived in Los Angeles determined to be as businesslike as possible with Hannah. But when she answered the phone for the first time since she left, she sounded so cautious that I was overwhelmed by a sudden surge of protectiveness, as if she was still a kid.

"It's me," I said. "Janie."

There was a brief silence. "What do you want?" she asked.

I looked around my hotel room, at the dingy cover of my bed, and the slightly damp carpet. The goodwill I had felt upon hearing Hannah's voice dissolved. What did she think I wanted from her? What did she think I would do? "I'm in L.A.," I said. "I came to see you."

Another pause: an intake of breath. "Are Mom and Dad with you?"

"No."

"All right," Hannah said, and her voice was firm and level. "I can see you, then."

That evening I waited at the beach across from my hotel, where Hannah had agreed to meet after dinner. Neither of us had suggested eating together. As it was, I had no appetite. So I went to the beach early, to stretch my legs and walk off my tension while I waited.

Clumps of seaweed and dead fish washed onto the shore and drifted out again. The water looked dirty, but I took my shoes off and stood in the damp, cool sand. Across the ocean, I thought, my parents were hovering somewhere in the distance, moving toward another continent. Beyond them, the sun was sinking into the horizon. "Five minutes," I said out loud, playing my father's game. I looked at my watch.

In the darkening light, I looked over the crowd of people beginning to gather up their things to leave. I saw Hannah coming from the landmark we had chosen as our meeting place, the foot of the stairs that led to Washington Avenue. The shock of seeing her was sudden after all. I pinched my arms. There she was, in front of me. She was dressed all in white linen, and her pants billowed out slightly in the breeze.

"Hey," she said.

All through her childhood, she had wanted to look like me: to wear the clothes I wore, to be my height, to sleep in my bed. I'd still thought of her as a little kid when I left for college, the shadow listening in on my phone conversations, trying to read my books, always wanting to know what I was doing that was more interesting. "Did Unni have to do it, too?" was her most common refrain. "Did Unni do it when she was little?"

She snooped through everything: she read my diary, put her feet in my shoes, she even spilled the small plastic bottle of perfume I'd made my mother buy me at the grocery store. She wanted to follow me everywhere. Sometimes when I said something, she mimicked me. My parents thought it was funny, but I wanted to hit her.

I caught her in my room once, sitting in my chair at my desk, in a dress my grandmother had sent me by ship from Korea. It was a dress I hadn't even gotten to wear yet. She had found my diary, which I kept hidden in my desk inside an old notebook. She had also found the key to my diary, which I kept hidden inside a lone sock in the back of my sock drawer.

She was sitting in my chair, bent over my diary with her crayons in hand. She had opened the diary to the page where I listed the names of all the boys I had ever had crushes on: a boy from my old neighborhood, a boy from school, the first boy to give me a flower, the first boy I had ever wanted to give me a kiss, and, since moving to Michigan, Jesus.

When I crossed the room and pulled the diary out of her hands, I saw that she had written her own name in crooked capital letters at the bottom of this list, and drawn hearts over the names of the boys. Furiously, I pulled the chair she was in to the middle of the room. I started chanting at her, partly in English, partly in Korean, partly in a wild sort of rhythmic gibberish. I danced around her, blocking her every time she tried to get up. It was a sort of wild imitation of a mudang, a shaman woman I'd seen in Korea once, who'd danced at a distant uncle's funeral.

When I finished, Hannah was shaking in her chair, crying.

"I curse you," I said, panting and exhilarated. I pointed my finger at her face, and she cowered, raising her hands to shield herself. "I call on the ghosts and skeletons and creepy things to find you and take you away." I laughed. When I snatched at her wrist to drag her out of my room, she screamed.

Once I was gone at college, she stopped wanting to be like me, and turned into someone else entirely. She stopped wanting what I had, and started acquiring the things I would never have. She grew taller, surpassed me, and people began to notice her.

My mother once said to me, "It is easier for some people to be loved than others." I don't remember the context, and am sure she did not mean to compare Hannah to me. But it applied: Hannah was easier to love. Even when we first started school in America, she made friends easily. I never really understood how she did it.

When she was still in high school I would come home and see how everyone looked at her, how strangers, even adult men, would pause in the street to look at her, and how easily she held their attention. I had always hated when people looked at me: it made me uncomfortable. Their interest made me feel suddenly awkward, as if I was under an intense light, onstage, jerkily moving around.

No one could call Hannah awkward, though. My parents' friends were always asking if she was a dancer or a gymnast. Now, against her loose linen clothes, her body was tan and glowing, and I was aware of the bags under my eyes, of being older, of having aged in the last few months.

"You look great," I said. "Good for you."

She smiled at me, as if that had been a peace offering on my part and she was deciding whether or not to accept.

I said, "Let's walk."

We walked up the beach, not looking at each other. She said, "How's your dissertation going?"

I shrugged. "Who cares," I said. "I've had other things to worry about." I was keenly aware that I was here at my parents' bidding. Meanwhile she had made a life for herself here. How had she done that?

She started to say something, stopped, started again. But before she could continue, a strange barking howl sounded directly ahead of us, drowning out her voice and startling us both. We looked toward the noise, and saw that a small crowd had gathered around a ditch. Surrounded by a semicircle of people, a seal was trapped there. It bellowed and flopped.

"Hang on," Hannah said. "Let me check this out." She walked to the ditch. "Has anyone sent for help?" she asked the crowd. They shook their heads, and began talking to her all at once.

"I think it's hurt," someone said. "I don't know how long it's been there," said another. Hannah waved them all quiet and pulled out her phone. She called Animal Control, gave our location, said a few more words, clicked her phone shut, and came back to me.

People kept coming up to us and trying to talk to her, but she said, "Help is coming," and nothing more. We stood, a little apart, watching the seal writhe. Its skin shone against the dull sand.

"A lot of seals have been beached out here lately," Hannah said, turning to me. "One even attacked a few fishing boats and a swimmer last week."

"Whoa," I said. "Why?"

"They have brain damage from the pollution," Hannah said. She shrugged. "It makes the males more aggressive, and it makes the females miscarry. They have seizures all day long. That's probably what happened to this one."

"That's terrible," I said. In the ditch, the seal sobbed. The crowd around us was growing. A woman pulled out her camera and started snapping photographs. The seal flapped closer to the shore, then reversed and began to flap back toward the ditch.

Animal Control came and trained a spotlight on the seal. The water, when it sprayed out of the hose, smelled filthy. The seal howled. She gasped in the frothy green water, the fierce blast propelling her forward. They will kill her, I thought. I turned to Hannah, but she had already taken several steps away, ready to move on. "Animal Control can handle it now," Hannah said, and started walking away before I could respond.

When we were younger, my mother had told us stories about the seal-people who could turn into humans when they came to shore. If they lost their seal skin they'd be stranded on land forever. My mother had told us a story about a seal-woman who had lost her skin one night and found herself stranded: unknowing, she married the man who had hidden her skin, and had human children with him. When one day she found her skin in the attic, she slipped into it and swam away, leaving behind her husband and children.

My mother had also told a similar story about a heavenly maiden whose clothes had been stolen when she came to earth to bathe. When at long last she discovered her clothes, she put them on and gathered up her children. Her husband, who had stolen and hidden her heavenly clothes, begged and wept, clutching at the hem of her dress as she rose to heaven.

Growing up, Hannah and I had played at being seal-women. We'd played at heavenly maidens. We'd played at abandoning each other, over and over again.

I followed my sister up the long steps to the street above the beach. "Are you seeing anyone?" I asked at the top of the stairs.

She shook her head. "Nope."

I was vaguely disappointed. I'd almost hoped that she was involved with a man. It seemed like something that could account for her cruelty. I said, "So Dad's sick."

She blinked. "What do you mean, sick?"

"Yeah. He has cancer. They sold the house."

She stopped walking, but otherwise she took it calmly. "Wow," she said. "What are his chances?" She looked at me intently, and for a moment I wanted to tell her everything. I wanted to describe how after his prognosis, my father had held out his fingers, spread out his hands before him and studied them, counting out the months. "I feel perfectly fine," he'd said then, laughing. And my mother and I had laughed with him, as if we all believed this new information was a joke that could be laughed away.

"I think that's something you're going to have to ask him yourself," I said.

She touched my arm. "Come on, Unni," she said. "Let's be friends." She smiled at me. As if all the trouble between us had been nothing at all. I thought of my mother weeping as she walked from room to room in our house. I thought of the voice mail I'd left Hannah after she'd abandoned us, and of the hours I'd spent waiting, afterward, worrying.

"What's going to happen to that seal?" I asked.

"I have no idea."

"Do you remember your friend's baby that fell out of the window?" I asked. "I went to the trial for the boys who did that."

"Oh yeah? What happened?" She sounded totally casual, and this made me angry. I'd been so sure that story had been connected to her leaving.

"The boys went to a juvenile prison," I said. "All three of them." I suddenly wondered if they had been separated in prison, or if they saw each other every day. I wondered how that made them feel. My chest hurt. "Did you care about that baby?" I asked. "Did you care about those boys?"

"Unni," Hannah said, the word for older sister: I could feel it pulling on me like a tide. She said, "I've stopped wasting time on things I can't save."

I wished I could tell her how anxious my parents had been, how much she'd been missed. I thought of my grandmother telling me to always keep my sister safe. I remembered our father bowing to his trees. "What do you know," I said, "about who you can save?"

10.

In sixth grade, Japanese cars flooded the market, and the auto industry in Michigan went into crisis. That year the father of a girl in my class killed a Chinese man; he claimed he thought his victim was Japanese. With six witnesses to the murder, the judge let him off with manslaughter and a fine.

When all this happened, I was in Mrs. Yates's class with my best friends, Allison and Heather. I had a crush on a boy named Curtis. He had told Erin Fuller to fuck off once during silent reading time, his voice slicing through the quiet of the room. I had looked up from my book just as Erin started to cry. Curtis was sent to the principal's office, Mrs. Yates ordering him out without even pausing to glance at Erin. I admired the way he got up and left the room, like it didn't bother him at all. Like he enjoyed it.

I didn't tell Allison and Heather about my crush on Curtis. I didn't tell them when he passed me a note in class one day that said, *I like you, do you want to go with me? Check one.* I didn't check either the yes or the no box, but put the note in my backpack and took it home with me, where I put it in my desk drawer to look at whenever I wanted.

At Allison's house we ate brownies and played with her Barbie collection. She had twenty-three of them, and each time I visited, it seemed, their collective wardrobe had increased. Some days we counted them. Heather had only three Barbies, in the outfits they'd originally come in.

Heather showed us porno magazines at her house, the ones her older brother kept hidden in his baseball card collection. Once, while Allison and I turned the pages, shrieking, Heather got on all fours and stuck out her chest. She raised her butt in the air and arched her back. She pouted. Her frizzy brown hair stuck out in wisps. "How do I look?" she asked. "Sexy?"

"Like a hooker," Allison said.

At my place, we played house. Allison was the mother, Heather was the older sister, and I was the baby. Heather always wanted to spank me, but Allison pretended to feed me from Hannah's old bottle, and stroked my head when I pretended to cry. We looked deep into each other's eyes, and whenever we did this, I felt vaguely ashamed. Nobody in sixth grade was supposed to play house, so we swore not to tell anyone. To seal the promise, we spent two weeks making friendship bracelets using my mother's special silk embroidery thread.

My mother used to embroider beautiful peacocks, roses, and cranes that she framed and gave to relatives. When I lived in Korea I had loved the pictures my mother made, and wanted to learn how. But after we moved to America her workbasket lay untouched until I brought it out. The basket itself had a peacock embroidered on the cover, and inside were nestled lovely spools of silk thread swirling around each other in bright whorls of color.

The first time I'd shown Allison and Heather, Allison had said, "Wow," and reached out her finger to touch the shining spools. I'd been proud then to have something special to offer.

In any case, the three of us were inseparable. During recess we played on the monkey bars and swings. "This is *reserved*," we said to the fifth graders who tried to use them. Sometimes we organized games of the Blob, which was our favorite game. We played the Blob on a field or court, and everyone had to stay within bounds. One kid was It. Whoever he caught had to join hands with him, and the kid at the end of the chain was whipped around by the arm of the Blob as he tried to grab whoever was still free. If you played long enough and there were enough kids, the Blob always became so large that it could reach all the boundaries, and the last person was always eventually cornered and caught.

I was really good at staying out of reach, but I liked being part of the Blob, too. I liked succumbing to the wave of motion passing from one end of the chain to the next. It was a powerful feeling to watch the ends on either side swerve and close in on someone, to feel the tug that ran through everyone's held hands. At those moments, I felt like the heart of something big.

One day Mrs. Yates asked us to hold on a minute before she let us out for recess. "You'll probably find out that there's been some trouble in Erin's family," she said. "Her father was involved in a fight, and a man died. The whole thing is a horrible shame."

Then the bell rang, and we sat in our seats, not sure if she was finished. Mrs. Yates looked lost in that unaccustomed silence.

At recess, Heather told us what she knew about Mr. Fuller. "He killed some Chinese guy," she said. She was perched on top of the monkey bars, her legs hanging over. "My father said the Chink had it coming to him."

I tried out a new flip on one of the single bars.

"Hey, Janie, no offense," Heather said.

Allison, who had been sitting on her own side of the monkey bars, quietly chewing her hair, let the strands fall limp and wet to her shoulder. "Oh, Heather, shut up," she said.

That same afternoon I had an appointment with an orthodontist to have braces put on. I didn't want them, but my parents said it was for my own good.

My teeth were so sore after the braces were put on that I didn't even want to stop at the supermarket, but my mother took me in anyway. When we walked past the card section, I thought of Erin. I couldn't help thinking of my own father's troubles when we left Korea, and I felt sorry for her, with her father in jail. I asked my mother if I could send her a card. I found a few that read, "Sharing Your Sorrow" and "In Your Time of Need," but my mother said they weren't appropriate.

At home I had to set the table for dinner, even though I could tell I wouldn't be able to eat anything. It hurt too much. My lips scraped along the wires that connected the metal brackets, and when I clicked my teeth together by accident, pain shot through my gums.

That night Hannah tried to sneak into bed with me, but my head ached and I felt hot, and I kicked her out when she tried to crawl in, burying my face in my pillow when she tapped on my shoulder over and over, whispering my name. When I woke up shivering the next morning, she was curled at the foot of my bed, wrapped up in all my blankets.

I was one of only a few kids who had braces in the sixth grade, and when Erin came back to school she called me Robot. Nobody really talked to her for the first few days, but when she started telling the story of the fight between her father and the dead man, they gathered round to listen. In her version the Chinese man knew karate and screamed, "Ching chong ching chong," when he attacked her father. The other kids laughed when Erin impersonated the dead man. In her story the dead man struck first: he hit her father while his back was turned. After that, some of the other kids in my class started calling me Robot, too.

It got worse. "Who's gonna kiss you?" a few kids chanted one day outside class. They took a show of hands. When Curtis raised his hand I started to smile, but then everybody laughed like it was a joke, and Curtis laughed with them. I was embarrassed to open my mouth with all the metal sticking out like wiring.

After that, Allison and Heather started turning away a little when I played with them, as if I wasn't really in their group. They organized a game of the Blob without me, and when we played they didn't try to catch me. I was the last person to be caught, but I knew it was nothing to be proud of.

Halloween was my favorite American holiday, but that year I went to school without a costume. "Only babies wear costumes to school," Allison said.

Heather agreed. "We should wait for trick-or-treating."

So on Halloween, as we stood outside the school waiting for the morning bell to ring, Curtis came up to me. He was wearing a blue robe and a pointy hat. "I guess you didn't wear a costume," he said.

I tried to smile back, but the insides of my lips scraped against the braces, and I kept my mouth closed. Then Curtis's friend Greg came toward us. He put on a mask, snapping the elastic behind his head. The mask was a great ugly face of a bucktoothed man with narrow slits for eyes.

"I'm Janie's boyfriend," Greg said. Curtis looked at me, then Greg, and laughed.

My father had seen this costume at the grocery store a couple of weeks ago and had wanted to complain. My mother had held him back and said, "*Please.*"

"It's wrong," my father said.

"Don't cause trouble," my mother said.

I'd read what it said on the package: "Chinaman Costume." My parents had already started walking away. As they walked, they bent their heads together angrily, forming a wall that shut us out. Hannah chattered along beside me, but I hushed her up and tried to listen.

"Haven't you learned anything?" my mother said. "If you have to cause trouble, we can go back to Korea where at least if something happens to you, we have family to help us." She stopped walking and faced him. She took a breath. "I want to go back," she said, as if she'd been waiting a long time to say it.

My father flinched, but did not seem surprised. "I have a job here," he said.

"We live in a place that sells Chinaman costumes." Her voice shook. I didn't know why she cared so much. We weren't even Chinese. "I want to leave."

"We're here now, and we can't just pack up and go," my father said. "I have this family to support."

"If you care so much about our well-being, then act like it," my mother hissed.

My father reached for her arm, but she wrenched away, and left us standing there, at the edge of the produce aisle.

My father stood, fixed in place behind the shopping cart. I tugged at his hand. "Daddy," I said. "Could we really go back?"

He smiled down at me. "I thought you liked it here," he said. "I thought you said it was better than Korea."

He'd been so angry when I'd said that. I didn't feel it was fair to use it against me now. It was cheating.

"Please?" I said. "Daddy?"

My father pulled his hand out of mine and rubbed his face.

In the meantime Hannah had run after my mother, and was trying to hug her around the waist. My mother pushed Hannah away impatiently.

"Never mind," I said quickly, reaching for my father's hand. "It's all right. We can stay."

My father looked down at me and smiled. Suddenly he drew himself up straighter and bounced once on his heels. He took my hand and growled a little, like a tiger, waving my hand. I growled back. We were tough.

And now in the schoolyard Greg was wearing the Chinaman costume. He said, "Don't you want to kiss your boyfriend?" He waggled his tongue at me from the hole in the mask between his buckteeth. Everyone was watching. I could feel their eyes on me, including Allison's and Heather's, waiting. I knew something had changed: I knew I had to say something in response to change it back. But I could think of nothing. Then the morning bell rang, and Mrs. Yates let us in. "Oh, what great costumes!" she said, as we filed by.

That night I waited for Allison and Heather to come to my house. Hannah left with her friends, a little band of witches and bunnies, bumping their pumpkin baskets excitedly against their knees. I was dressed as a bunch of grapes: I had spent three hours pinning the balloons onto my all-green clothes, and had painted my face purple. But Allison and Heather never came.

The next day I didn't try to talk to either of them. At recess I went by myself to the edge of the schoolyard and searched for late-blooming flowers to braid into a wreath. My mother had taught me how to make them, and I had taught Allison and Heather, and then we had agreed to keep the method a secret after we saw how the other girls wanted to learn, and how our knowledge made us separate. As I linked the flowers together I wondered who I would be friends with now, what I could offer that anyone might want. I didn't mind being alone: it wasn't that. It was the humiliation that bothered me: that I had been singled out as the one to make fun of and pick on. I didn't know if there was any recovering from that.

I looked up to scan the schoolyard, to see what everyone was doing. A group of my classmates had gathered, and they were slowly making their way toward me. They were between me and the school, and when I saw them coming I started heading back to the main building, trying to loop out so I could avoid them, but they spread and caught me easily. They formed a semicircle around me. Everyone was there. My entire class.

I stood there and faced them, and in my head I told myself to think of Queen Min, who had been the hero of the girls in my grade school in Korea. We'd learned that she'd been torn apart by Japanese soldiers when she refused to accept Japan's occupation of Korea. In response they'd hacked her to pieces, and then although she'd kept her legs closed, they'd pried her open and hacked her to pieces there as well. They'd lit her on fire twice. I told myself now that to Queen Min, this would be nothing. I pretended my classmates were Japanese soldiers, and I was a queen, and I stood there and looked at them without flinching. To stay detached like this seemed like its own kind of power.

"Does Janie have no one to play with?" Erin said. "Did she come out here to cry?"

"I'm not crying," I said. I stared at her so she could see for herself. Allison and Heather were standing next to her, and Allison looked away when I tried to make eye contact.

Allison and Heather had stickers of scorpions stuck to their right hands. They weren't wearing their friendship bracelets. I was still wearing mine. "Why are you doing this?" I asked. Neither of them replied.

Greg asked, "Who did you go trick-or-treating with last night?"

"I went with my mom," I said. I knew the moment I said it that it was a mistake. Heather snorted. My classmates laughed.

"You should have called," I said to Allison. "You said I was your best friend." I hated myself for saying that. It sounded like begging. Allison flinched, though, and avoided the furtive, hurt glance Heather shot at her.

"It's not true," Allison said. "I never said that."

Erin stepped forward. She reached out and pushed my face with the palm of her hand, hard, so it hurt. "Look at Janie's face," she said. "It's as flat as paper."

My classmates laughed. "Why don't you go back to Japan with

the rest of the robots?" Erin continued. She knew I wasn't from Japan.

"Why don't you go back to jail where your father is?" I said.

Erin gasped. Her face screwed up tight and small, and she reached her arm back. When she swung, I caught her right arm and then her left. I held her arms back as she tried to hit me again. I remembered the story she'd told about her father and how the Chinese man had yelled, "Ching chong ching chong," and for no reason I could think of, I yelled this at her as loud as I could.

"Ching chong," I screamed. "Ching chong ching chong ching chong." When I saw the fear in her face, I laughed.

"Let me go," she yelled. She started to cry.

"Let her go," someone said from the group. I looked up to see who had spoken and saw the faces of all my classmates watching me, appalled.

Then the short bell rang, announcing the end of recess. I shoved Erin away, rushed past the kids who surrounded me, and ran. I wanted to get away from them all, to run past the school and into the woods, and I wanted to keep running until I got home. I wished I was big enough, giant, to scoop up my parents and Hannah and to keep on running until the kids and the school were far behind me.

Behind me, Greg yelled, "Get her!" I pumped my legs faster and faster, past the trees, then the wide lawn of the field, and I was on the sidewalk. I was exhilarated: I was faster than them. If I could push my legs a little harder, I would be able to lift off the ground and fly away until the school was only the tiniest speck. If I could make it to the bench outside our classroom, I would be safe.

I looked behind me. Only Allison was close. It felt good to run. I almost forgot I was being chased. I almost laughed. They were still yelling, "Catch her!" The bench was there, sitting calmly against the wall, only a few steps away. I began to slow down.

And then I felt Allison's hand between my shoulders. My head snapped back, and I fell forward. I couldn't stop. I threw my hands up to block the wall, but it was coming too fast, and I felt my palms tear as they hit the brick. My head bounced when it hit the wall. I lost my body. The sun flickered. The world wobbled. The next thing I saw was someone's shoe, and then Greg's blurry face peering down at me.

I sat up. My hands rose to my face. Blood spilled into them, filling my hands and dripping onto the ground. There were little white pieces like pebbles, like sand, floating in the blood, and I cupped my hands together, trying to keep the pieces from washing out.

I am not going to cry, an urgent voice said from inside my head. *Don't cry.* The voice startled me. It seemed completely separate from me.

Someone's hand gripped my arm. "Let's get you cleaned up," a woman's voice said, with authority. I didn't know who she was, this adult who had appeared from out of nowhere, but I felt my legs pushing themselves up in response, and in my head, the voice ordered again, *Don't cry.* But just beneath my stomach I felt a wail beginning to rise like a wind, and to my shame it rose and rose, apart from me.

The woman kept a firm grip on my shoulder, and walking me into the school, said, "Let's go."

Then I sat in the principal's office for an hour, bleeding slowly into a box of Kleenex until the secretary came back from her lunch break and called my mother.

"The first thing she needs is a dentist," the secretary said when my mother walked into the office.

My mother looked at me, checked herself mid-step, and nodded. She walked past me to have a brief conversation with the secretary, and thanked her for watching over me. Then she very calmly took me by the hand, and led me out of the school and into the parking lot. There, she knelt and looked at my face; she reached out and touched my cheek, softly, softly. Her face was quite still as her fingertips ran down my cheek. She was smiling, as if nothing so terrible had happened, as if everything was all right. I felt such a rush of relief then that I began to cry.

My mother leaned forward and held me, kneeling in the gravel. When I finally stopped, she pulled away and touched my face again, still smiling that same beautiful smile, and I thought in that moment that things would be okay. We got in the car, and she drove us straight to the dentist. She did not ask me then, or ever, what had happened.

I couldn't feel anything. Everything had gone numb. It was Dr. Stanley's day off, so he had to open his office to handle my case. Darlene, the hygienist, held my hand. She was beautiful, with long blond hair, and she looked like a beauty queen, like no one I'd ever met before. When Hannah had first seen her she'd asked if she was the tooth fairy. Now, I squeezed her cool hand shyly. Darlene told me that once when she was little, she had knocked three of her teeth clear out of her mouth. She smiled; with her left hand she pointed at them: they were perfect. "See? If they could fix me, they can fix you," she said.

For a moment I almost believed her. But when I looked in the mirror Darlene gave me, I almost dropped it, the face looking back was so unfamiliar. There was a lump on my forehead and my lips were too big. Everything was muddy black. When I opened my mouth, wires stuck out of my shredded gums: my front teeth had disappeared.

Dr. Stanley came by, then, and I lay back and let him work on me. "Don't spit for the next few days," he said, as he finished. "Or you might end up spitting teeth." My teeth had been knocked back up into my head. That was why I couldn't see them. It was better to leave them there, he said, to work themselves down on their own. We would have to wait and see.

Back at home I held ice packs to my face and felt like a hero. I hadn't done anything brave, but as my parents fussed over me, I was aware that I was precious to them. Hannah watched us and whimpered. I let her crawl into my lap.

Just before bedtime, I began to throw up, and that knocked loose a tooth that had been crammed halfway up my gums. It fell suddenly and hung, crippled and dangling. When I felt it, loose as a string, my mind went very quiet. I was calm when I went to my parents to show them, my mouth dribbling blood and puke. They took one look at me and got straight out of bed.

We dropped Hannah off at Mrs. Chong's house on our way to the hospital. She was the only other Asian in our town, and sometimes she watched us when my parents were busy. Her furniture was covered with thick, uncomfortable plastic, and she liked to give us her children's old games to play with, dilapidated and always missing some crucial piece.

"I don't want to," Hannah wailed, clinging to me in the car

when my parents came to take her out, but my parents were firm, and she was pulled out and handed over, screaming.

A t the hospital, the doctor was brusque. "Why didn't you bring her in right away?" he asked. My mother started to answer, but he waved her off. "We're going to have to run some tests and take some X-rays," he said. "Head injuries are very dangerous." He said this angrily, and then turned to me, taking three quick steps forward so that he stood between my parents and me. When he looked at me, though, his face was soft, the anger tucked away.

"Are you ready for some scans, kiddo?" he asked, his voice totally different.

I nodded, and the movement made the room whirl.

"Come with me, then," he said. "We'll bring you back to your parents in a little bit."

"Okay," I said, and for whatever reason, I wasn't nervous. I followed him.

He took my hand and led me to another room where a nurse helped me change into a paper dress that opened in the back. It reminded me of the paper dolls I used to play with, of the dresses my mother had cut out of colored paper. After I was dressed, the nurse took me into a bright room where she told me to lie down on a belt that would feed me into a tunnel. "You're going to hang out in a machine," the doctor said. "It won't hurt, so don't worry; it's just something that will make sure you're a-okay. You won't feel a thing."

I nodded.

"You can close your eyes, but don't sleep," he said. "Can you do that for me?"

"Yes."

He patted me gently on the cheek, with the tips of his fingers, like he thought it might hurt me to be touched.

From the outside, the scanner looked like a tunnel glowing spooky blue from within. It was something out of television or outer space. The belt pulled me slowly along, and as I was fed into the open mouth of the cone, I thought how I would tell everyone about the way I entered the machine. I was in a cocoon of light. *I was held in a cocoon of blue light,* I would say. I could imagine their disbelief, their envy. *No really, I was.*

Then I realized with a dim shock that there was no one to tell. With all the light moving through me I felt invisible. It was warm in there, and the blue glow steeped into my skin. I imagined I was disappearing. I thought of my parents, waiting somewhere outside. I thought of Hannah sitting on Mrs. Chong's plastic sofa. When I closed my eyes, the light leaked through my eyelids. Even the dark was soft and blue. I imagined my parents, pale and green under the fluorescent lights, clattering on the cold linoleum of the hospital. I felt warm and safe, and I imagined I was being transported. I was being beamed up to my home planet. On my home planet, everything that had been broken would be healed. I would emerge whole, my face and teeth intact.

Afterward, the doctor told us I had a concussion from the accident that would keep me dizzy for the next couple of days. My brain had bounced and bruised itself against my skull. He showed us the X-rays, pointed to the fissures in the bones of my face. Then he looked at my parents. "Could I have a moment alone with the patient?" he said.

I expected them to protest, but the nurse opened the door to usher them out, and they left. As soon as the door shut behind them, the doctor turned to me. "What exactly happened?" he asked.

"A girl pushed me," I said, wondering if I was in trouble. I wondered if my parents had been taken to the waiting room, or if they were just outside the door. "It wasn't my fault."

"Of course it wasn't," he said, leaning forward. "What I want to know, Janie, is how another little girl could push you so hard that you got hurt this badly."

"It was an accident," I said, feeling strangely flattered that he'd remembered my name.

The doctor shifted his weight from one leg to the other. "Look," he said. He lifted his chart and tapped it. "Do you get hurt like this often?"

I thought of scraped elbows and knees, and the time playing tag when I had slid four feet in gravel and scraped all the skin off my butt. Treacherously, I thought of Hannah and the pitcher of glass she had dropped on my foot. I thought of my parents making us pick branches from the backyard to switch us with when we misbehaved. I stopped abruptly.

"Not really."

"Janie," he said my name again. "You can tell me. How did this happen?"

"During recess at school," I said.

"Did your parents have anything to do with this?" he asked. The light glinted off his glasses. "Do they hit you?"

I was tempted to nod. I thought of the time my mother had

117

grabbed my hair in her hand and shaken me back and forth; the time my father had thrown a book that caught me on the side of my head. I remembered the sharp booming sound that filled my head when it made contact, and how the sound echoed in my ears for days.

I knew enough about America to imagine reporting them to the police then. *You're not allowed to do this in America,* I'd say. *It's illegal.* In those daydreams they always ended up crying and apologizing, and I took them back after they promised never to hit me again.

But this was different. The doctor thought my parents had done this to me: my smashed face, my broken teeth. I felt suddenly afraid of my thoughts, of the knowledge that my parents were not safe from me, and I could do them harm.

"You're shaking," the doctor said. He reached out his hand and stroked my shoulder very gently with the backs of his fingers. "Tell me. Who did this to you?"

What would happen if I said my parents had done this to me? Would someone come to take me away? Would I be sent to a different school? I imagined living in this doctor's house, being his daughter, sleeping in a pink canopy bed.

I pulled away from his hand. "We were racing at school," I said. "It was an accident."

"What happened?" he asked.

I shrugged. "Allison and I bumped into each other. I guess we were going too fast."

The doctor shook his head slowly. Then he threw back his shoulders and laughed. "All right," he said. He opened the door and called my parents back in. When they entered, he smiled at them and wagged his finger at me. "You be more careful, young lady, you were lucky this time."

. . .

On the ride home, I told my parents the story I'd told the doctor. Allison had bumped into me while we were racing. I had tripped and hit the wall. All of it had been an accident. Clumsiness. Bad luck. Even from behind, I could see some tension in my parents' bodies ease away. I basked in the warmth of their relief. I almost believed what I said was true. We were going home, and I was safe from the glow of the houses lining the streets outside.

We stopped by Mrs. Chong's on our way home to pick Hannah up, and when we arrived she was still awake, wide-eyed and silent. In the car, she pressed against me, mute, her head burrowing against my shoulder. I put my arm around her and told her things would be okay. It's over now, I said. Go to sleep.

I began to understand that night that my parents could not protect me, and that I could never let them know I knew this. Still, it was a strangely beautiful night, one in which I felt particularly close to my family, grateful to have them, relieved to be intact. When we got home, by some unspoken consensus and for the first time in years, we all huddled up together in my parents' bed, Hannah and I cushioned between my mother and father. That night we were especially gentle with each other, careful and loving, as if each of us had some secret hurt that could not be touched. In the dark, my mother's arm formed a careful circlet around me, Hannah's legs entangled my own. "Good night!" we called to each other. "Good night! Good night! Good night!" I could feel my mother's pulse beating gentle and measured through her wrist against my cheek. I listened to my family breathe, steady and warm. I fell asleep quickly, shielded by the fortress of their bodies, their fragile bones.

11.

Hannah and I sat in the lobby of my hotel: I had refused to visit her apartment, and had not invited her to my room. Instead, we sat in adjacent armchairs, making awkward conversation.

"I'm back in school," Hannah volunteered. "I'll be finishing up the rest of my credits at UCLA in a year."

I looked at her feet. Each toenail was perfectly painted a dark shiny blue. I said, "Why didn't you call? Couldn't you have done that just to tell us you were alive?"

"I wanted to," she said, and she pulled her feet up onto her chair and tucked them under her legs. "But then you would have told Mom and Dad where I was, and it wouldn't have worked."

"What wouldn't have worked?" I asked. "Dad was worried sick. Literally. Stress causes cancer, Hannah. It makes the tumors grow."

Hannah held up her hand. "I can't play that game," she said. "You can't blame me for that. I've been working. I'm putting myself through school."

"What, do you want a prize? Everyone does that, Hannah. It's called being a grown-up. Plenty of people manage to do it without having to disappear."

"Unni," she said. "I wanted a chance to be my own person. I wanted to be independent. Can't you cut me some slack?"

"Running away from home and then secretly going back to school doesn't make you independent."

"And neither does doing everything to please your parents."

"I don't do everything to please them," I said. "I just try to be decent."

"I'm trying to make it possible for us to be friends now, but this always makes it so difficult. It's never just us."

"You could have said that back then," I said. "Before you broke all our hearts."

"I never meant to hurt you."

"But you didn't care that you did."

"I had to leave. You all wanted me to be someone I wasn't."

"So what, Hannah? I don't even know what you mean by that, but even if it's true, so what?"

Hannah's smile was twisted. "Other families aren't like this, you know. Not everyone is like you." She shook her head. "Anyways, you left first," she said. "When you went off to college you said you weren't going to come back, you said we were on our own."

"I never said that."

"You did. And you meant it. You said you were sick of being controlled all the time, and you were done being told what to think. You felt the same way as me. You said you hated it at home."

"Everyone says things like that when they're teenagers. It doesn't mean anything, Hannah."

She leaned forward. "Maybe, but you meant it." The look on

her face made me uncomfortable. "When you came home in the middle of your sophomore year, you were different; you were dating that guy, and you wouldn't talk to any of us."

"That was a hard year."

"You left first. It was you."

"I went to college," I said. "Jesus Christ, Hannah. Did you expect me to stay home and wait for you?"

"You know what I mean," she said. "And here's the thing: when it didn't work out with that guy, you came crawling back to us, but I knew better. I knew you'd have left us then, if you could have."

I stiffened. "It was more complicated than that," I said. "You were too young to know anything about it."

Hannah looked me straight in the eye, and smirked. "I know enough," she said.

My sophomore year of college I'd dated a guy who hit me. He was the first guy I ever slept with, and the marks he left took days or weeks to fade. Sometimes, days later, he'd softly push back my clothes, at my neckline or my sleeve, and stare at the disappearing bruises. Sometimes he would lick them. He touched me so gently in those moments, and it was the gentleness that actually scared me. I could never reconcile it with what else I knew.

So yes, I'd come home and been secretive. What could I have said? It all ended when one day the guy put his hands around my neck and choked me. I'd wanted him to stop, and I tried to tell him so, but when I opened my mouth to speak, his hands were around my throat, and I wasn't able to breathe.

My eyes had watered, and I reached up my hands and tried to pull his off, but he was looking at the ceiling, and wouldn't look down. His hands tightened beneath mine. I stared up at his chin, trying to pull back his fingers. He blurred a little in my vision, and in that moment I knew more clearly than anything that I could die, that this guy could kill me. And then I passed out.

When I woke he was gone and I was tangled up in sheets that smelled like him. My neck was sore, and his fingers had left puffy pink marks up and down the sides. Over the next few days they turned purple then black and faded away beneath the turtlenecks I wore.

After that, things changed. We stopped speaking, and he never hit me again, but he lived in my dorm, ate in my cafeteria hall, and I thought I could smell him everywhere. I stayed in my room as much as I could: I skipped my classes and meals. I couldn't breathe correctly, and worried he'd damaged my windpipe. I hated him for making me afraid; I hated him for not coming back. I only felt safe when I went home to be with my family.

I looked at Hannah. She understood nothing. "We thought you were dead," I said. I got up. "I'm done," I said, walking toward the elevator.

"Where are you going?"

"I have to get away from you."

Hannah stood and followed me.

"Go away," I said. "You're not six years old anymore." I clenched my hands.

A white-haired man approached from the lobby and sprang into the elevator when it opened. With great gallantry, he held the door and smiled. "Going up?" he asked.

I nodded. "Good-bye," I said to Hannah, but she followed me in.

The man pressed the button for his floor, but I did not step forward and press mine. We ascended sixteen floors. When the door opened, the man held out his hand to signal us out. Wordless, we stood our ground, looking away from him, looking away from each other. There was a moment of baffled silence, and then awkwardly the man lurched forward and exited. The elevator door closed. We began to descend.

"I thought we were talking," Hannah said. "I thought we were finally getting somewhere."

"It's too late."

"You don't believe that," she said. "Why did you come here if you believed that?"

The elevator door opened. We were back on the lobby floor, and a family with two young girls crowded into the elevator. Again we rode up, and again we waited on a floor that was not mine. The girls looked back over their shoulders at us as they walked away.

"Why did you come here?" Hannah asked when the elevator door closed. She folded her arms. "I can ride this thing forever."

I folded my own arms. "That makes two of us."

As we rode up and down in the elevator, neither of us willing to concede, I wanted to tell her that she could not always win. I stared at the Stop button on the elevator. I thought about hitting it and beating the crap out of her. I imagined us emerging from the elevator bloody and bruised. The thought was satisfying.

Finally, I hit the button for my floor. "I told Mom and Dad I'd find you," I said.

Hannah shrugged, that familiar motion.

"They went crazy over you," I said. "You ruined their lives."

"Okay, enough," Hannah said. "No one can really ruin someone else's life."

I wanted to tell her that she had ruined my life for the last year. Instead, I said, "Dad didn't get treated for cancer because he was waiting for you to come back."

"Don't put that on me," Hannah said. "I never asked him to do that. It's not my fault."

The elevator door opened.

"Yes." I stepped out of the elevator. "It is."

Undeterred, she followed me out.

"Don't follow me," I said, but she pushed herself into my room behind me.

"Get out," I said. "Nobody invited you in here."

"Whatever. So where are Mom and Dad now?"

"Korea." I was suddenly tired. "They'll be landing at the airport soon." They would be deplaning, collecting their four suitcases between them: that was what they had distilled from twenty years. That was what they'd been able to take with them.

Still, they'd have family to meet them. My grandmother and uncle, my father's cousins, and my Komo's family, too, except for Gabe, who'd been killed in a car accident while he was in college. I'd been in high school when it happened, and even though it had been years since we'd seen them, his death had been a shock to me. It was so sudden and violent, he was alive and then not, and his death made me aware of the fact that we had shared blood.

My father had told us the news in a grim voice. "I don't understand," he'd said, and the admission surprised me. I wondered what he wanted us to say. My mother went to him and took his hand.

She said, "Darling, it was an accident. Just a terrible accident."

I'd wanted to say something comforting, too. I had never seen him look so sad or defeated. But before I could say anything, Hannah laughed. We turned to her, astonished, but she kept laughing. She showed us all her teeth like a cat.

I looked at her now. I reminded myself she was not to be trusted.

"I'm not going to let you hang this around my neck for the rest of my life," she said.

I stood with my arms folded. When my father had first told me all his test results, before we knew the full prognosis, I sat down on the sofa and had nothing to say. I held up my hand when he began to list all the places they'd found the cancer. "It's in my liver," he said. "And I think maybe my lungs. Is that right?" He sounded baffled, almost amused.

He'd looked at my mother then, and she smiled at him encouragingly, but that lasted only a moment. She left the room hurriedly, pretending she had something else to do, but we heard her weeping through the walls.

My father had turned to me and smiled, after glancing after her in a dazed way. "I've lived a good life," he said. "Haven't I?"

I shook my head. "Don't say that."

"I'm happy," he said. "It's been a good life."

That night I looked up the disease while my parents were sleeping. Less than one percent of patients with my father's kind of cancer survived one year. I logged onto numerous groups, searched for miracles, and tried to find survivors. I told myself they were out there. It didn't matter how many out of one thousand or ten thousand survived. As long as one person could, as long as my father did, it would be enough for me. But I couldn't find a single one.

Hannah interrupted my thoughts. "So what happened to you your sophomore year in college?" she asked. "Are we ever going to talk about that?"

"It's none of your business."

Hannah smiled, a little twist of her face. "I wasn't the first one to give up on us," she said. "I just want you to admit it."

"But it's not true," I said. "You're wrong."

"Fine." She sighed. "So tell me: how long does Dad have?"

"That's a messed-up question."

"Is he terminal?"

I hated her for using those words. "Look," I said. "Don't worry. You don't have to come."

"Yeah, right."

"Seriously. They just wanted me to tell you they sold the house, and they're gone. They wanted you to know. They're done with you."

She didn't even blink. "I see," she said, and then she squared her shoulders and nodded.

I wanted to laugh. When we were little girls, I'd told Hannah that she was adopted, that she wasn't ours. "That's not true," she'd insisted, tugging at my sleeve.

But now, she nodded thoughtfully. She couldn't possibly believe it. It was such a stupid lie. We stood, staring at each other, tense, as if the moment could go either way.

"I guess I'll go then," Hannah said, and turned toward the door.

I felt a momentary triumph. She paused, her hand on the handle. She turned back to me and smiled. "You're just like them," she said. Then she turned away slowly, and walked out of my room. I watched as she turned the handle and stepped into the hallway. She was slow enough for me to go to her, slow enough for me to call her name at least five times before the door closed behind her and she was gone.

12.

My favorite story of all the stories my mother told me growing up was about a beautiful girl named Simchung. When she was born, her mother died, and her father went blind from grief. Because of this, he had to beg for his living, and as he went from door to door he also begged the village women to nurse his newborn daughter.

Simchung grew up into a dazzlingly beautiful girl who took such tender care of her father that she won the admiration of her entire village. "She is beautiful enough to marry a prince," they said. "What a shame her father cannot see how beautiful she is."

One day, while her father was walking the roadways begging for coins, he fell into a ditch. Simchung, at home, preparing dinner, knew nothing of this. That evening, when he didn't return, she grew frantic with worry. Anything could have happened, but she could only sit at home and wait.

Meanwhile, a passing monk on his way to the temple happened upon her father, and pulled him out of the ditch and took him to the temple. The monk gave Simchung's father dinner and a bed to sleep in for the night. Before going to bed, Simchung's father confessed to the monk how much he wished he could regain his sight. Then he could work and earn money and provide for his daughter, and she would not need to spend her entire life looking after him.

The monk listened to the blind man's story, and told him that for a donation of three hundred bags of rice to the temple, he and his fellow monks would make the necessary prayers to the Buddha to restore his sight. Simchung's father wept when he heard this: he knew he would never be able to beg that many bags of rice.

The next morning, after having breakfast with the monk, Simchung's father returned home to his daughter's anxious welcome. He recounted the tale of what had befallen him, and what the monk had said about the three hundred bags of rice. From then on, Simchung could think of nothing else.

Weeks later, a sailor came to their village. He was searching for a maiden willing to sacrifice herself by throwing herself into the ocean to placate the Dragon King. This would secure passage for his ship. When Simchung heard of this sailor's mission, she called him to her house, and agreed to go for the price of three hundred bags of rice to be donated to the temple on her father's behalf.

The sailor agreed. He was regretful: usually the women who agreed to make such a sacrifice were old or unattractive, with nothing he saw to offer the world. The loss of such a beauty was a waste and a shame, but there was nothing to be done, and so the next morning, he came to fetch her.

"Where are you going?" Simchung's father asked, eating his breakfast. "Who is our visitor?"

When she told him of the deal she'd made, her father threw himself at the sailor's feet, weeping and pleading for him to reconsider. But it was too late: the deal had been made, the bags of rice already purchased and given away.

So Simchung left her father weeping in their house, and followed the sailor to his ship. They sailed for several weeks, and each day the sea became more and more dangerous. Finally, a day arrived when the waves grew as tall as houses, and the sailor came to Simchung and told her the time had come. They had arrived at the place above the Dragon King's palace where the sacrifice must take place. And so Simchung fixed her dress and tied back her hair, and said that she was ready.

The sailors onboard wept as she walked past them: they had never seen a girl so beautiful. Yet they buried their fists in their mouths and watched her leap, praising the filial love that led her to death. Then they watched the waves crash over her. They watched the waves grow calmer and calmer. She was gone.

But that was not the end of Simchung: in stories, it never is. A week later, the King's courtiers were sailing the seas when they saw a giant lotus blossom floating on the surface of the water. It was the finest anyone had ever seen. As they approached, they were struck by its unparalleled beauty and sweet scent. They took this flower as a present to the King.

The King, delighted, ordered that this blossom be put on display in the middle of his palace hall so that everyone could admire his treasure. As the court stood around the flower admiring its beauty, the flower opened, and everyone gasped, for hidden inside was the beautiful maiden Simchung, asleep.

The King fell in love with the sleeping girl instantly. Believing her to be a gift from the heavens, he proposed marriage to her as soon as she awoke. The resulting wedding was the largest anyone had ever seen, and guests came from far and wide, from all over the kingdom to pay tribute. At the banquet there were fifty types of kimchi and fifty kinds of rice, and the dishes of meat and fish and fowl and vegetables were uncountable.

No one had ever seen a more beautiful or radiant bride. So when she broke down in tears during the banquet, the King was shocked. He insisted on knowing the reason for her unhappiness. Simchung, miserable, confessed that she felt guilty for this new-found happiness, when her father, all alone and blind, had no one to take care of him.

To make her happy, the King arranged a feast, and invited all the blind men in the realm to attend. To ensure they would all attend, an announcement went out: the feast would last one hundred days, and each guest would be honored with riches and granted audience with the King.

Thousands of blind men arrived for the feast, but Simchung's father was not among them. With each day, she became more convinced something had happened to him. She was horrified to think that perhaps he had died, and there was no one to tend his grave. She grew sadder and sadder each day, and sat silently at the head of the table. On the final day of the feast, one last man arrived, barefoot and dirty. His hair was unkempt, his clothes torn and ragged, his beard long.

This was Simchung's father, but she did not recognize him in his dirty clothes and long hair. She had always taken such good care of him. So he was seated with everyone else at the table, and the King asked him what he most wished for, and said he would try to grant the wish. At this question, the man began to weep. He said that he had come for the feast, since he'd been hungry for so long, but his dearest wish could not be granted: all he wanted was to hear his dear dead daughter's voice again.

As he spoke these words, he heard a familiar voice. "Father," it cried.

He leaped up, calling Simchung's name, and like a spell, the darkness fell away from his eyes. For the first time, he beheld his daughter. She was running to him, and had thrown herself into his arms even before he had finished speaking her name.

In elementary school, I tried to tell this story to my American friends. I was surprised when they smirked. This made me feel worse than their disgust at the food we ate in my house, or their laughter at my parents' accents. Still, I made my mother tell me the story whenever I could, and I played at being Simchung with Hannah.

Hannah told me later, after she was already in college, that she'd never liked the story. "Why would you want to be like her? She's just some spineless girl," she said.

"What are you talking about?" I said. "She's a hero!"

"You're such a martyr," Hannah said, rolling her eyes. "Seriously, how do you buy everything that's fed to you?"

That was how our arguments went after a certain age: our disagreements about one thing were always really about something else. She said she had only pretended to like that story because I loved it so much. "It teaches girls to kill themselves," she said. "It teaches them that their lives are just a debt they have to pay back to someone else."

"I don't think that's what it teaches at all," I said, caught off guard. "You're overanalyzing." The thing was, I loved that Simchung gave up her life, and in doing so, saved her father.

I yearned for the moment at which everything the father had lost was returned to him, when everything was restored and multiplied. I recognized that Simchung's life could not really begin until that moment, until she had made that happen. That made sense to me.

I had always retained a keen sense of what had been denied our family, of what we had lost. After we moved to America I kept track of the twists I imagined my life would have taken if we had remained in Seoul. I wouldn't have struggled so much with everything; I might have been popular; I could have done better in school.

I imagined the other side as well: if we'd stayed in Korea my father might have been thrown in jail. He might have been tortured or executed. The government might have seized everything and sent the rest of us to the countryside to live off apples and the kindness of our relatives.

As I grew up the story lines kept diverging, and I tried to map out all the different paths our lives might have taken if certain circumstances had been altered. This habit contributed to a sense of mine that my current life was not quite solid, not quite real. That might have been why as a mathematician, I chose topology as my field, studying how certain objects that intersect in three-dimensional space don't in four-dimensional space.

I was aware that my father had come to the United States to work as an engineer, but before that, he had been considered the most promising young mathematician in Korea. So this was another story line that I filed away and tended carefully: the life we would have had if my father had been able to fulfill his potential. In these scenarios, there was never any question that he would have been great; there was only the fact of this future having been denied him.

When I went to grad school in what had once been his chosen field, I knew I was living a phantom version of his dreams. This thrilled me, as if I'd found a way into one of our parallel lives, and reclaimed something that had been taken away. And then, slowly, I began to understand the other side of that dream. I could not take him with me. That was the price: I had to live his dream alone.

Still, I thought about what Hannah said. Why had my heroes been Mother Teresa, Florence Nightingale—why had I prayed for my own crippled person, my own terminally ill or unlovable person to take in and love, with such fervor when I was young? I wondered if Hannah was right. I wanted to remind her that as children we had fought to play Simchung, that she had always been happy when I let her take the title role. I could still see her, acting out the moment of sacrifice as she jumped off the back of our sofa, arms out, eyes closed—glowing with the thrill of that plunge into the imagined abyss.

13.

I left Los Angeles without seeing Hannah again. I walked up and down the beach my last morning there, listening for seals. I felt angry and ragged, as if my sister had tricked me into saying things. I thought of that guy from college, whose name I still couldn't say without feeling nauseated. He had taught me that I could count on no one but my family.

The year I'd dated him, I had to come home to Michigan when an infection began at the tips of the roots of my teeth and spread to my jawbone. I never knew how much my parents had known or guessed back then. We never talked about what was wrong: I tried to keep everything from them, afraid of what it said about me.

The infection, I was told, was a result of the accident long ago, when Allison had pushed me into the wall. That had actually surprised me. The body remembers old wounds. It stores them away, in your blood and your bones, long after you believe they have healed.

. . .

I cried when the plane to Korea from Los Angeles took off, and was surprised by the tears and unable to check them. I turned my face to the window. The woman sitting next to me offered me Kleenex after Kleenex, and I took them without acknowledging her, ashamed and terrified that she might ask me what was wrong. I could feel her looking at me. Once she let her hand flutter questioningly onto my shoulder, but I shrugged it off and moved as far away from her as I could in my little seat, leaning my forehead against the window. I pressed my hand against my mouth and closed my eyes, and after a while was able to stop.

When the plane finally landed in Korea thirteen hours later, it was the dead of night. My uncle was waiting at the airport. He stood behind the gate, in the front row of the crowd gathered there to greet the plane. It was the same airport where I'd waited for him years ago, when he hadn't come. In the years between, he had never called us, and we had never called him.

As he approached now, he nodded at me, and I bowed my greeting. He took my suitcase, awkwardly raising his hand as if he might pat me on the shoulder. He let it drop without touching me. I followed him then, in silence, to his car.

It was a long journey to the house my parents were renting in the countryside. First we had to pass through Seoul, which had become completely unfamiliar to me. There were so many new buildings and flashing lights—even the traffic signs, now in both English and Korean, were new. It did not feel like a place I had come from, like anywhere I'd ever lived. I sat with my nose almost touching the window, watching it roll by.

"Sleep," my uncle insisted each time I turned to look at him.

I did not know if he thought I was tired and should rest, or if he didn't want to talk to me, or if there was some bad news he was trying to hide. I wanted to ask how my parents were doing, and I also wanted to hear his voice after all this time, but I felt clumsy and confused, as if the affection I felt for him was unseemly or misplaced. I had missed him, and had never forgotten him. But whenever I turned to him he looked uneasy, and looked out his window, away from me, and did not speak.

I was quiet, too, watching the lights of the city until we had passed the tight streets of crowded buildings, and left it all behind, everything coming farther and farther apart until even the streetlamps were gone. We went a while longer, and stopped at a gas station: a pocket of light surrounded by darkness. A man filled the gas tank and gave my uncle a packet of tissues, and we went on. The road turned to dirt, and then it was completely black except the light the car cast ahead of us. For the rest of the way, we drove like that into the dark.

I saw the glimmer of trembling light that was my parents' house from a distance, even before my uncle pulled onto the road that would take us there. A low fog clung to the ground, but above it the air was clear, and behind the tiny light of the house I could see the shadows of mountains in the distance.

My parents were renting a place that had been built in the traditional Korean style, complete with a curving roof. When we pulled up, a door was flung open. A figure stepped out and started walking in our direction: a shadow moving through the haze. Then the figure waved, and began running toward us. It was my father, in his old blue coat and a brand-new baseball cap. I stood next to the car, watching him come toward us.

"Shake," he said when he reached us, holding out his hand. As he pumped my arm up and down, some of my anxiety dropped away.

"You look good," I said.

"Do I?" He smiled broadly.

I nodded. "You look great, Daddy," I said. "You look better than you did when you left."

Then my mother called my name from the open door. She stepped into a cloud of lamplight. "Hurry up and come in," she said. "It's chilly outside!"

As we went in, she gave me a quick kiss on the cheek. She put her hand on my uncle's arm. "Thank you," she said. He flinched a little, but followed her into the house, dragging my luggage behind him.

"Go," my father said. "I want you to see the house." He was smiling, expectant.

Inside, it was small and clean. Everything was bright: the wood floors, the small kitchen off to the side, and the sliding paneled doors made to look like old-fashioned Korean paper screens. My father stepped in behind me, his hand warm on my back. "Do you feel the heat?" he asked. "Coming from the ground?"

I could feel the warmth penetrate my socks through the wood floor.

"Yes," I said.

"It's a traditional Korean heating system," he said. "Let me show you how it works." He took several sheets of paper from the table that stood in the middle of the room and flourished a pen. "Now," he said. He motioned to the sofa at the back of the room. He sat beside me, immediately beginning to sketch. He drew a picture of a house and a space beneath it. He explained that it was one of the most efficient heating systems in the world. "It's uniquely Korean," he said. He drew a fire under the house, and mapped the tunnels winding together beneath the house, directing the heat from under the floor. "Sometimes traditional is best," he said.

I smiled, and studied the drawing.

He turned to my uncle. "How was the drive?"

"Dark," my uncle said.

My father nodded, and waited for my uncle to say more. My mother came in with a pot of tea on a tray, and my uncle rose—I thought to help her, but then I saw he'd gotten up to leave.

"No, stay," my mother insisted. "Have just one cup."

"Please sit down, Uncle," I said, trying to help. "I haven't seen you in so long." My uncle glanced between my mother and me and reluctantly resumed his seat.

My mother smiled at him encouragingly.

This seemed to alarm him, and he fidgeted. "Can I smoke?" he asked.

"It's not good for my father," I began.

"It's okay," my father said. He leaned forward and, putting his hand on my uncle's shoulder, said, "Go on."

My uncle's hand shook as he lit his cigarette. He took three quick, nervous puffs, and we didn't ask any more questions, just watched him for the next several minutes as he relaxed, blowing long streams of smoke into the air. He did not touch his tea, and we did not talk. When he was finished, he stubbed out his cigarette onto the tray with the tea things on it, and stood up again to leave.

We rose, too, and followed him to the door. When he stepped into the darkness he did not look back: we waved, though we couldn't see him through the darkness, and didn't know if he saw us. My mother called out a last-minute message for my grandmother, but he gave no sign that he'd heard as he pulled away.

"What happened to him?" I asked, watching his taillights fade from view.

Neither of my parents answered.

"Is he always like that?"

My mother shrugged. "Your Halmoni says he's better now than he was," she said. "It's a blessing he's doing this well."

We went back in and sat quietly for a while, and then my mother asked, "So how is your sister?"

I'd told them on the phone that Hannah was in school, that she looked well, that she wouldn't be able to come to Korea. They had taken it all with a resignation that alarmed me, as if they no longer had the energy to worry about anything other than my father's health.

"She looks well," I said. They looked so expectant that I wanted to give them something, so I lied. "She said maybe she'll be able to visit after the semester is over."

"Does she have our number here?" my mother said.

"She has our e-mails," I said firmly. "She didn't want our number."

My mother sighed. Her lip trembled, and my father reached over and rubbed her leg. She put her hand over his, and tried to smile. "She will regret this," my mother said. "She is hurting herself more."

The house we were staying in stood at the foot of a mountain, and over breakfast the next morning, my father pointed out the window, and described the lay of the land. To the south there was a small river, to the east the rice paddies, with their shallow, gleaming surfaces punctured by slim, graceful shoots. And to the west, between two fields, was a man-made pond the landowner had stocked with fish. My father described this all with great enthusiasm, getting up from the table to go to the window and point.

"Eat," my mother insisted, laughing. "Tell her whatever you want, but eat."

While he was still explaining, a large black car came up the gravel driveway, spraying pebbles and dust.

"That's your grandmother," my mother said. She sounded surprised. "I didn't expect her until this afternoon."

We rose together, and my mother told me that my grandmother had gotten in the habit of dropping in on them without calling ahead. They had hidden the extent of my father's illness from her, but she suspected they were lying, and now she came unannounced, as if she meant to catch them at something.

We went out to meet my grandmother and my uncle, who had driven her here. I bowed, greeting them both formally.

"Umoni!" my mother cried. "You shouldn't have come so early. It's too exhausting."

"How else was I going to see my firstborn grandchild? Were you going to bring her to me?"

"Of course," my mother began, but my grandmother waved at her to be quiet.

"It's no matter," she said. "Let's go inside. There's no reason for us to be talking outside in the cold."

"Yes, Halmoni," I said, thinking that it was somehow reassuring to watch her boss my parents around. As if some order was being restored.

Inside, my mother cleared off the breakfast table, and my grandmother took both my hands in hers and squeezed. Then she stood back and appraised me. "Hm," she said.

She readjusted my posture, pushing my shoulders back, my

lower spine in. "How is your father feeling?" she asked. "Does he eat well? Does he sleep?"

He was standing right there, but I answered anyway. I was struck by how she seemed more herself than she had the few times she had visited us in the States. There, she'd been unsure and wavering, and I'd thought she had grown different with age. Here, she was in her element, and it was clear that she had retained some essential energy, a force that I remembered from childhood. Here was the one person, I thought, to whom my relationship would never change.

She grilled me about my father's illness. My parents had told her it was nothing. From the way she pressed and retreated, prodded and pulled back, I realized that she was trying to reassure herself. If it was bad, she did not really want to know.

When I had satisfied her about my father's health, she pointed to the kitchen where my mother was still cleaning up. She said, "It's bad manners to let your elders clean up after you."

So I went in and took over for my mother while my parents and my grandmother talked in the other room. My uncle was quiet, but I heard him get up and pace around the room.

After I had cleaned up, I brought out fruit and tea. "Let Jee-hyun come and stay with me a while," my grandmother said. "If you'd brought her to Korea earlier, she'd be married with children by now."

I cringed. In the timeline of Korean things, I was late to marriage, late to everything. In the States, only two of my friends were married. But I hadn't had a boyfriend in years, and this embarrassed me.

Thankfully, my grandmother didn't pry. Instead, she turned to my father. "The most important thing now is your health," she said. "These other things will work themselves out."

"Absolutely," he replied. "But really, I'm feeling much better." He described the hikes he'd taken recently. He talked about the freshness of the air, how he felt rejuvenated here. "I'm doing great," he said.

"Good," my grandmother said. She turned to me and smiled. "You've given him energy," she said. "He looks better than I've seen him yet."

This made me happy, and my father nodded. "It's true!" he said.

None of us mentioned his treatment or his actual illness. Instead, my grandmother launched then into a list of all the ways she had stayed so healthy for the last fifty years, and named herbs and tonics she had brought, with long instructions in the order and frequency with which he should take them. "And insam, of course," she said. "With some natural raw honey. And push here, with this finger on this point in your hand. And this point in your leg. Ten or twenty times a day, push hard." She reached over and pressed.

My father cried out.

"Is it tender?" my grandmother said, with satisfaction. "Keep pushing there until it doesn't hurt anymore. Are you paying attention, Jeehyun? Will you make sure your father does this?" She sat back. "Do as I say," she said, "and you'll live to be one hundred."

A few days later, my parents and I drove out together to go to my father's treatment in Seoul. On the drive there, everything seemed beautiful. My mother pointed out cranes nesting in the trees, the shining glass surface of the paddies, the rice stalks waving in the wind.

When we reached the city, I was glad for a chance to see it in daylight. There were so many cars and so many people. Neon signs in both Korean and English stacked up the sides of the build-ings. The weirdest part was that everyone was Korean: everyone looked like me. I wondered if this had taken my parents by sur-prise as well when they first arrived, after so many years of look-ing different from everyone around us.

The hospital itself was impressive and immaculate, with soar-ing ceilings and granite floors. Men in suits whisked back and forth. They looked alike, sharp, with somewhere to go.

"Hurry," my father said. He took me by the elbow and pulled me along.

For all the bustle of the lobby, we were the only ones to get on the elevator. We went to the fourth floor, which was drab and empty, and smelled of disinfectant and something else familiar that I couldn't place. Overhead, the fluorescent lights backlit every-thing with a garish glow. My father, undeterred, led us through the hallways to the treatment room, which was crowded with beds, but otherwise bare. None of the other patients had arrived.

"Huh," my father said, shrugging as he settled himself onto one of the empty beds. "I guess we didn't need to worry about being late." There was only one chair beside my father's bed, and I hov-ered as my mother sat down.

Then a nurse entered, and briskly measured my father's blood pressure. When she went to wheel an IV stand over, my father stopped her. "Wait," he said. "This is my daughter." He pointed at me. "She came from America to see me."

The nurse smiled, and after arranging the IV stand next to my father's bed, she brought an extra chair over for me. I sat next to my mother as the other patients wandered slowly in, chatting and introducing themselves. The small room seemed to expand as they entered.

One man came with someone who seemed so clearly to be his son, but it turned out that the patient was actually the younger brother of the two. He was only forty, but he was gaunt and balding, and in recent months people had started calling him "grandfather." He laughed at the mistake as if it was the funniest thing in the world.

The family members who'd accompanied the patients remained pretty quiet, but the patients traded stories about what they were in for, and what kinds of things they were doing to stay healthy. This talk of illness made me uncomfortable: I had brought my math notebooks with me to the hospital, hoping my father would be able to go over them with me, but when I pulled them out of my backpack, he waved me off. He was listening to the conversation of the other patients, leaning so far forward that the line of his IV was stretched taut.

I hadn't done any work on my thesis since going to Los Angeles, so I opened my book and looked at my notes. I took out my colored pencils, and I tried to concentrate, but I couldn't help listening, instead.

"My third relapse," one person said, and a murmur went around the room.

"Metastasis," said another, and an immediate chorus went up of patients calling out which organs their cancers had spread to, and what that meant, and how their treatment was working. They talked about pain management and what worked best for them.

"I haven't taken anything," my father said. "No painkillers for me!"

The others were astonished. "Not any?" they asked.

"Not a single pill."

I beamed at him. I was proud. Even here, he was special. Tough. Once everyone was finally hooked into their IV drips, they settled back and the giddiness passed. The room became much quieter. I watched my father lie on his bed, and I was reminded of the few times he'd stayed home with me when I was sick. It had always been my mother who took care of me through the actual illness, and she was the one I wanted then, her cool hands feeling my forehead or smoothing my sheets. My father was for the recovery. He was pure excitement. He would climb into bed and read *The Little Prince* to me. Every time he got to the part about the astronomer who couldn't be taken seriously because he looked like a clown in his native clothes, he'd throw back his head and laugh.

My mother scolded him then, because he would forget to let me rest. He'd wake me when I fell asleep, exclaiming, "Listen to this!" Then, realizing what he'd done, he'd encourage me earnestly and loudly to go back to sleep. But he could never resist his favorite part, about how the Little Prince's planet was so small he could watch forty-four sunsets a day. "That'd be so great," he'd say, reading that page over again. "Just imagine it!"

Now, while the other patients quietly rested, he fidgeted.

"Could I have my phone?" he asked my mother. "I want to call Mr. Lee." His voice was very loud. He turned to me. "Hey, do you remember him?"

Looking significantly at the patients lying with their eyes closed now, at their quietly reading families, I whispered, "No."

"Sure you do," my father said heartily. "Mr. Lee! He bought you Little Bear, remember?"

I kept my voice low. "Daddy," I said, "shouldn't we keep our voices down?"

He looked around, blinking in surprise. "Oh, they don't mind," he said. "Do you remember how you cried when you lost that bear? We had to search for it for days, and even after we bought you that stuffed whale, you weren't satisfied."

I did remember. I shrugged. "It wasn't Little Bear," I said.

Mr. Lee agreed to come right away, and as my father snapped his phone shut, I could tell he was gratified by how quickly his friend had agreed. When he arrived, I didn't recognize him at all. He was dressed in a suit, and his hair was dyed blue-black. It swept over his forehead to hide a receding hairline. He greeted my father with a handshake.

"You look just like your mother did at your age," Mr. Lee said, shaking my hand next. "Do you remember me?"

I shook my head.

"Impossible!" he cried. "How could you have forgotten? You ruined all my books in one day." Then I knew who he was. I had heard this story before. When I was about two years old, my parents left me in his study to sleep while they visited him, assuming I would cry for them when I woke. I slept the whole time, or so they thought, but when they were ready to leave, they came to fetch me and discovered me sitting in front of his bookshelves. All the books from the lowest shelf were pulled down around me, their pages torn out and scattered everywhere.

"I don't think that was me," I said now.

"Oh, it was you," my mother said grimly.

Mr. Lee laughed. "I would never have imagined you would turn out so well," he said cheerfully. "I hear you're a scholar now. Is that your work?" He nodded at my notebook.

I decided I liked him. I liked the easy way he teased me, as if I was someone close to him. I liked the way he put his hand on my father's shoulder. No one in America had been close to my parents like that. Once, this man had been young with my father. Leaning over my father's bed, he said, "Remember when we jumped out of a plane and landed on those thorny bushes? Remember when we had to run up that mountain in twelve minutes?"

"That was pure hell," my father said. "Military service was the worst thing that ever happened to me," but he was laughing.

"Just remember," Mr. Lee said. "If you survived that, you can survive anything."

He stayed for lunch, which we ate while my father was still receiving treatment. He kept my father laughing the whole time, and then he left. I watched him go. He'd been close to my father, I thought. They had done their year of mandatory military service together. I'd seen pictures of my father during that time, crisp in his uniform, his hair buzzed short, the expression on his face serious and unsmiling. He did not look like the father I knew in those pictures, but like a sculpture. The lines in his face were too harsh. It wasn't until after he married my mother that he began to look happy in photographs, his face softening and opening up with the years.

He had met my mother shortly after his service. My mother had been an organizer at her school for the student democratization movement, and my father was on the fringes of the group. He went to the demonstrations, and shook his fist and yelled, along with everyone else. He actually had no memory of the first time they met. They'd been at a demonstration, and he was standing close to my mother near the front line when a stray rock thrown by another student hit him in the back of the head. She saw the rock ricochet off his head, watched his legs give way and collapse beneath him.

She lunged forward, grabbing my father's arm as he toppled. She scooted under it to prop him up. This was the first time she had touched a man who was not related to her by blood. He was incoherent and mumbling, and he let her drag him away from the crowd. When she'd gotten them away from the main area of conflict, an old woman watching from the front of a teahouse with a broom in her hand waved them over as they approached. She ushered them in.

My mother maneuvered the weight of my father's body into a chair in the back of the room; once she had him propped up against a wall, she took the chair next to him. The woman brought two washcloths and told my mother to wipe off her face. She had caked toothpaste around her eyes and mouth before the rally to combat the tear gas that she knew would be sprayed over them. My mother did as she was told.

Then, carefully, avoiding eye contact with the old woman, she wiped off my father's face. Her hands were shaking. Her knees. She kept seeing the snap of my father's neck when the rock had hit his head, the buckle of his knees, so quick and awkward. When it happened, something inside herself she could not name had mirrored my father's fall, dropping like a rope within her.

When she was finished cleaning his face, she touched her hand to the back of his head and found the bump there. Her hand came away sticky with blood, and she wiped it off with the cloth. She stood and thanked the woman for helping them. She gave her a little money, and asked her to give my father some tea and something to eat when he woke. Then she left him there, propped up against the wall, unconscious.

Outside, the demonstration was already over. Some students

were being dragged away in handcuffs, some were on the ground covering their heads as the soldiers kicked them. The rest were running in all directions. My mother walked calmly through the chaos, her hands in her pockets, her mind humming.

In the next few weeks, she found out more about my father. He was an orphan, with only one older sister to whom he was devoted. He was very serious and very poor. He was friends with other poor young men who were equally intense.

Once she had discovered all this, she stopped prying and made no attempts to contact him. She told herself she just wanted to make sure that he was all right, that her efforts had not been wasted. So she was surprised when, a full year later, he turned up as a new employee at the place where she had recently taken a job. When he showed no recognition upon meeting her, she met his face with an equally blank one. Still, they were alumni of the same college, and she was very pretty. It took only a few weeks for him to ask her on a date. She refused. He asked again. She refused, with some irritation. Perhaps it was the assuredness of her refusals that intrigued him, but whatever the reason, he was smitten.

On their fifth date, my mother finally told him she was the one who'd rescued him the day of the demonstration. He was astounded. He said that when he had woken from his stupor, he remembered nothing. The old woman at the teahouse told him his sister had brought him there. My father was not a superstitious man, or a stupid man, but the rock had perhaps knocked some sense out of him. He had been convinced that somehow it was his sister, miles away, who had saved him.

My mother was not particularly surprised that he had no memory of her face, no memory of her body against his, but his attributing her act to someone else filled her with outrage.

"I will never marry you," she declared, though the question had never been raised.

And at that moment my father realized he had to have her. That was the beginning of his campaign to win my mother's hand. As for my mother, it marked the moment after which she would always think of him as a man who owed her his life.

We went to meet my father's doctor after the chemo, and I sat next to my father on the exam table, swinging my legs.

"I have some surprising news," the doctor said as he came in, peering at us over my father's folder.

"Tell us," my mother said.

The doctor looked down at the file again, and shook his head. "The cancer has shrunk," he said. He sounded baffled. He pulled an image from the folder and laid it on his desk. "The tumor in your stomach," he said, "has shrunk two-point-five centimeters—in half since you first came here. In just two weeks."

We craned our necks forward, staring at the picture, dazed.

"The tumors in your lungs are incrementally smaller," he continued, "and the one in your liver has decreased by about forty percent."

"What does that mean?" my mother said.

"To be frank, it is very irregular," Dr. Kwan said. "It is what it is," he said. "I wouldn't necessarily get my hopes up, but it is certainly encouraging."

I had read about stories like this when I'd searched for miracles. This was how it always began. I opened and closed my hands. The tumor was halving, disappearing. If it shrank 2.5 more centimeters in two weeks, the doctor said, it'd be gone. Even if it didn't,

I thought, even if it just stopped growing now, my father could be okay. He would survive.

My father reached out to shake his doctor's hand. His face opened into a wide, dazzling smile. "Maybe you'll get to write about me in a case study," he said. "Maybe I can make you famous." He laughed. The hope I felt when I heard my father laugh like that terrified me. It frightened me more than anything had since Hannah had first gone missing.

On the drive home, we were very quiet. We didn't want to disturb anything with talk. Outside, fields of rice paddies rolled by, the water shining like glass beneath the midday sun, scores of white cranes picking their way through the stalks of rice.

When we were a few miles from home, we stopped by a shop to buy seedlings. The shop was a little box set on the side of the road, a convenience store alone in the middle of that countryside surrounded by paddies and mountains. We walked up and down the aisles of seedlings, shaded by large umbrellas, and we bought trays of tiny plants: organic tomatoes, peppers, mint, lettuce, and radishes.

My father had always dug our gardens himself, but this time he just marked the perimeters and I did the actual digging. The seedlings smelled fresh and pungent. My father patted plant after plant into place, his knees pushing into the ground. When he was finished, he stood up, his hands and knees caked with dirt. He patted brown handprints down his shirt, and I thought of my mother having to wash them out later. He saw me watching in disapproval, and laughed. He said, "Let's go. I want to show you the rest of the property."

He led me in a loop around the pond, which was very clear and stocked with all different sizes of fish. Its walls had been built up with rocks, and the surface held the outlines of the mountains around us. We crossed a small curving footbridge and watched the large dark shadows beneath the surface slice calmly through the water. The fish swam back and forth, slowly.

Beyond the pond was a field, and past the field ran a river lined with trees. My father led me to the path. Along the edges of it, the grass grew long, as if to mark the border. The long stems clung to our pants and our arms as we walked by. The reeds there were thick with insects. I slapped at my arms, at the wet grass sticking to my legs. Pointing to the river, which ran alongside our path, my father said, "I put a watermelon in there yesterday, as a surprise. Let's go down and get it."

When I was little, my father used to put watermelons in the ocean. At the end of the day he'd break it open, and shivering dry in the setting sun, we'd taste the surprising coolness of the fruit after a day in the water.

"Don't eat too many seeds," my father always said, "or a vine of watermelons will grow out of you."

"More likely you'll wet your pants," my mother replied.

Now, on the edge of the riverbank, my father took off his shoes and rolled up his pants. He walked up and down looking for the watermelon. He plunged in. Knee deep in the river, he peered into the running water.

There were rocks on the bottom of the river. My father wasn't supposed to cut himself because of his weakened immune system. "Be careful," I said. "Come back. I'll do it."

But he was already in the water, holding his pants high in his fists, picking past branches and rocks like a long-legged bird. The current swirled around his legs.

"Could somebody have taken it?" he asked. "I left it right here."

"Hold on," I said. "I'm coming."

He splashed ahead. "I found it!" he said triumphantly. The melon had rolled a little bit away, and caught itself against a branch. When he reached down to take it, he let go of his pant legs, which unfurled and fell into the water. He held the watermelon up high and shook it in triumph. Then he splashed back toward the shore, laughing, the hems of his pants drowning against his knees.

14.

My Komo interrupted our breakfast one morning, just as my grandmother had when I first arrived. We hadn't heard her car pull up, and when she appeared at the threshold of our house and stood, peering around, we jumped up, startled. We looked at each other as if we'd been caught doing something she shouldn't have seen.

I recognized her immediately; she was exactly as I remembered her: angular, unlovely, and somehow striking nevertheless.

"I didn't mean to interrupt your breakfast," she said, as we bowed our greetings.

"Let me set a place for you at the table," I said, motioning toward our breakfast. "You should join us."

My aunt shook her head. "We have our breakfast by six a.m.," she said. "When your father and I were children we woke even earlier than that. Our parents thought anything later was laziness. I guess he's gotten out of the habit. But go ahead, finish your breakfast."

"We were just finishing up," my father said, even though when I looked at his plate he had barely eaten anything. "I'm done."

"Maybe you can finish up what you have left?" I said, but he pushed his plate away.

"Come, Noonah, sit down," he said, smiling.

I looked at my mother, but she didn't even flinch. She motioned for me to help her as she began clearing away the table.

"He didn't eat anything," I whispered.

"Let it go," my mother hissed back.

In the living room, my aunt had seated herself beside my father. "How do you feel?" she asked. She peered at him anxiously. "Did you stay up late the other night waiting for Jeehyun to come in? I hope not."

My father smiled. "It was fine, Noonah."

She looked unsure. "The body heals while it's resting," she insisted. She turned to my mother, who was serving the tea, and said, "He looks so tired. And he ate hardly anything."

My mother raised her eyebrows but said nothing.

My aunt sighed and turned to me. "So," she said. "Jeehyun, what's it like to be back in Korea?"

I shrugged. "It's good," I said.

She nodded. "My sons didn't like Korea at all when we first came back."

"Oh, I like it," I said. I wondered if I should mention Gabe now, and say I was sorry he had died in that car accident.

"Well, they didn't," my aunt continued. "But I prayed for them, and prayed for them, and in the end it all worked out."

"That's nice," I said, still unsure about whether I should say anything about Gabe.

"You have to pray," my aunt said. She looked at my father. "Your father," she began, "has made some mistakes. And he has this illness now, which only God can take away. Your father turned away from God, and now he must find his way back."

I shook my head, and looked from my mother to my father. I wondered what they expected me to say. "That's not exactly how people get cancer," I said. "Anyway, I don't think that is a kind of God I'd be willing to pray to."

"Even to save your father?"

"I don't actually think my father has made such big mistakes."

"Oh? Let me assure you: mistakes have been made. Years have been wasted."

"Noonah," my father said, but she cut him off with a curt wave of her hand.

"First," she began, "he married too early. I told him, establish yourself first: you have too much potential to throw away on a girl, on these petty responsibilities. But he'd never had responsibilities," she continued. "I'd always shielded him from that, and maybe that was my mistake. And so everything I had hoped for and waited for and sacrificed for, he decided to let go."

I stared at her, mesmerized. She had not changed since her visit years ago, when she barged into our house in Michigan and tyrannized our family. And just like then, my parents sat quiet and powerless, allowing her to do so.

"And then"—here my Komo shot a look at my mother that was filled with unmistakable venom—"that act of idiocy I have never understood. That foolish, stupid pamphlet, just like a schoolboy. If I had been in Korea at that time it never would have happened." She slapped her hand down on the table. "He wasted his whole life," she cried. "He fled like a dog, and laid aside his talent, and lived like a nobody, this mediocre life that anyone could have lived."

She caught my eye and held it. "It is a sin to abandon your talents," she said. "Do you understand? It is a disgrace against God."

My father's eyes were fixed on his teacup.

"God can go to hell," I said. I thought of my aunt nursing this bitterness all these years. "That's the sort of thing, what you just said, that can make somebody sick."

To my surprise, my aunt looked stricken. "I know," she said, her voice suddenly low and grave. "I know it is." It was as if something had shifted in that second, as if she had let go of all that rage. She took a deep breath. "And God isn't only vengeful. He can heal, too. Have I made him seem as if he only punishes? Is that how you see him? Is that why you don't pray?"

I glanced at my parents. They were silent, their faces guarded and neutral.

"I don't think about whether he's vengeful or jealous or any of that. It's that I don't believe such a thing as God exists." I tried to make my voice as gentle as I could. "If I believed in God, I would pray to him. I would do anything to save my father."

My father reached over and squeezed my hand. My aunt watched him do this, and sucked in her breath. "Loving your father, wanting him to get better, that's Jesus," she said. "That's Jesus Christ."

Her voice was strained, and in that moment I felt sorry for her. She had given too much to my father growing up, it was true. She'd been mother and father and sister to him. And because she had given too much, she demanded too much in return. It could never be paid back: nothing my father could do would ever be enough for any of it, for their poverty, their isolation, or her fierce guardianship over him. He could only disappoint her for the rest of their lives.

My poor father, I thought. *My impossible-to-love aunt.*

"All love is Jesus," she said. "Don't resist him. He is all things good."

"Not for me, he isn't," I said. "For me, love has nothing to do with Jesus. And it never will."

My aunt stayed another hour after that, and we all tried to move the conversation to safer topics. But when finally she left, our house felt strangely empty, as if she'd taken something with her as she went. We tried to recalibrate: my mother said my father and I should go for a walk to clear our minds. She said, "I've had to go hiking with your father every day. He's been wearing me out. Now that you're here, I can rest." She laughed, and touched my father's arm, and I knew she was telling him then that the visit from my aunt had done her no harm.

And so my father and I went out together. The air was cool, and we walked toward a trailhead that was hidden by a stand of trees.

"It's like a secret entrance," he said, as we sneaked through the trees and onto the path. "I wish I'd been able to stay in Korea and buy a place like this," he continued. "When I get better, I'm going to buy land out here in the country."

"I think that'd be nice," I said. I watched my father surge ahead. He looked so energetic that I couldn't help doing calculations in my head. Four of the five to eight months the doctors had given him were nearly up. But he was still nearly as healthy as he had been when they said that. That meant he could make it another five to eight months, I thought. All he had to do was stay right where he was, and we could make it forever: month to month, year to year, just like this.

"Look," he said, pointing to a tiny tree frog in our path. We stopped and squatted, watched it hop and disappear into a pile of leaves. The air smelled of pine and earth. I hoped that here in these mountains, my father would begin to get better. Would this have been what it was like to grow up in Korea, I wondered, daily walks, a sense of space?

My father reached out and tugged at the branch of a pine tree. "The trees in Korea look different, don't they?" he said. "Even when they're the same kind of tree."

"I guess."

"I should have brought you and Haejin back to visit."

"It's nice to be here now."

"I shouldn't have written that pamphlet."

This topic had never come up before between us. We had never acknowledged why we left Korea, or that I knew anything about it. We were in unmarked territory.

"I was proud of you for taking that risk," I said.

My father shook his head. "It was a waste," he said. "Nobody read it, nobody cared. I was a fool, and it didn't help anyone."

"I'm glad you did it," I said. My father had never talked to me like this before, and it frightened me. "And we were better off in America."

"Do you really think that?"

I shrugged. "We had more freedom. Our horizons were broadened."

He laughed. "Was it worth it?"

"Yes," I said. "Definitely."

"I am glad you think so." He sighed. "I wanted to accomplish something with my life," he said. "I hoped to do more."

"You still can."

He shook his head. "At my age, you've already caught up to your dreams," he said. "You've already passed them by." We were walking faster, and both breathing hard. "That's why I want you to push yourself," he said. "That's why you have to work hard now."

We hiked on, until we turned a bend that led us straight into a meadow. The sunlight was dazzling in the long grass, playing off the way it bent to the slightest breeze. "I always wanted to write a book," my father said. "Maybe I can do that, when this is over. When I have time."

"Yes," I said. "You should."

We had come to a small grove of trees marked off from the waving grass by a trampled circle. My father stopped here and said, "This is where the deer come to rest." He smiled. "Perfect for us." He lowered himself onto his back and lay down. I sat beside him, and he groped for my hand. He brought it back to rest with his on his chest. He covered his face with his hat.

"A book," he said, from beneath his hat. I could tell he was smiling. "I could do that."

I sat, looking at my father with the hat over his face, watching the rise and fall of his breath, thinking of a book filled with all the things I still didn't know about his life. I thought: *Let him get better.* I lay down beside him.

On my back, squinting against the light, I thought I could see the air moving. On the tree above us, a lone leaf quivered recklessly out of sync with the rest. When we were children, my mother had told us how trees grow: about the roots gripping the ground, the stable trunk, the branches, the separate leaves. She told us about veins we couldn't see carrying sap to all the branches, the chemical processes that turn light into sugar, chlorophyll infusing each leaf with green as it unfurls.

She had told us that beneath the ground, where no one could see, some trees gripped each other's roots in the ground like so many held hands. Mahogany did it. Aspen. Gnarled wood grasped gnarled wood until one tree's roots were another tree's roots. In times of drought they passed water, when there were fires they passed messages of danger. Burning, an aspen would send the alert root to root so that even if it died itself, the other trees could bring up sap to save themselves from danger.

"Even plants live longer if they're closer to their families," she'd said.

Next to me, my father stirred. "Tell me what you're thinking," he said sleepily.

I turned to look at him. The trees were bending over us, blurring in the hot sun. "I think that heat warps the space-time continuum," I said.

"Heat?" he said. He laughed. "Do you think it speeds it up or slows it down?" He lifted the hat from his face, peered around, and chewed on another piece of dried fruit. Down went the hat again.

"It definitely slows it down," I said. "And when it's hot enough, you can see the air bend. Look over there at the trees."

My father cast aside his hat and propped himself up on an elbow. He looked at the trees and smiled. We watched the leaves shake. He moved his hand through the air. "What else?" he said. "Do you think there's anything that can stop time?"

"Maybe the past," I said. "Do you think maybe time is expanding all the time, like space, and can only expand so long before it collapses back into itself, and we can only use up so much time before we end up getting pulled back by the force of it? Like the past gains gravity?"

My father started laughing. "No," he said. But then he was

quiet. He looked around, at the mountains in the distance, at the trees. "But sometimes I still feel so young, like nothing's changed and I still have so much to do. And then I remember I've had a whole life." He stretched his hands above him and then clasped them beneath his head. "A good life."

The trees swayed above us.

I closed my eyes. I thought, *let the tumor shrink*. My grandmother had taught me to pray like this: chanting the repetition of my dearest wish. I thought maybe the universe had been saving up its magic my entire life for *this* wish. *Let him get better,* I thought. *Let him heal, let him heal, let him heal.*

"I think joy can stop time," my father said. "I think joy can do the trick." Satisfied with this answer, he nodded his head, lowered himself back down, and closed his eyes again.

I turned to look at him, my father half sunken in the grass, the blades pushing up around him. The sun in his eyes, the light all over him, and the grass, and the arms of trees meeting overhead. He was smiling with his eyes closed, pleased with his answer, pleased with himself. I felt the weight of it upon my chest. Yes, I thought. Joy can stop time with the force of its insistent, incomprehensible weight.

15.

In the following days, which my father jokingly called "the tourist season" at our house, guests came early and stayed late into the evening, sitting in bunches in our living room or out on our porch. They hugged my parents and talked about their youth, the mischief they'd caused and the dreams they'd had—it was like a reunion. One woman said it had been years since she'd laughed so hard. The presence of these people made me realize how different our lives had been in America.

They brought gifts upon gifts including bags of books that filled our one bookshelf double stacked, and spilled onto our table and a corner in the floor. Most of them were about spirituality or alternative treatments and miracles. My father would go through all the books and sigh, wondering in mock despair when anyone would ever bring him a comic book, and then our house was overrun with them, my father greedily reading them at night after our visitors had left.

My parents' friends told me my father was a hero. The best and smartest of them all. My mother, who had always bristled at such praise—since she had paid the price—smiled indulgently. Those nights, my parents seemed to expand, to become larger versions of themselves, more real somehow.

In the kitchen I cut up fruit and listened to everyone talk. "What a good daughter!" the adults cried whenever I walked in bearing trays of melon or peaches or cut-up pears. I blushed. Here everyone called me Jeehyuni, the diminutive, the little girl name, but it didn't bother me. Instead, I felt cared for, and safe. It made me wonder if I would also have been a different person had I grown up in Korea: more confident and easygoing.

Most days when things were quiet, my father would go outside wearing a hat, his trowel in hand. I sat by the window and watched him; other days I went out and helped. He looked like a child then, sitting back on his heels, examining the plants. And time passed as it had when I was a child—without distinction, as if nothing would ever end and the days were years, and the hours whole days.

One day I came indoors muddy from working outside by myself, and my mom and dad were lying together on a single sleeping mat, which they had dragged out into the middle of the living room. They were heaped under the blankets, whispering and laughing. I checked myself at the door and stared. They looked like children sharing secrets under the blankets. When they looked up and saw me, they laughed. After a moment they rolled out of the sleeping mat and pulled it back into their bedroom. I could hear them still laughing there.

The only thing that bothered me those days was that I'd told my parents I'd been sending Hannah regular updates about my father. I had meant to. I had meant to write to her, to tell her my parents wanted her to come out here after all. When my parents' friends asked about Hannah, I told them that she was in Los Angeles studying biology, as if there were no problems between us.

I told myself Hannah wasn't thinking about us either, and that she could always write me if she wanted to know how we were. I spent time with my parents and all our guests. I worked on my dissertation. I felt I could only do one thing or the other: that dealing with Hannah would make everything else impossible.

But some days I watched my father go out to the river and sit back on his heels, watching the water, and I thought of Hannah and felt like I was committing a crime.

The day our garden yielded up its first pepper, my father's cousins came to visit. These were the cousins my father and aunt had gone to live with when he and his sister were orphaned, the cousins whose father had made them eat in the kitchen with the servants because they were poor relations. After my parents had married, my father never returned to that house, even to visit. We'd never gone there for holidays when we lived in Korea, and I had never even seen a photograph of the place, though every once in a while my father had described the grounds there, the lake, the mountain, the trees.

Now his cousins arrived with baskets of fruit and packs of aloe drinks. "Jeehyun is here!" they cried, and pushed each other aside to embrace and greet me. My father showed them the pepper, and with our smallest knife he cut it into six little pieces.

"Delicious!" they exclaimed, nodding at each other and chewing theatrically. We all laughed. My father's cousins had always been kind to me. They'd been proud of him ever since he'd placed first in a nationwide exam at the age of fifteen. They'd adopted him into their clan without question—but my aunt had been left out.

"And who made sure he won that prize?" my aunt had complained to my mother. "Who took him to the library and tutored him and fought for them to let him go to school when they said he wasn't smart enough? No one else cared for him in those days."

"Your father has been through so much," his oldest cousin, the head of the family, said, launching the rest of them into stories about the "old" days, when my father had become sort of a mascot to them. He'd won competition after competition: I knew the story. He'd gone to college at the head of his class. He'd been in newspapers. He had been a self-supporting student who worked on the side and sent his money home to his sister, as well as a little for his uncle and cousins, not because they needed it, but as a symbolic gesture of gratitude.

For a while my father smiled through the stories, content to relive his former accomplishments, the potential he'd had when he was young. Then he said, "But Jeehyun is the genius now. She's getting her Ph.D. at the University of Chicago! She'll be a baksa in math!"

They looked at me with approval, and said I must have gotten my brains from my father. "You're going to fulfill your father's potential," Big Cousin said, patting me on the shoulder. "That's why we have children, after all." He looked thoughtful. "It's a shame," he said, "that the country was what it was when your father came of age. He could have done great things."

"He's done enough," my mother said.

"Yes, he has," Big Cousin agreed. "But we expected more." He turned to me again. "Not just from your father, but from our generation, I mean—we thought we'd do big things."

"Big changes have happened," my father said. "More than we thought possible."

"Not enough," Big Cousin said.

My father shrugged. "But it's not the end." He smiled. "Our children will make us proud." He stood up. "Anyway, enough of that. Does anyone want a tour?" he asked.

We walked around the grounds, then, saving our garden for last. As my father talked, he let slip what the doctor had said—about the shrinking tumors, the decreasing cancer markers. We'd agreed not to mention this to anyone, as if it was a secret and something fragile to be protected, so I was surprised. Later he said that his cousins didn't count, since they were family. But soon enough both my parents were telling everyone who asked that the cancer was shrinking, that it was too early to tell, but surely it was a good sign. The exhilaration of saying this out loud was addictive: it seemed more true each time.

That afternoon I was full of hope, and wrote to my advisor in Chicago. My father's praise was still fresh in my mind. He thought I would accomplish something. He was proud of me. "I'm making progress," I wrote. I detailed a few new results I'd been able to get since arriving in Korea.

"I brought all my books," I remarked to my father after my e-mail was sent. "I brought my notes and latest results, and I made some new sketches today. I thought we could go through them now that I've been here awhile."

"Yes," he said, smiling. "That would be great. But maybe later."

"Sure, like when?" I asked.

He patted my hand. "Not now," he said. "I'll let you know."

I was disappointed, but I felt placated when my advisor responded to my e-mail within the hour, saying he was very pleased, and that we should talk.

"These are great results. Very exciting!!!" he'd written.

I noted the exclamation marks, and wrote back immediately. I said that yes, we should talk very soon. I wanted to tell my father about this exchange, but he had fallen asleep in his armchair. *I am doing this for you,* I wanted to say. I felt a terrible pang remembering how my parents had told me this when I was growing up, *It is for you we work this hard. It is for you we do everything.*

When he woke from his nap, he said, "Let's play cards." So I didn't say anything about my work or my advisor's e-mail. Instead, I got out the deck and dealt. My father lost four times in a row. I was shocked. He had always won at card games, at chess, at anything involving strategy, but he didn't seem too worried.

"I wish I could go home," he said, laying down his cards. I thought he meant back to Michigan, back to our home there, but he started talking about an orchard, south-facing windows, the sound of the wind rushing through from the mountains, and I knew he was talking of his old ancestral home, the one he'd once told me he no longer remembered. Still, when he sat back in his comfortable chair and talked about his childhood, about walking across hills in the snow, and the games his sister had made up to get him to walk when he was too tired, when he talked about the hunger that gnawed at his belly for months, I leaned forward and listened.

I wondered why he wanted to go back there now, after so many years. "I like it here," I said. "I think this is a good place." I was inexplicably jealous of his ancestral home, that place that still called to him, that I had never seen.

At dinner that evening, I noticed my father didn't eat much. As soon as we'd cleared the table and had our tea, he said, white-faced, "I don't feel well. I think I should take some painkillers."

"Are you sure?" I asked. His face was set, and his skin had a yellowish cast to it, but I didn't want him to take any pills. He hadn't taken one yet, and I didn't want him to start now. "They're not good for you," I said.

My father said nothing, but took my hand and put it on his abdomen, right under his ribs, which I could feel beneath my hand. My fingers fit into the grooves of them. My father said that when he breathed, he tried to push his energy through the areas where the cancer was.

"I used to be able to feel it going through," he said. "At first there was a block, and then it cleared, but now the block is back again."

"You're just tired," I said. "It's because of the chemo."

"No," he said. "I'm sure."

"It's nothing," I said, as dismissively as I could. "I feel different because the tumor is shrinking."

My mother interjected, "If you need a painkiller, you should take it."

"Give it a little longer, Daddy," I said, but he shook his head impatiently.

"I don't feel well," he said, and rose. I thought he'd go to the cupboard to take the painkillers, but he walked right by them. Without saying good night, he went into his room and shut the door.

My mother and I stared at the shut door. We heard him shuffling around. We heard him lie down.

I took up my notebook. I couldn't concentrate, but I didn't want to go to bed either.

After a moment my mother said, "How is your work coming along?"

"It's been going well," I said. "But it's also been harder than I expected."

"What's been hard about it?" my mother asked.

"Well, it's like building a house before you know what it will be. Or how you will build it. And with what."

"Why don't you do something you are better at?" she asked. "I always thought you should have changed your major to history back when you wanted to."

"I'm not actually bad at this," I said. I wanted her to believe in me. "As painstaking as it is, I like drawing and thinking about objects that exist in a kind of space that is itself just an abstract concept. It's like drawing an imaginary place. Anyway, I'm hopeful."

My mother sighed. "Then get it done," she said. "Don't waste your time." She looked at the closed door to the room she shared with my father, and then she looked at me, straight on, a hard, inscrutable look that traveled down to the very tips of my toes. "Your father is doing worse, if you haven't noticed," she said.

"He's just tired today," I said.

"It's time for Haejin to come."

"I'll try to get her here. I've been trying."

"Are you sure you're trying hard enough? Does she know the situation?"

"That's not fair."

"Okay, then tell me—what is she doing? What does she say?"

"It's Hannah," I said. "You know how she is. She doesn't say much."

"You need to get her to talk. We need you to get her here."

"How can you forgive her for everything she put you through?" I asked. "How can you pretend nothing happened, and keep asking me to beg her to come?"

"She's part of this family. Nothing else matters."

"She could really mess everything up."

"Shame on you," my mother said. "You can't throw away a sister."

"I'm not the one who threw anything away," I said, standing up. "I've been here since the first day, I've done everything you've asked me to. You can't blame me for this."

"Sit," my mother said.

"I won't," I said. "If you want her so badly, then call her yourself. I'm going to bed." And I left my mother sitting there. I went to my room and shut the door.

I lay in the dark for a long time: long enough to hear my mother go to bed, and to hear my father shifting and turning through the night, my mother's worried voice asking how she could help. I wanted to get up and tell him to take the painkillers if he needed to, that I was sorry I had been selfish, and that I knew it was unfair. But I wanted to believe it meant something that he hadn't taken the painkillers after all, and so I lay in bed and did nothing.

The next morning my parents were late getting up for my father's doctor's appointment in the city. I set out breakfast, slowly, clumsily. "We'll drop you off at your grandmother's for the morning, and your uncle will bring you home," my father said.

"Okay," I said. I wasn't sure why he didn't want me with him. Whether he was letting me off the hook, or trying to shield me from bad news.

He must have guessed what I was thinking, because he said gently, "Jeehyun, I think you need a break this time. You don't have to come along."

"Okay," I said, again.

We drove to my grandmother's house in silence, through what felt like impending doom. When my mother pulled over to the curb to let me out, my father opened the window and stuck out his hand. He smiled. "Shake," he said.

M y grandmother had lined up apples on her kitchen table: I was horrible at peeling fruit, and she was going to make me practice. "Skill in everything," she said, handing me a slender knife.

We sat at her kitchen table, facing the apples. Her current house oddly lined up with my memory of the house she'd left many years ago: the painting of the three mountain peaks had been over there, the picture of my grandfather sitting sad and stern still propped up in the center of the living room, the daenjang pots lined up side by side on the balcony. Everything seemed an echo of the past, down to my grandmother, sitting at this very table, showing me the right way to peel an apple. Growing up, I had always used a carrot peeler, and when I used a knife the skin did not come off thin enough in one continuous peel.

We peeled and ate the apples slowly, and when my grandmother grew bored of trying to improve my technique, she turned on the television. Today the lead story was about a girl who had recently been discovered living the life, they said, of someone who'd lived a hundred years ago: no electricity, no running water, no contact, really, with the outside world.

The girl's speech was hesitant and quiet. Like someone who is used to talking to only one person. She had always lived here, she said, since she was a child. Her father had brought her out here after her mother died, and she didn't remember anything else. They lived so far away from everything. Still, her father had taught her how to read. He had taught her how to draw water from a well, had told her to hide from strangers.

Her clothes were of an ugly, loose, coarse linen that billowed about her. Behind her was a glorious garden, spilling out of itself. Behind that, the woods. Then the camera was off the girl, and onto the two hikers who had found her. They were solidly of this world. They smiled into the camera; they talked, interrupting each other, eager, excited. They were proud of themselves for stumbling upon the major discovery of the year, they said. There was not even a path to the house—they had simply gone off exploring, and had discovered the hut and the girl within it.

Then the camera panned to the small hut the girl had lived in all her life. She was a true Korean, the reporter said. She was what a Korean woman might have been generations ago, untouched. The hikers wanted to take her to Seoul to be interviewed and made famous, the reporter said, though her father, lurking somewhere off camera, refusing to be seen, did not approve.

But the reporter was adamant. The hikers were sure. The cameras zoomed in on the girl again. Her face was broad and coarse, and she was built stocky and low to the ground. I tried to see something different in her wide features, some lingering aura of another time. She was not beautiful, but she was evidence that time can stand still. Except of course time had caught up with her.

My grandmother turned the television off and sighed. "Children aren't obedient to their parents these days. When I was a girl, that's all we had: the ability to honor our parents."

During the Japanese occupation, she said, everyone was forced to take a Japanese name. They were made to give up their given names, and those who refused were punished.

"They wanted to make us forget," my grandmother said, "but at home we spoke Korean. I spoke Korean with my friends."

She looked at me sideways. "Your father's family refused to take a Japanese name," she said. "Did you know that? They were offered status as Japanese aristocrats, and they turned it down. They were punished." The coil of her apple peel broke. She set the fruit down, the knife beside it. "We are nothing but our history," she said. She sighed and looked at me. "Your parents had no sons. It's up to you to be a son to them."

"But I can't."

"You must. Your line ends with you."

I shook my head. History was treacherous: a tangled path back to what, I didn't know. "There's Haejin," I said.

"Haejin," my grandmother said. "Where is she now? What is the trouble between you?"

"That's between her and our parents."

My grandmother shook her head. "I don't believe you," she said. "That's not the whole truth."

I looked at my hands. I thought of the night Hannah was born, and what my grandmother had told me about the girls in our family, that one of the sisters was always lost. She had made it true, I thought.

"What really happened to my auntie?" I asked.

It was as if I had slapped her, the question shocked her so much. She drew a sharp breath. "She died."

"But of what?"

"Illness. She was very sick."

"What kind of illness?" I persisted. "No one will ever tell me."

My grandmother narrowed her eyes and looked at me until I lowered mine. For a moment I felt ashamed of myself. After a long silence, she said, "To ask an old woman about her dead child is reprehensible. If you want to know, ask your mother."

As indignant as I was, I was also afraid that I had wounded her. Anyway, I knew the truth. I did not push it.

Later that afternoon, my uncle came by and picked me up. He drove me home in silence. The gloom that had been pressing on my chest since last night had been growing more insistent, and under its weight I was content to let the silence stand. When we got to the house, I got out of the car and waved once, but didn't bow or speak. My uncle didn't comment, but waved back and drove away, and I stood in the cloud of dust and felt pleased that no effort had been made between us. It felt like a kind of honesty, and at the same time, I felt let down and lonely. I thought of all the people who loved my parents, and visited us weekly. I thought of the comfort they brought, and the comfort my uncle used to bring me, when I was a child. You can really lose people, I thought.

At home, I couldn't concentrate, so I went outside and worked in our garden. I weeded all the innocuous-looking green shoots that if left to grow would take over our plants. I staked all the tomatoes to long slender rods to hold them straight so they would not drag their leaves on the ground. The sun beat down on my back as I raked the dirt again and again until it was fine and soft beneath my fingers.

After that, I tried to take a nap; I thought of hiking in the mountains, but went for a walk down the long deserted highway that our house led out to, instead. I walked and walked. For a long time there was nothing. Then I crossed a bridge. On either side of the road from there were rice paddies and workers bending over the rice plants with their pant legs and sleeves rolled up.

I wondered how long it would take me to walk to the city. I counted the white cranes picking their way through the paddies on their long, careful legs. I wondered if my parents were already on their way home, and if I stayed out long enough whether they would pass me on the way back. When the sun had dipped down below the tree line, I turned and headed for home. It started to rain.

By the time I was halfway home, I was soaked through to my underwear. The rice plants bent under the onslaught, and the shining clear water of the paddies turned brown with mud. The cranes had lifted off while I wasn't looking and were already gone. I thought of my parents driving back in the storm, and wondered if they had passed by without seeing me. I hurried then, but when I returned the house was empty.

The rain stopped before my parents returned, and when they came I was standing in the dusk in front of the garden staring at the plants that had fallen into the mud.

"How did it go?" I asked.

My mother didn't respond, looking away from me as if she hadn't heard my question. My father glanced at her, and said, "It's not so bad, Jeehyun. There's no reason to worry."

"You have to tell me things," I said. "I always think the worst, since I never know what you're hiding."

"The cancer has stopped shrinking," he said.

"Oh."

"Don't worry too much, Jeehyun. At least it's not growing, either."

"What does your doctor say?"

There was a silence. "He thinks it will grow again," my father said. "He thinks it will grow back faster than before."

"I see."

"He might be wrong," my father said very gently. "Right now, I feel perfectly fine."

I nodded. I wanted to say something encouraging to him. When my father had planted our first garden in Michigan, I had thought the plants grew because he told them to. "Oh, Daddy," I said.

My father reached down his hand and patted me on the shoulder.

"Let's just have dinner and deal with this in the morning," I said.

"We ate on our way," my father said. "That's why we were so late. At least we can stake some plants this evening. Let me go and change, and then I'll come out and help you."

And so I waited, staring at the ground. He came out in loose linen pants and tennis shoes, and stood, his hands on his hips, his back absolutely straight. He looked at the tomatoes, which were in disarray. "I'll get some sticks," he said.

I watched him. I did not want to garden anymore, or to go on walks, or anything at all. I wanted to lie down in the dirt and sink. But he paused at the edge of the river, waiting, and I watched. The water in the river was high, rushing, insistent.

When he returned, his walk was energetic. Mud snaked up his ankles. He bent down and began planting the stakes he had gathered. He had found the straightest fallen branches, and stripped them clean.

"Get me some rope," he said, beginning to pull up the collapsed plants. I went indoors to get some twine.

When I entered the house, my mother was mixing fruits and vegetables in a blender. "Nutrition," she said. "My friend who's a nurse said this would be good for him, for all of us."

She smiled at me, and handed me a pair of scissors to cut the twine. She knows, I thought. And she is smiling and calm. She is preparing everything like always. I smiled back at her. I said, "Great."

Outside, my father had propped the plants up to the stakes, and was waiting for me. I handed him the twine, and moving slowly, my father gently tied each tomato plant to a stake. He was so meticulous and careful; the tomatoes nestled against their vines. I thought of our garden that had frozen over in Michigan, and wondered what the next family to live there would do with what was left. It seemed astonishing that anything there could remain, now that we were gone.

As my father finished staking the tomatoes, my mother came out with two cups and ordered my father and me to drink. We both downed the concoction and praised it to my mother, who smiled extra wide. We were acting for each other, showing each other we were all right. And I felt reassured by this, as if it was true, that if we were all standing here, drinking smoothies and gardening, nothing could be so terribly wrong.

My father adjusted his posture so he stood a little taller. "Shall we take a walk around the pond, quickly, to stretch our legs?" he said. "Yubbo?" He held out his hand to my mother. "You, too, Jee-hyun," he said. "Let's go."

The pond had changed since the afternoon: the dim evening light had turned the water greener, and the flowers around it seemed brighter. Scores of tiny silver fish were visible just beneath the surface of the water, and beneath them the heavy shadows of the large, dark fish.

We stood out there and listened to the sound the water makes when it is almost still: the barest of ripples lapping against the edge of the bank. My mother put her arms around herself and leaned against my father, who tilted his head to one side so it was resting on hers, and I knew they were listening, too.

16.

The next morning, my father ate a large breakfast and said, "Today I want to climb to the top of the mountain."

"Won't it be too much?" my mother asked.

"It will be all right," my father assured her. "Right, Jeehyun?"

I promised my mother not to let him overexert himself. We would turn back, I promised, before he wore himself out.

"I don't know," my mother said. But she looked at the empty plate in front of him, and I knew she was telling herself he must be feeling better if he'd eaten so well. So she let us go.

We started off in high spirits. The trail at the bottom of the mountain was muddy from the last week of rain, and at first our feet slid and gathered weight as we made our ascent. We tried to be good-humored about it, making jokes as we pulled our feet out of the sticky ground.

On our way up, we overtook a group of thirty or so women my grandmother's age, all dressed in the same outfit. They were wearing bright yellow T-shirts and identical calf-length black pants. They were noisy as sparrows, chattering and heaving their way up. Their walking sticks kept getting stuck in the mud. When we approached they stood to the right, single file, and let us pass.

The ground hardened after about half an hour, and we started to hike faster, though it was hot. We took frequent breaks on the benches, and once while we rested, the group of grandmothers passed us. My father seemed to gain energy from this, and a moment later we zoomed on ahead and passed them again. They laughed as we did so, calling out encouragement.

It took us a long time and was strenuous going, and we didn't talk much, just took our breaks when they were possible, resting and eating our snacks. When we finally reached the peak in a burst of energy, we were panting and hot. Below us stretched hills and hills. The country spread out before us. The wind brushed our faces. The sun was already low and sinking in the sky. The entire day was nearly gone. In the distance, we could see houses in the valley, spaced far apart. "Is one of those ours?" I asked, pointing.

My father leaned forward. He was panting a little. "There's our river, our little stream. But I don't see the pond, do you?"

I squinted. "No."

"Then I think our house is behind those trees over there." As he pointed, he leaned forward and his arm brushed my shoulder. It was so thin. His sweat smelled different: there was something metallic in it. Underneath his hat, my father had been losing his hair. At home, it covered the floors and matted on the bottoms of our socks—we were always picking it off and sweeping it up.

"I think it's about time we get started down," he said. He stood up and held out his hand to help me. I thought his face looked haggard.

"Yes," I said. "Let's go."

But then he turned and pointed to a path that was not the same as the one we'd come up. "Want to try another way down?" he asked.

"I don't know," I said, but I looked at his face, and it was eager. Suddenly, I wanted us to have an adventure: some evidence that he was still all right after all. "Okay," I said. "Let's do it."

The path he had chosen to take us down was more gradual, and seemed to go on for a long time. We made many winding little turns, alternating between trees and vistas. After a while I looked over at my father, and saw that he had turned pale. I asked how much longer he thought we had to go.

"I don't know," he said, pausing, his hand against a tree. "Let's rest a moment."

I pulled out my cell phone; I was not surprised that it had no reception. I looked at the sky. The sun was starting to fall, and I didn't want to get stuck out here in the dark. There were no other people on this path, and this worried me. I thought maybe we were going the wrong way, but I wasn't sure we'd be able to make it if we went back up and headed down again.

"The sun is setting," my father said, stepping out onto a rock at the side of the trail, where the trees fell away. He pointed at the horizon. And there it was, setting gloriously against the mountains, against a stream, over rice paddies I'd never seen before.

"Daddy, I think we're lost," I said. "We might be on the wrong side."

He nodded. "How much time do you think until the sunset?" he said, looking at the sun, and glancing at his watch.

"Not much," I said. "Should we go back up?"

He shook his head. "I'm tired," he said. "Let's just go down."

"Do you want to wait here? Should I run up and get help?"

"No, no," he said. "It will be all right." He touched my arm. His hand was warm; he was smiling. "Let's sit here and rest a moment." The evening light was soft and set the trees around us aglow. Even the rock we were standing on seemed to radiate the sun's fading light. "Jeehyun, how long?" He nodded at the sun.

I shielded my eyes. Half of it was already gone. "A couple minutes?" I said. "Maybe less."

"Less," my father agreed. He didn't look at his watch. "There isn't much left at all." We watched the sun disappear. The trees lost their glow.

"It's dark," I said. "Daddy, let's go."

"Just another second," he said. We were quiet. "Your mother and I went to a temple yesterday," he said. "On the way back from town."

"You did?"

"Yes. We drove up a beautiful path to get there," he said.

"Did you meet any monks?"

"Yes, we met the head monk, and when we were having tea, he said to me, 'Don't fight nature, everywhere is nature, and everything is nature.'"

"I wish for once they could just say whatever they're trying to say."

"I liked him," my father said. "I wish I could have talked to him longer. He was very old. He said, we fight so much in the world about what's ours and what's not. Who belongs where. America and Korea are different countries, and North Korea and South Korea are different countries, or one country divided in half, however we want to think of it; but he said always remember, one country, two countries, three countries, it doesn't matter: we are just one world." My father laughed. "He's right, you know. We're just one world."

"That's interesting, I guess."

"And afterwards I wrote all our names down to be painted onto the tiles of the temple's new roof."

"Did you make a donation?"

"Yes, of course," he said. "So all our names will be there, in a row up there next year. Haejin's, too." He laughed. "Whatever happens, we'll be together on the roof of the temple next year."

"We'll have to go and see it together then."

He didn't respond for a moment. "We should have gone on this walk two weeks ago," he said. "It wouldn't have tired me out as much then."

"It's a hard hike," I said, making my voice as bright as possible. "I'm tired, too."

"I wanted to come today," my father said, "because I thought it might be one of the last days to do it."

"Don't say that," I said. "You're doing fine."

"I meant before it gets too hot," my father said, gently. "There's no way we'll want to climb the mountain once the heat wave comes."

"Right," I said, calming down but still uneasy. I didn't like the feeling that my father had more to say and wasn't saying it. "Daddy, let's go," I said. I wanted us to get home safe.

We finally made it home around ten p.m., more than twelve hours after we'd set out. My mother rushed out the door before we even reached the walkway. "What happened?" she said, taking my father's arm. She turned him to face her, and looked full into his face: taking stock. When she was satisfied, she turned to me with a grim, hard look.

Inside, our dinner was still set out on the table, but it had long gone cold. All the little side dishes sat reproachfully there, the fish casserole, and three little bowls of congealing rice.

"How could you be so irresponsible?" my mother said. She helped my father out of his jacket. "How could you be so late?"

"We got lost," I said.

"It's my fault," my father said.

"I don't want any excuses," she said. "Your father missed his dinner today, and he's exhausted. You know how important it is for him to have regular meals and rest. You're not a child anymore. Whatever happens, it is on your head."

"I'm all right," my father said. His voice was weak, and filled me with remorse. "Truly, it's my fault," he said.

"Go to bed, darling." She gave him a push toward their bedroom, then turned toward me. She said, "I called Haejin while I was waiting for you."

"What?" my father cried, stopping on his way to their room. "How is she? What did she say?"

"She is coming in two weeks," my mother said. "She bought a ticket. Go to bed, I will tell you about it in a moment." Her voice was impatient, edged with anger.

I knew how exhausted my father was when he obeyed. "You'll tell me in a minute?" he said.

"Yes," she said. "I'll be right there."

He shuffled to their room. My mother turned back to me. She said, "I called her when you didn't come. I thought she should know that you and your father were lost—who knows where."

"It wasn't my fault," I began.

"Quiet," she said. And then, "I waited here all day, wondering what had happened, wondering if I should call the police, whether

I should wait. I sat by the phone, and then I sat by the window, and then I called your sister." She said fiercely, "How could you?"

I wondered what Hannah had told her. "I'm sorry," I said. "I didn't mean for you to worry."

"I don't want to hear it," my mother said. "I have wasted enough time." And she stalked to her room, and shut the door between us. I stood in the living room, staring at my parents' room for a good long while. I wondered what they were saying to each other. I listened for voices, but I heard absolutely nothing from their room.

The next morning, my father seemed all right. I was relieved. I had been unable to sleep worrying about him, and what he and my mother knew about what I had said to Hannah in Los Angeles, and how I had kept her away. But he said nothing about it.

"When Haejin comes," he said, "I want to celebrate. I was thinking we could go to the Muju Firefly Festival together."

"I don't think that's a good idea," my mother said.

"What's the festival?" I asked.

"You were exhausted just driving to Seoul," my mother said. "And remember how you wore yourself out yesterday?"

"I want to go," he said. "I'll be okay."

"It will be too hard on you," my mother said.

"Hello?" I said. "The festival?"

"Someone told us about it at the hospital," my father said. "He said it was magical. I thought it would be good for when Haejin comes. Remember how you used to catch fireflies in the backyard?"

I nodded.

"You used to make wishes on them," he said.

"No we didn't," I said. We'd wished on stars back in the day, not fireflies.

"No?" He sounded confused. "We used to catch them and make wishes on them," he said. "Didn't that happen?"

"I don't know," I said. I was sure we hadn't, but his confusion confused me. "Maybe we did."

In the following week, my mother was busy planning Hannah's arrival, and my father was busy making plans for the festival. He spent hours on the computer looking things up. He was so excited I couldn't help getting excited, too, even though it made my mother anxious.

I wasn't sure, but I suspected that Hannah hadn't said anything to my mother about our conversation in Los Angeles. I told myself it didn't matter: I'd told Hannah our father had cancer. It wasn't as if she hadn't known.

At the end of that week, my mother took me aside. "Don't encourage your father about Muju," she said.

"It might be good for him," I said. "He's looking forward to it."

"He's doing it to please you."

"Why would he think I wanted to go to Muju?"

"He thinks this will bring us all together."

"The firefly festival?"

"Yes," my mother said, laughing a little. "But it will make him sick." Her voice broke, and she turned away.

After that, I couldn't muster the same enthusiasm about the trip. I watched my father, and I saw how sometimes his hands trembled when he unfolded the map of Korea, and how it fluttered like a leaf between them. He began to sleep longer than he had, getting up later and going to bed earlier.

Meanwhile, news came from Michigan that our house had sold. The buyer was willing to take all of our bedroom furniture. From afar, we gave the agent permission to sell everything still in the house in an estate sale. Around that time, a strange and unrelated thing occurred. It was announced on the news that the father of the hermit girl who'd been discovered in the mountains had been killed. While his daughter was in Seoul, becoming famous, he'd been robbed and murdered in their solitary mountaintop hut. The hermit girl, newly orphaned, was stranded in the city, surrounded by well-meaning, guilt-ridden strangers, and besieged by reporters. She was all over the news, glimpses of her stricken, bewildered face that had not yet learned how to prepare another face to present to the world.

I was surprised by my interest in the hermit girl: how much I longed to make some connection between her story and my own. Like the rest of the country, I wanted to claim her as mine. I thought of her father, hidden with her in the mountains for all those years, and how he'd been found out at last. His daughter had left, and strangers had come to steal whatever was his. There was no safety in the world: no hiding.

I thought of the temple tiles my father had written our names on to go up on the roof next year. What else lay hidden in the mountains? I wondered. What else lay hidden in our bodies and souls?

17.

When Hannah finally arrived, she was as lean and stylish as
the last time I'd seen her, pulling behind her a soft and nubby dove
gray suitcase. In her hand was a photo album, which she held out
to us as we went to meet her.

"I brought pictures," was the first thing she said, and my mother
checked mid-step, so that my father and I surged forward, and my
mother was left behind us, on the patio, holding the door.

"Pictures of us, from before," Hannah continued, slowing down.
"I took them with me to California," she said, presenting them like
a gift.

"I didn't know you had those," I said.

"How would you?" she asked. She met my eyes. In that moment,
I knew at least that whatever she had told my mother, she hadn't
revealed that I'd told her not to come, that I'd said she was unwanted
here. Perhaps she had told her nothing: perhaps they hadn't talked
about me at all.

I looked at my father: his face was aglow. His hand gripped

my sister's shoulder. Hannah seemed to shrink away from his touch the tiniest bit. But he ignored this, or didn't notice, and pulled her forward by her shoulders then, into an embrace. Her arms came up, and she hugged him back. He was not one to hug others, we had never been that kind of family, and something about his doing so now both moved and angered me. In this unexpected pose they both looked fragile.

I reached out and took her suitcase, and she pulled her hand away quickly as she relinquished it, as if she was afraid.

My mother, who had been waiting all this time, stepped out of the house. "Come in," she called. She waved at the cloud of insects hovering in front of the door. And my father, a kind of light working on his face, took my sister's hand in his own and led her in.

"We're all tired," my mother said, once we were inside. "Unless you need anything, let's just go to bed for now, and talk in the morning."

"That sounds good," Hannah said.

"We're not going to ask her what she's been doing all this time?" I asked.

"Later," my father said. "There will be time for everything later," and he touched her arm.

"You'll sleep in that room," my mother said to Hannah, pointing at my room. "With your Unni." She leaned forward and gave my sister a kiss on the cheek. "Sleep well."

That night, Hannah slept on a sleeping mat next to mine. The heat came up through the floor and warmed us. We didn't say anything to each other. I wanted to sit up and turn on a light, and draw her the diagrams my father had made on my first night here: I wanted to tell her how our mother had ironed her clothes under the mattresses with her sister. I wanted to ask her if she'd wondered about us, and if she'd really believed me when I told her not to come.

Instead, I listened to her breathe. She was only an arm's length away from me. I could almost imagine that our breaths rose and fell in unison. We had not slept in the same room like this since we first moved to America. We had listened for ghosts then, her hands clasped around mine. *One if you're sleeping, three if you see a ghost.*

The next day, relatives and several of my parents' friends descended upon our house. They were all anxious to see Hannah. First my grandmother and uncle and my father's cousins came. Hannah sat in an armchair, her legs crossed at the ankles, her hands clasped together.

"She's so ladylike," my grandmother said, talking about her as if she was a doll. When anyone had a question to ask her, they looked to me to translate.

"She could be Miss Korea," my uncle said, looking her over shyly.

My grandmother said to her, "If you only learn how to speak Korean, you will be the perfect granddaughter."

Everyone called her Haejin. For most of her life, only my parents had called her that. I remembered that my grandmother, who had had to live with a Japanese name for her entire childhood, had not been publicly called by her own name until she was an adult. Even now she would not tell me what her Japanese name had been; not even my mother knew.

For the most part, Hannah played along. She smiled and nodded at everything that was said to her. She laughed when they told stories of when she was a baby. My parents passed around the photo album she'd brought to our guests. It was filled with pictures of us from childhood. "She brought it all the way from California," my father said.

And then, "Tell Uncle what you're studying," my father said. "Tell Auntie about your senior project."

And Hannah, leaning forward with a serious look in her eye, talked about wildlife rehabilitation—in English—while my father nodded his head enthusiastically and translated from time to time.

"Actually," Hannah said, looking at me, "I'll finish my studies this year and then I'll probably go to grad school."

"Another baksa in the family," Big Cousin said, laughing out loud. "I am jealous of you," he said to my father. He turned to me. "And how is your research coming?" he asked. "Will you win a Nobel Prize, or will your sister beat you to it?"

I squirmed. I hadn't been spending enough time on my work, and I was aware of falling behind. Recently, I'd found it increasingly difficult to find my way back into my own ideas.

Hannah surprised me by interrupting. "I was thinking maybe for my grad work I'd study biodiversity in Korea."

"That's what I would study if I had the chance," my mother said approvingly. "What would you focus on?"

Hannah talked about the wildlife that had been killed during the occupation and the war. About Agent Orange and what it had done to the forests. She talked about the wildlife flourishing in the DMZ, how it might be the only place in the world where Siberian tigers still lived.

"I want to go there and see things," she said. "I want to learn more."

I realized that Hannah actually knew things about this place.

I had thought that she had cut herself off from us entirely, but there were these threads she had thrown out in our direction, and followed. She had been tracking us, paying attention, when I thought she was wholly gone.

Still, we kept our distance from each other. If our parents noticed, they said nothing about it. As for Hannah, she and my parents acted as if the last year and a half of estrangement hadn't happened. They were polite and careful with each other, and if Hannah was a little reserved with them, my parents were tentatively affectionate. No one asked any difficult questions. We acted as if no such questions existed.

Hannah and I still hadn't really spoken when we went with my parents to the city for my father's chemo session that week. There was a new group of patients in the treatment room. They were not particularly talkative, but sat quietly in their beds from the very beginning. My family followed suit, sitting around my father's bed while he laid his head back and dozed.

Afterward, we went to the doctor's office and waited. My father was unexpectedly radiant, smiling at my mother, then me, then Hannah. He was proud to have his whole family with him.

My father's doctor did not notice. He greeted my mother and father, and glanced briefly at Hannah and me. Then he said without any preparatory remarks, "It's growing, just as I expected."

We took this in.

"About thirty percent in just two weeks," the doctor continued, "which is faster than I anticipated."

My father's face was frozen in place; I could not even look at my mother. His expression reminded me of myself when I was trying not to reveal a wound. I wished I could protect him from this conversation.

It was Hannah who spoke. "Ask him how he suggests we move forward," she said.

I asked the doctor her question. I added, "Can we switch to another kind of treatment?"

The doctor shook his head. "All we can do now is slow the growth," he said. "It will do no good to change the treatment." He turned to my parents. "I thought I was clear about that."

My father nodded, and I realized that they had already had this conversation. My parents had brought us here knowing what to expect. My father cleared his throat. "And if I discontinue treatment?" he said.

The doctor blinked. "I wouldn't recommend that," he said blankly.

"I've heard people can survive on alternative treatment or no treatment at all," my father said. "Do you know anyone who's done so?"

"Yes," the doctor said. "I know one man who left and tried alternative treatments and survived. But there is no medical reason for that to have happened," he said. "No one knows why that person survived. It might have been the medicine; it might have been a miracle." He shrugged.

"Do you know anyone in my situation who has survived on chemo?" my father asked.

The doctor shook his head. "No. But you have to consider the fact that it may actually make you more comfortable," he said. "Even if it doesn't meaningfully extend your life. We're aiming for palliative care now."

"I see," my father said.

"Ultimately," the doctor said, "the decision is up to you."

Then he told my father that the doctor from Texas who'd referred my father to him in the first place was in Seoul for a conference. "He asked about you," the doctor said. "I was sorry not to have better news to report."

"Thank you," my father replied. Then there was another moment of awkward silence, before the doctor wished my father luck in a way that made it clear that he did not think that there was much hope of anything.

We drove home very quiet, though my father continued to attempt cheerfulness. I could not join in. We were alone, I thought. Medicine had given up on us. We'd been cut loose.

At home, my father asked if I would e-mail the cancer specialist from Texas who was currently in Seoul. "Why would we do that?" I asked.

"Just to tell him how I am," my father said, smiling. "Since he's here, don't you think he'd want to know?"

"He already knows," I said. Didn't he remember how impatient that doctor had been with us? How he'd told us this was the only chance we had? This afternoon his own doctor had just said there was no hope. I wanted to shake him for not learning to stop going to these people for answers.

"Maybe I could take him on a tour," my father said. "Maybe I could show him the city."

"You can't take anyone on a tour," I said. "You're exhausted all the time."

"I think I should send him an e-mail," my father said. "Will you draft one for me?"

"That's not what he's here for," I said. I couldn't bear the thought of his disappointment when the doctor rejected him. "He doesn't want to see you. He can't help you. None of these people think you will make it."

My father smiled then, shrugging, and that smile shamed me to my core. "What do you think he can do for you?" I began angrily.

Before I could continue, Hannah stepped in. "I'll send the doctor an e-mail," she said. "It's no big deal." My father turned his head and smiled at her gratefully. "I'll do it right now," she said.

"It's a waste of time," I said, but they ignored me. Then she and my father turned their backs to me, wrote their e-mail, and sent it off. In the end, the doctor from Texas never replied, but it didn't matter. We never spoke of it again.

That same evening, I heard my father ask Hannah if she thought he should stop chemo. He asked her quietly and seriously, and she did not flinch.

She answered like an adult, "What are the risks and benefits?"

My father drew a chart and began to diagram his decisions. I bit my tongue and went into the garden to pull all the stubborn weeds that had put down deep roots since Hannah had arrived.

They were still going over it at dinner, their heads close together, neglecting their food. My mother sat calmly enough, occasionally commenting on trivial matters and pushing more food onto their plates.

"Why wouldn't you continue?" Hannah asked.

"I'm tired," my father said to Hannah.

I interrupted. "You still look good," I said.

"I can't taste my food," my father said. "Everything tastes like metal."

We fell silent.

"I care about quality of life," my father continued. "I don't want to be on chemo just to live an extra month."

"Does chemo decrease your quality of life?" Hannah asked.

My father shrugged. "I have headaches," he said. "Everything tastes wrong."

Hannah looked down at her plate. A few years after we first moved to America, she had started refusing to eat Korean food. She wanted hot dogs and grilled cheese and ice cream. She wanted American-people food. By the time she went to college, Asian food had gotten trendy, and I'd noticed she'd started eating it again. Now she seemed fine with everything.

"Once the tumors start growing, it's unlikely the chemo will be able to shrink them again," my father said. "But the doctor also says it's the best thing left to do. It's the only thing he thinks might slow the growth."

"What about alternative options?" Hannah said.

My father listed the names of two people who specialized in desperate cases; both of these alternative practitioners had saved relatives of my parents' friends, after their doctors had given up.

"But the doctor said alternative options have an even lower chance than chemo of working," my mother said.

My father snorted. "The doctor says there is no chance of the chemo working now." He shook his head. "So how can there be less hope than that? How can there be negative hope?" He laughed.

I tried to laugh, too, but I felt gutted. Negative hope.

Hannah cleared her throat. She looked down at her plate. We all looked at her. "You know there's this bird," she began, fiddling with her chopsticks, "that I'd like to track down while I'm here. It's native to Korea, and happens to be the only known species that can survive a certain fatal fungus."

I'd heard cancer described as a kind of fungus spreading within the body.

"What happens after the bird is infected?" my father asked.

Hannah settled in her seat and set down her chopsticks. "Well, it usually dies," she said. She leaned forward now. "Let me tell you how it happens."

Hannah had always been a storyteller. She'd scared her friends with ghost stories, she'd made them cry playing house because someone in the game, the baby, the mother, the sister, would always die.

She told us now that as the fungus spreads, the infected bird becomes covered in a sort of mold, and can no longer fly because its feathers grow stiff and heavy. Its beak begins to soften, and when it tries to peck insects out of trees, the beak bends and becomes deformed. Even its claws begin to rot and fall out one by one. Most of the birds that get this disease, she said, starve to death. Not even their predators will touch them. "When my professor lived in Korea she discovered one of these sick birds," Hannah said. I noticed as she spoke how in control of my parents she was, how completely they were her audience.

"Is your professor Korean?" my father asked.

Hannah nodded. So her professor had found a bird covered in this mold; it had fallen at the foot of her tree. She picked it up: the fungus felt like moss against her hand. The bird blinked a crusted eye.

She took the bird inside and put it in a crate. She did not give it food; she did not try to wash it. She knew there was nothing to be done. Still, she wanted to keep the bird warm overnight, and to keep it company while she could.

The next morning, it was on its feet, shuffling against the edges of its box. It was agitated, but stronger than it had been the day before. So Hannah's professor took it outside and left it where she had found it, at the foot of the tree. All day the bird knocked its mangled beak wearily against a nearby rock until the rotten parts broke off in long, painful slivers, leaving only the soft tender core.

At night, she gathered the bird and took it inside again. The next morning, the bird lay in the box and did not move. She gave it water. It slept. She thought it would die. The next day, however, it was up again, plucking out its own feathers, pulling out the stubs of its claws with its soft core of a beak.

She gave the bird more water. She gathered insects and worms. She could not bear what the bird was doing to itself. It looked like suicide. But then, Hannah said, the bird did not die. Every day her professor gave the bird water and fed it, and day by day the beak hardened. Slowly the feathers and claws grew back. Later she learned that if the bird had neglected to tear out a single feather, or left a single claw, the disease would have returned. But each rotten part of itself grew back new, and the bird lived and recovered, and flew away.

When Hannah finished this story, my mother stood up. "So," she said. "I am glad you are here. And I am glad you have learned how difficult it is to survive."

18.

In the coming weeks, Hannah and I took turns tending to the garden, taking walks with our parents, serving fruits and drinks to our guests. My father gave up chemotherapy and started a course of alternative treatment that involved special meals, fresh-pressed juices, and hundreds of pills. Once he started, it felt oddly as if nothing had changed from when he was receiving chemotherapy. My parents had heard stories about friends who had stayed alive this way, and it felt easy to transfer our hope from one method to the next, as if this might work for us, too. In any case, we did not talk about it very much.

Instead, my mother prepared all my father's special juices and meals. She did our laundry, she cleaned our house. Every day at every meal, before she began to eat, she touched my father's hand quickly, as if she wanted none of us to see. Astonishingly, my father began to seem better. He seemed to be gaining strength.

He even brought up the approaching Muju festival, which he

hadn't mentioned at all since Hannah's arrival. I thought he'd forgotten or given it up.

"Will you go?" he asked Hannah, after describing what it was.

"Sure," Hannah said. She grinned.

I expected my mother to protest, as she did when my father first brought it up, but she just pursed her lips and said nothing.

I turned to my father. "Maybe it's too far: you don't want to get worn out," I said.

"No, I feel good," he said. He jumped up and down. "See?"

He looked so light on his feet. "I want to see the fireflies," he said. He smiled at me, his face hopeful and bright.

"And after the festival, I'm going to stay longer," Hannah said. "I cleared it with school; I'm taking a leave of absence, and I can stay as long as you need me."

"That's great news!" My father stuck out his hand at her, beaming. "Shake," he said.

"Can you really take that much time off school?" my mother asked.

"Sure," Hannah said. "I'm doing great right now, it'll be fine."

A period of unprecedented calm followed. We filled the days with family walks and visits from friends. In the evenings we played card games and planned our trip to Muju. Hannah and I began, tentatively, to hang out. We gardened side by side; we went on hikes. We were reserved still, but more relaxed. I began to think that maybe this was just how it would be between us. That nothing was resolved, but perhaps even that was all right.

All this might have continued if it hadn't been interrupted by my Komo's next visit. This time she brought my cousin Keith, and together they swept into our house. He had grown into a totally different person from the boy he'd been in America: tall and lanky now with a pleasant, thoughtful face.

Hannah did not recognize them at first, and greeted our Komo the same way she greeted everyone here, with a deep, stiff bow, jerky with her hands at her sides.

"Haejin," my aunt said. There was some quality to the way she said my sister's name that made me look up. She came forward with both arms outstretched in a theatrical gesture.

Then Hannah knew who she was. She stepped away. "Don't touch me," she said, surprising us all.

My aunt shrugged, lowered her outstretched arms, and stepped around Hannah. "Don't worry about her, my dear," she said to my father, taking his hand. "I know how children are."

Keith looked down. His face was quiet, thoughtful even. From what I knew of him as a child, I would have expected him to be watching with a smirk on his face. I would have thought he'd say something snide.

"When are you going to get a job, Jeehyun?" my aunt said, turning to me as we arranged ourselves at the kitchen table. "Don't you think it's time you supported yourself?"

"She does," my mother said, coming in with the first tray of tea, and setting it down. "Jeehyun has always had fellowships and full scholarships for school."

"She gets her brains from our side of the family," my aunt replied.

My mother snorted, tried to cover it with a cough, and gave my aunt her tea.

My aunt said, "I wish that you were settled. How can your father feel easy in his mind knowing you haven't established yourself in any way?"

This was something I had worried about. I looked up at my father, and he winked. I felt immediately better.

"It's a tough life," I said.

"In my time it was nothing to joke about," my aunt said. "Two unmarried girls whiling away their time out here in the country-side when they could be making themselves useful."

"Ah," my mother said, coming in with the tray of honeydew, Hannah with empty hands following behind her. "You forget, we don't believe in being useful."

My aunt looked up at my mother, anger gathering in her face. "Yes. That's what I came here to talk about," she said.

"Haven't we already had this talk?" my mother asked, sweetly. She sat down very gracefully, with great care, and folded her hands in her lap.

My aunt reached out her hands, and nodded at the fruit tray. "Let us pray," she said. My mother did not protest, but gave my aunt her hand. I wondered if my aunt really prayed over all her snacks, or if this was meant solely for our benefit.

I was gamely reaching for Hannah's hand when she rose from her chair. "Jesus fucking Christ," she said.

"Haejin," my mother said, but Hannah was already heading for the door, which she slammed behind her on the way out. There was a shocked silence, and then my aunt bowed her head again as if nothing had happened, and continued praying. I saw her fingers tighten over my father's. When she was finished, she raised her head and looked at each of us in turn.

"Maybe I should go after Hannah," I said to my mother in a low voice, but she shook her head.

"Let her go for now," she said.

"It's a shame that girl doesn't have better manners," my aunt said. She speared a piece of melon and put it in her mouth. "Never did."

My parents were silent. "I think she's all right," I surprised myself by saying. "She's gotten along great with everyone else until now."

"It doesn't matter," my aunt continued, "I came to talk about other matters. I've met a minister who has offered to come out here once a week to pray for a cure for you."

"That's very kind of you, but it's not necessary," my mother said.

"It might help," my aunt said. "Many people have been healed by faith."

At this point, Keith sighed loudly, and I turned to him. "Would you like to go for a walk?" I said. "I don't think we need to be here for this."

He looked at his mother, and nodded quickly. "Yes," he said. "Please." So we left our parents to have their conversation about prayer and sickness and God.

When did you get to Korea?" Keith asked as we circled the pond. He still spoke English fluently, but had acquired an accent.

"Just a couple months ago," I said. Hannah was nowhere to be seen. Where had she gone? I wondered. Perhaps she had gone up the mountain; perhaps she'd gone down the country road to look at the fields.

"Are you glad you stayed in America?" he asked. "For college and everything, I mean."

"I don't know," I said. "I can't imagine anything else. What about you?" Perhaps Gabe's accident wouldn't have happened if they'd stayed in America. But Keith just shrugged.

He rubbed his hand over his chin. "You know," he said, "your father is my favorite relative. It's too bad he's the one who got sick. He's the best of everyone."

"Thanks."

"Seriously," Keith said. "He's a decent guy. One of the only decent guys in my family." And he laughed. He reached down and picked up a handful of stones, flinging them one by one at the fish.

We talked then, about his move to Korea and how disorienting it had been for him. "That's the first time I understood what you and Haejin must have gone through," he said. I nodded, surprised to hear my sister's name on his lips. Aside from that, though, we didn't talk about her or about Gabe.

We paused for a moment to admire the shining surface of the pond, and just then, a beautiful long water snake slithered through the water and slid across the rocks at our feet.

"Look at that," I said, touching Keith's arm and pointing. He jumped.

"Don't worry," he said, shaking his arm as if to rid it of my touch. He picked up a stick. "I'll take care of it."

"Oh no," I said. "Don't." But he had already leaped forward, and was bashing at the snake with the staff. The snake writhed under the blows, stuck between the rocks, which glistened like glass.

"Stop," I said, and I stepped forward, but something stopped me from touching him again. "It's bad luck," I pleaded. All the creatures that lived on this property were our creatures. This pond, this mountain, this air were all supposed to make my father better. "Leave it alone."

"Don't worry, I won't let it get you."

"Please," I said, but maybe he misread the panic in my voice because he thrashed even more wildly at the snake until I finally couldn't bear it. I grabbed his arm and pulled him away. The snake curled in on itself and slid backward into the water. It drifted away from us limply, its body bending in the water. It coiled and uncoiled, and it was unclear whether this was a live motion, or the water pushing against it.

I couldn't believe that the snake had been so easily killed. *I should have stopped him,* I thought. *I shouldn't have let something like that happen here.* I did not notice that we had begun walking toward home until we were almost back.

nside, my father was sitting at the table, eyeing a cup suspiciously. Keith and I hesitated at the door. My aunt was watching my father intently. He picked up the cup and downed it.

"Thank you, Noonah," he said, when he was finished.

"Remember," my aunt said, pulling back slowly, "four people from our church were cured by this. And daily prayer." Then she turned to us.

"Did you have a nice visit?" she asked.

Keith nodded. She smiled. She cocked her head at me. "You're no beauty like your mother," she remarked.

I heard my mother suck in her breath.

"It's probably better," my aunt continued. "Humility is important."

"Thank you," I said. "They tell me I look like you."

My aunt laughed. "You're thicker than I was at your age," she said dismissively. "Of course I changed after I was married and never got my figure back. Not that my children ever appreciated it." She fixed Keith in her sights. "At least not him."

I sat with my aunt and cousin for another hour before they left. I watched their departure with relief, and went for a walk as soon as they were gone.

Our garden was the same as always, the plants a little wilted in the midday sun. I knew I should water them, but I walked past. I avoided the pond, and went to the river instead. I walked toward the mountains.

As I approached, I saw Hannah coming down the path, and I went out to meet her.

"Hey," she said.

"Hey," I said. "You were smart to leave."

She smiled a little, but she didn't ask what had happened. Together we walked back to our house. When we entered, my parents were still seated at the table, all the uncleared tea things between them. My father was slouched in his chair.

"You sent her money for years," my mother was saying. "Money we didn't have, money I denied our children——"

My father sat up suddenly as we walked in, and hit the table with one hand. The little forks on the plate of fruit jangled. "Enough," he said.

I jumped at the noise, but what frightened me was the expression on his face. It was not angry or impatient—there was no emotion in it. Just weariness and dread. "Please stop."

That night, after everything had been cleared away and washed and put back, in the dark through the wall between our two rooms, I could hear my mother, sharp and clear, "Why should we have to see your sister? It's not as if she ever has anything good to say to us. Even your daughter hates her."

And then my father, blurred and indistinct, his voice pleading.

I rolled over so I was facing Hannah, but she was on her back, perfectly still, asleep. Her sleeping roll was so close to mine that I could feel the heat of her body. Her lips were slightly parted, her blanket rising and falling with her breath.

The next morning my parents were acting cold to each other, and Hannah was sullen.

"What should we do today?" I asked brightly, hoping I could cheer everyone up. Hannah flicked her eyes at me and gave the slightest shrug of her shoulders.

My parents were similarly listless, though beneath their listlessness was a lurking anger I didn't quite understand. Hardly anyone spoke at breakfast, and even our movements were clipped and silent. It went on like that all day, as if this combination of exhaustion and wrath had been simmering under all those days of quiet in our house. It might have burned itself out if not for the appalling weather, but as the pressure grew in the air outside, my parents grew more irritable. The house already felt claustrophobic when the monsoon began in torrents, in floods, as if the sky was a bowl of overturned water.

All day it rained. The roads to our house got washed away. We were stuck in that downpour of rain together, and none of us had anything good to say. I fretted: if something happened to my father, how would we get him to a hospital? I watched my parents, I watched Hannah, I watched the rain. I remembered that my grandmother had told me that in the countryside corpses rose from the ground during monsoons.

Too many people had been improperly buried during the Korean War. Near the sites of big battles, corpses would float to the surface, released from the grip of the earth. They would float down the streams that washed away the streets. When the rains abated, someone would have to go around collecting those bodies deposited in people's backyards, most of them just bones and skulls. In the quiet tension of our house, I almost expected such a catastrophe. I almost wanted the corpses to rise.

My parents stared moodily at the rain, which brought tiny frogs, hopping across the street past our house. The frogs traveled single file like they were in a miniature parade. They were as small as marbles. From a distance, they looked like blown leaves being pushed ahead by the rain. They made little paths in the mud, small roads to somewhere else. And it rained on for days.

My father became finicky. He spent more and more time in his room; he became peevish and hard to please. "I don't have enough room in my stomach to eat as much as you feed me," he complained.

Every day during the rains I went outside and worked in the garden to try to keep the tomatoes and other plants from washing away. Each morning the pepper plants were overturned, the tomatoes drowning. I drove the stakes back into the ground, cutting the old ties that floated in the water and tying the plants back up. As I worked, my feet sank into the mud and were held there by the weight of the earth. When I came back in, Hannah was reading on the sofa. My parents sat mutely, staring out of windows, typing on their computers. It made me impatient.

"How come this is all we ever do?" I said.

My parents kept typing on their separate laptops. Hannah kept reading. Those days, my parents stayed home and did not drive into the city. I took my notebooks into my room and worked on the floor. I wrote long notes to my advisor and received long notes back that felt like my only link to the outside world. I lived almost entirely in my own mind, and I tried to think only about my work. I was reminded how reassuring it could be to live in the world of abstract ideas: how it untethered you from the physical world, and cut you loose from reality.

When I emerged from my room, my mind was bleary and unfocused. But I noticed at mealtimes how my father ate less every day; he took his pills one by one, and grew weaker.

Finally the rains ended; not everything was ruined. The garden survived. One sunny morning, my father opened all the windows. The heat had lifted somewhat, and we went outside and walked around. Things felt better.

That night my parents said they wanted to play cards. We pulled out our table and chairs onto the porch, under the starlit expanse of sky. We brought out tea and fresh sliced peaches, and from the trees there came the tentative calling of the frogs. The river was engorged on the recent rains, and it roared by as loud as we'd ever heard it. We had to raise our voices over it.

My father's favorite card game was a partners' game, and I was partners with my mother, Hannah with my father. My mother and I kept winning, by a lot, and my father shouted and laughed every time a point went against them. It was such a relief to be outside, laughing and talking again.

"Hannah," I said, "do you remember when you were little you used to say that four was the perfect number for a family?"

"Did I say that?" she asked. "I don't remember." She sounded a little stiff.

After a while my mother said to Hannah, "Are you sure it's all right to miss the rest of the semester?"

"Of course," Hannah said. "I would have come sooner if Janie had told me how sick Dad was."

It took a moment, but I could sense the shift in the silence, as if it everyone was suddenly paying attention.

My father lay down a card. "What do you mean by that?" he asked.

Hannah shrugged. "If I'd known, I would have come right away."

"Jeehyun never told you?" my mother asked.

Hannah shrugged again.

"I did tell her," I said. I gripped the table.

"You said he was fine," Hannah said. "You said it was under control."

"Why are you doing this?"

"You lied to me," Hannah said. "You didn't tell me how sick he was."

"You knew," I said. "I told you everything."

"You told me he wasn't that sick."

"I told you he wasn't dying."

My father took in a sharp breath.

"She disappeared," I said. "She didn't call."

"I can't believe this," Hannah said. "Unni, you lied. You kept me away."

"No one kept you away," I said. "You're the one who deserted us."

"Jeehyun," my mother said, "Haejin. Stop." But it felt good for us to be fighting for once, and I didn't want to stop.

"Do you see how they're afraid of offending you?" I said. "Do you see how carefully they treat you?"

My father reached out to Hannah and put a hand on her shoulder. Hers, not mine. "Let's not fight," he said. "You're here now."

I kept going. "You have no idea what it was like for us while you were gone," I said.

"Enough," my father said. "Jeehyun, enough."

"It wasn't my fault," I said. "Daddy."

He didn't respond. The moon shone on his face, and he turned away from me. My cards were still in my hand.

Hannah spoke. "I'm sorry, I shouldn't have started this," she said, but she was talking to my father. "It's not worth fighting over."

I looked at my parents, and then back at Hannah. She looked so smug, and I wanted to hit her. She didn't get to be magnanimous, I thought. She didn't get to win. "You knew I was lying," I said. "You knew Mom and Dad wanted you here, when I told you in L.A. not to come. You knew the whole time we were waiting for you."

"Jeehyun," my mother said sharply, "there's no reason to ruin our first nice night in weeks."

"I won't let her blame me for this."

"Janie," Hannah said, and her voice was very patient, as if she'd already won. "You said they didn't want me. You said they were done."

"You knew better," I said. "Mom and Dad called you every week. Jesus, Hannah. I flew out there."

"And then you told me not to come," Hannah said. "Why would you do that?"

For a moment I just looked at her. Then I put my cards down. "Because you wanted me to," I said. "Because you deserved it. Because you knew better and still you chose to believe it." I looked at Hannah, at my mother, my father. "Aren't you going to ask her?" I asked them. "Don't you want to know how she could disappear without one word of reassurance? Don't you want to know how she could put us through something like that?"

My mother was silent. My father was silent.

"Isn't that the million-dollar question?" I asked. "The thing no one has been able to ask since she miraculously came back? Can you answer it, Hannah? Can you tell us anything that would make us understand?"

"You told me not to come," she said, very softly.

"You chose to let us suffer."

Hannah shook her head. "I would have come," she said. "I'm here."

"Yes, and you were welcomed here with open arms. But you should have crawled here on your knees and asked forgiveness when you found out Dad was sick. You should have come whether we wanted you or not, because you couldn't bear not to be here. That's what you should have done, Hannah. I gave you that chance, and you stayed away."

"Jeehyun, enough," my father said.

I ignored him. "You didn't love us enough."

My father's hand hit the table. "Enough," he said. "Please stop." His face was white, and his hand was clenched, as if he was bracing himself against some terrible pain.

"Yubbo, don't get excited," my mother said. She touched his arm. Then she looked at us. "I think this game is over," she said. "It's time for us to go to bed."

Hannah was silent, and I, too, was quiet, stricken by my father's expression. Hannah looked at no one as we cleared the table and brought in the table and chairs.

When we had gone inside and said good night to our parents and went to our room, Hannah closed the door and stepped onto my sleeping mat. She whispered, "I have something to say to you."

"Please don't step on my sleeping mat," I said. Then I looked at her face. "Okay," I said. "Let's go outside."

We sneaked out of the house together. The river was still roaring. I watched Hannah's face from the corner of my eye. It grew darker as we stepped farther away from the house and toward the pond, and then her face was lost in shadow, and we walked on. When we reached the pond it was very still, lit by a sliver of moonlight that cut across its surface and trembled there.

Hannah was the first to speak. "That was a great performance you gave tonight," she said. "It was really well done. How you threw me under the bus. You've never done that before."

"You attacked first," I said. "You cornered me."

"Whatever," she said. "Fuck you."

"No, seriously, you shouldn't have started it," I said, but her words stung. I felt ashamed. "And whatever code existed, you broke when you left the way you did, when you didn't answer my phone calls begging you to call back."

"So you said."

"It's not that I don't want things to be better between us," I said. "I want to move on."

"But you still need answers," Hannah said. "Why I left, why I don't love you enough, why I am the way I am." She laughed, a short, terse laugh.

"I do."

"It's a little late for this conversation is all I want to say. It's a little late for your curiosity."

I thought of her spit bubbles as a child, how they had held me hostage. I thought of life this past year, without her. I stepped toward her. "Listen, sometimes I've wished I could run away from everything, too."

There was a moment of silence, and then Hannah laughed again. I could sense the tension in her laughter, in the way she held her body. "Jesus Christ," she said. "You really are a piece of work. When you're the one who said never to tell."

"What are you talking about?"

"Don't pretend you don't know."

"I'm not pretending."

She turned to face me, and her eyes were red. She did not relax her glare, and she reminded me suddenly, strongly and completely, of my mother. "You told me not to tell anyone what happened to me, and you were my *sister*. I trusted you."

"Okay, you're freaking me out. I still don't know what you're talking about."

"He touched me," Hannah said. "He touched me and all of you knew it, everyone knew and all you said was be quiet, don't talk, don't say anything."

My entire body felt the shock of it. "No," I said, with such force that I staggered forward. It was so sudden, the realization so complete: it was like hitting a wall, like the bones of my face rearranging themselves completely and forever. I knew.

"It was Gabe," I said. "Oh God." My reaction was instantaneous. I began to cry in front of my sister for the first time in years. But even then I didn't really know what he had done, what I had told my sister to hide. That he had hurt her doll? That he had touched her how? She had been clothed when I found her. She had been *fine*.

I couldn't think straight. "Hannah," I said, "I didn't know."

She shrugged. "Anyway, that's that."

"What did they do? How did they touch you?"

"It's too late to talk about this now," she said. "When it happened, you told me to keep quiet."

"I thought all they did was mess up your doll." I rubbed my face with my hand. "Please tell me," I said, but I was frightened. It was too much to deal with on top of everything else, too long ago to do anything about.

I started to pace, walking up and down a small section of the dirt path.

After a moment Hannah came to me. She reached out and grabbed my arm. "Stop it," she said. And then, "Don't worry." Her voice was calm. "It was like a hundred years ago."

I shook my head. "No," I said. My voice broke. "Tell me what I can do."

"Nothing." She let go of my arm. "It's too late."

I stopped pacing and faced her. I wanted to say something, but I felt what she said was true. Too many years had passed, and too much distance had accumulated between us. So we stood there in the darkness together, and I was quiet. I stood beside her and watched the moonlight skim over the water, silencing each question that was no longer my right to ask.

19.

For several nights after that, I slept in the living room and let Hannah have our room to herself. My parents didn't comment on the new arrangements, and neither did Hannah. During the day, our house was quiet. Neither of my parents brought up the conversation from the card game. I wondered what they thought of what I had done.

One day my father brought up his plans for the firefly festival in Muju again. He hadn't talked about it for so long that I had assumed those plans were off, but when he mentioned it, we all agreed we would go. Two days before the festival was to begin, my mother and Hannah went to the grocery store together: they didn't invite me. I stood in the kitchen grinding down carrots for my father's juice, feeling left out. No one had spoken much to me in days, though they'd started tentatively talking to each other, and my feelings were hurt. *Let everyone hate me,* I thought.

My father came to the entrance of the small kitchen and stood, watching me. I did not turn around. "I don't want to go anymore," I said.

He sighed and came next to me. "I want to change our mood," he said. "I want us to be more cheerful."

He smiled at me hopefully, but I didn't smile back. *I am tired of always being wrong,* I thought. *I am tired of always being the one to give in.*

"Jeehyun," he said.

"What?" I didn't turn from the juicer. I pushed in another carrot and ground it down loudly. I pushed it all the way down to its core.

My father waited. I turned off the juicer, wiped my hands. "What?" I said again. The roughness of my own voice startled me. "I'm making your juice."

"I just want to talk," my father said. "How is your work going?"

I turned back to the juicer and began taking it apart into its component parts. I scraped all the carrot shreds into the trash.

"It's going fine," I said, and it was true. My work had actually been coming along great. "I thought you were more interested in it than you were though, I guess."

"I am sorry," he said quietly, "that I haven't been able to help you."

"I didn't need your help, I just thought you could care. Just drink your juice," I said. "I'll clean this up."

"Jeehyun," he said, taking his cup. "Wait a second, and come in the other room with me." And he went into the living room. I followed him, and watched him seat himself stiffly. He frowned at his juice, swirled it a little, as if it were a glass of wine. He took a sip and made a face. "I can't follow things so well anymore," he said. "I can't concentrate." Absently, he picked up my notebook from the table.

He opened it. Then he took another sip of his juice and looked up at me. "About your sister," he said. "Don't be so hard on her."

"I'm not the one who's hard." I squeezed my hands together. "Do you ever tell her to go easy on me?"

My father shook his head and smiled. "You're the one I can explain it to," he said.

"It's not fair."

He tapped my notebook. "An equation with no roots has no solution," he said.

"No," I said. I was tired. "It's not my fault that we don't have roots." I didn't want to fight with him while he was drinking his medicine. It was bad luck.

My father reached forward and put his hand on my arm.

"We have roots," he said. "Everyone does."

I shrugged his hand off, but where his hand had been, my arm was still warm. "I'll bring you the rest of your pills," I said.

That afternoon, my father sat at the table looking over my notebook. When I came back to check on him, he looked up and smiled. He tapped my notebook. "This is great!" he said. "Really great." He stood up and stretched, as if looking over my work for several hours had energized him. "I could kind of follow most of it," he said. "It was exciting. And the new sketches you've made of the discs intersecting in four-dimensional space are really beautiful," he said. "If I didn't know it was math, I'd think it was art."

I soaked in his approval. We spent the rest of the afternoon wandering around the property and napping. I woke up first and took out my notebook again. I was surprised to discover that it looked different to me this time. I began to see connections I hadn't seen before, a way to break through where I'd long been stuck. Something seemed to open up to me then: a path I might clear for myself if only I could follow it.

That evening, I was almost cheerful. I smiled at Hannah and my mother when they returned. While my family prepared dinner, I e-mailed my advisor in Chicago and told him what progress I'd made. I worked late into the night.

The next morning, my father slept in. It was the day before the festival, and we were preparing for the trip when he called out to my mother. She sent Hannah to see what he needed. A moment later, I heard her call, "Unni," in a low, urgent voice. I set the silverware down in a heap on the table. I moved toward my father's room. Before I reached it, a bad smell hit me. The first thing I saw was a heap of vomit next to my father's mattress on the floor, and my father's head next to it. He was on the ground, his hands on either side of his head, which was pressed sideways into the ground. He was trying to push himself up.

"I can't get up," he said, panting. He looked up at us, his eyes wide and startled.

I moved quickly toward him, looking away from the vomit, looking only at his eyes, at his head pressed awkwardly against the ground. "Sure you can get up," I said. I reached out my hand. "You just need a little help."

He took my hand in his, and I pulled. But he just lay there, on his side. Nothing happened. There was no strength in his arms. I tugged again. He moaned.

"Should we call Mom?" Hannah said. "Are you sure we should move him?"

He turned his head to look at us. His eyes were very wide. "Let me get up," he said. "I don't want your mother to see me like this."

"Get behind him," I instructed my sister. "Try to lift him from the middle."

So we all pulled as hard as we could, and then as he was rising, Hannah braced herself, scrambled for footing, and slipped on the heap of vomit by my father's pillow. She went down with a thud, and my father, wobbling, clutched at my hand for one breathless moment, then wavered and fell.

He fell forward toward me, and horrified, I stepped back. I will never understand how I did not catch him when he reached his arms out to me, how I did not step toward him, or beneath him, how I did nothing to break his fall, but stepped away.

For one terrible moment, I thought he would hit his head on the floor, but he fell on the mattress, his body folding beneath him like a marionette bending at the joints. As I knelt down to help him again, he began to tremble.

"Help me," I cried to Hannah, who was still on the floor.

I knelt down. I turned him over so he wasn't lying on his face, and then he lay crumpled on his side, twitching, his eyes unfocused.

I cried for my mother then, yelling her name in a panic like I was a child. There was a clatter in the kitchen, then her footsteps running toward us. She pushed me aside as she entered, and went straight to my father, gathering him up in her arms.

"Call an ambulance," she cried. "Call your uncle. Do something!" But I just stood there. I could not move. I could not take my eyes off him. I had let him fall. I had let him down, and I still could not believe what was happening.

It was Hannah who went to the phone and called my uncle. I

could hear her speaking her frantic, awkward Korean from my parents' bedroom as I watched my mother rock my father in her arms.

We drove to the hospital—my father strapped in beside my mother, his seat reclined all the way back, almost to my lap. Twenty minutes into that drive, another car turned unexpectedly in front of us from a small dirt road. My mother swerved to avoid it, and Hannah and I reached out simultaneously for my father's shoulder. Our car spun halfway and stopped, and we sat there, stunned and disoriented. It was so sunny outside, the road ahead of us so clear. Then my mother turned the car in the right direction and kept going.

A little later, my father woke up. "What's going on?" he asked. "Where are we?" He turned and looked at Hannah and me. "I must have fallen asleep," he said. "Are we going to Muju?"

My mother reached over and put her hand on his leg. She said, "We're going to the hospital. Just sit back and rest."

I pressed my forehead against the cold window. The hills, the paddies, all of it shining and glorious under the sun. And at any moment anything could happen and change: a car could appear from nowhere and run you down. This was how life worked, and we had no control—your foot could slip, your heart could stop, one cell might mutate again and again—and suddenly you had this disease that could grow in your body until everything was powerless to stop it.

In the hospital my father lay in his bed; my mother had gotten him a private room, and it was very clean and empty. The floor shone. The doctor was a short, squat, oily-looking man. "How long have you had blurred vision?" he asked my father.

"You've had blurred vision?" I asked.

"Jeehyun, be quiet," my mother said softly.

"About a month," my father said.

"How long have you been disoriented?" the doctor said.

"I'm not sure."

"How long have you had difficulties with cognitive processes: difficulty concentrating, finding it hard to read, forgetting words, being unable to add or subtract numbers?"

"A while."

I stared. My father had never said anything about forgetting words, being unable to add or subtract numbers. How long had he been losing at card games? I tried to count back.

The doctor stood up and turned away from my father. He addressed himself to my mother. He said my father had had a seizure: a tumor had spread to his brain and swelled. "He had better stay here from now on. We will be able to deal with such emergencies as they arise." He didn't say anything about the possibility of my father improving. Then he left, and we could hear his shoes tapping the floor as he walked down the long hall.

"Don't worry," my father said, looking up at us, an IV hooked up to his bed. How quickly he had become one of the patients, in his blue gown, lying in his bed with rails. It hit me how frail he was: how taut his skin, how yellow his eyes. I had not noticed until now.

Later, my mother and I sat out in the hallway in two chairs we'd brought out from my father's room. We were watching him in shifts; right now it was Hannah's turn.

In the hallway, a girl walked slowly with her father. Perhaps she was my age, or maybe even younger. Her face was sunken, but some sheen of youth still clung to her skin. Her hair was thin and fell limply around her shoulders. Back and forth she walked in her hospital gown, long and blue, stamped with the hospital's logo and address, rolling her IV before her.

Through her gown, I could see all her bones, her shoulder blades, her collarbone, and the sharp, dangerous points of her elbows. She shuffled her feet. She might have been pretty once, but now she had thin, colorless lips and enormous watery eyes. The bones of her face were too sharp. But they might have been lovely. She might have been beautiful, before the illness had wrecked her face and made it look so tired.

Her father murmured beside her, stroking her hand. His whole body was turned toward her, his shoulders, his head tilted in, even his feet shuffling sideways so that his toes pointed toward hers. His hand on her back looked strong. I wondered if the girl was dying, if she had hope. I wondered if we were all using up the same hope.

"I can't do this. I want to run away," my mother suddenly said. She twisted her hands in her lap. "I want to get in the car and drive." And suddenly, so did I. I wanted to run away from all of them, from the guilt I felt every time I looked at Hannah, from my mother's haggard, worried face and the memory of my father's mouth twitching, saliva coming out the corners.

When I was little, my mother used to leave the house after a fight with my father and say she was never coming back. She'd drive away in tears, both Hannah and me begging her to stay. Sitting with her now, I could imagine her leaving, and Hannah with her. "You can't trust me," I wanted to tell her. "I can't be counted on." I had let my father fall. I had let everyone down.

. . .

Every morning, the nurses came and weighed my father, took his vitals, his blood pressure. All day long they measured him, then had nothing to say. All day long I thought of my sullen response when he'd said he wanted to go to Muju: *I don't want to go anymore.*

We sat by his bedside and tried to talk. My mother called her relatives, his relatives, their friends, and we listened to her explain again and again that we were at the hospital now, that something had happened.

The day of the firefly festival came and went. My grandmother and uncle tried to visit, but my mother sent them away.

"In Korea it's not appropriate for someone your grandmother's age to have to face an illness in the husband of her child," she said when I asked why. "It's a burden for both parties, it goes against the order of things." So my grandmother sent messages and food through my uncle, but she did not come again.

My father tried to be cheerful, and we tried to be cheerful with him. But every time I left his room I saw things I did not wish to see. I saw whole families weeping, men, women, children. I saw a man lose his balance and swing in a long arc across the room, spinning until the IV pole tipped and took him with it. He lay splayed against the floor, a trickle of blood collecting near his face while nurses rushed to help him up. And there was so little blood, as if he had nothing left in him to lose.

My Komo and her cousins piled into the room later one afternoon while my father was sleeping. When they arrived, my aunt's eyes were brimming with tears, and Big Cousin's wife was openly weeping.

"How is he?" she asked in a voice loud enough that it woke him. My father opened his eyes, and tried to sit up. Hannah and I stepped forward to help him. He did not like other people seeing him in bed, or watching him while he slept.

He smiled at my Komo and reached out his hand. He wanted to shake hands with everyone: he thanked them for coming to visit. "I'm doing just fine," he announced.

Big Cousin asked in a low, stricken voice if it was true he'd had a seizure. If it was true he had a tumor in his brain.

"Sure," my father said. "But it's no problem."

Big Cousin's wife howled, then covered her mouth. My father stared at her, startled at the noise. Then he caught my eye and began to grin. He winked. He turned to my mother and said he had to go to the bathroom, and she jumped up immediately to help him.

As they passed us, I saw my mother's hands tighten around my father's shoulders.

"Your father and I were very close," Big Cousin told me as we waited, as he'd told me every time he visited us.

"It's so terrible," his wife said. "It's so terrible to lose him like this."

"We're not losing him yet," I said. How dare they do this?

"We lived together as children, you know," Big Cousin said. "We were like brothers."

"Yes, I know," I said. I bit my tongue—I didn't say I also knew the stories they never told: that when my father's mother was dying, they had not given her money to go to the hospital. They'd had the money to give, but she had died without so much as a doctor's visit because they hadn't thought her condition seemed serious enough. "He's spoken of it," I said.

Big Cousin looked pleased.

We sat chatting long enough for Big Cousin's wife to notice my father was still in the bathroom and wonder if anything had happened, and then he emerged from the bathroom, trailing his IV. He looked incredibly weary. I was worried: he usually made such an effort.

We must have all thought the same thing, because Big Cousin rose and went to my father. He raised his fist. "Fighting!" he said. He growled. My father laughed.

"Come on," his cousin said, hitting him on the shoulder so that my father nearly lost his balance. His IV shook on the pole, the bag rattled. My mother grabbed him by the shoulder, and Hannah and I leaped forward. We glared at Big Cousin, but his eyes were fixed on my father's.

My father smiled. He growled back. They both laughed.

Satisfied, Big Cousin took my father in an awkward embrace. "Good boy," he said. "Good boy." My father, thus released, stumbled to his armchair, lowered himself down with the help of my mother, leaned back, and closed his eyes.

Later that day, my advisor sent an e-mail. "I've read your results," his message read. "I think we can fast-track you to finish next year. But in the meantime you'll need to fill out some paperwork and demonstrate that you can complete all your non-dissertation requirements in time. Why don't you come here for a few weeks in person so that we can sort this all out?"

I read the e-mail again. I had never imagined I could finish early, and since I'd come to Korea had assumed I was falling behind. I looked around the computer room and wished there was someone to tell.

"But I can't," I said out loud. I started to write a response explaining that I couldn't leave now, but I couldn't bring myself to send it. I looked at a calendar. *Maybe I could go for two weeks,* I thought. *Just two weeks.* This was the one thing I'd wanted to give my father.

I thought about my notebook, filled with ideas and symbols and sketches that I'd thought would build a bridge to my father's past. I did the calculations. All I had left aside from my dissertation were my language requirement and the minor thesis portion of my qualifying exam. That would take three weeks at most to prepare. I'd messed so many things up, but if I went to see my advisor, I could come back with a date and a promise: I could tell my father I'd complete my Ph.D. within the year.

I erased the e-mail saying I couldn't come, and bought my ticket. "I'll come Monday," I wrote, and hit Send.

For dinner that night, my father's cousins and my aunt said they would keep my father company while my mother, Hannah, and I went to have dinner in the hospital cafeteria. We took the elevator down to the basement level, which was lined with restaurants and stores. It didn't look at all like a hospital there, but like a mall.

We went through the cafeteria line and found a table together. There were so many people down there: I wondered what they were all doing.

"Can you believe your father's relatives?" my mother said. "We're going to have to find a way to deal with them, and with all the visitors. Though it's nice to get this break down here." She sighed.

I couldn't bear to make small talk. I was anxious about my decision. I dreaded telling them, but my stomach was queasy and insistent.

"I'm leaving," I blurted out.

"To go where?" my mother said blankly.

"I'm going to Chicago."

Hannah didn't react. My mother blinked. "You can't go," she said. "You can't do that."

"My thesis advisor e-mailed me," I said. "I need to."

"No," my mother said, shaking her head. She started to cry into her soup. "Why?"

"I'm only going for a little while," I said. "Twelve days. I have to work on my dissertation."

"Twelve days," she said.

"Yes," I said. "I have to."

She turned to Hannah. "Tell her to stay."

"How does she have the right," I began, but Hannah interrupted.

"Unni has to do what she has to do," she said. And then, "It's her life."

A loud sob burst from my mother. She wiped her face with her napkin and blew her nose. "He may not live a month."

"He could still get better."

She shook her head.

"Anyway, that's why I'm leaving tomorrow," I said. "So I can leave soon and come back soon."

"You tell your father, then," she said, straightening up and suddenly livid. "Tell him what you're planning to do."

"I was going to," I said.

. . .

Afterward, Hannah and I went for a walk around the hospital. On the street, we passed a couple from the hospital: the woman was wearing the same pajamas that all the patients wore. She was holding on to her husband's arm. They were moving very slowly and not talking at all. On the sidewalk, some women were squatting, selling cabbages, apples, chestnuts, and a few pairs of pants. We walked right past the grandmothers, who called out to us in Korean. We spoke English, and I wondered if anyone would guess that we were from the hospital.

"It's hard to be around someone dying," Hannah said, out of nowhere.

"Don't say that about him," I said.

"He knows he is, you know."

I shook my head.

"I get why you're leaving," she said after a while. "I don't blame you. But, Janie, he's not going to last long."

I didn't respond; I just kept walking, and my sister stayed with me.

In the end, I couldn't bring myself to tell my father I was leaving until the day I left. If no one had said anything, perhaps I would have just stayed on, pretending I'd never planned to leave.

But an hour before the bus was due to leave for the airport, my mother approached me and said, "You can't go."

"Stop," I said. "It will be fine."

She started to cry.

"Jeehyun," my father called from his bed. I went over to him. "Why is your mother crying?" he asked.

"It's nothing," I said. "You know how she is."

"Wife," he called to her, lifting his head from the pillow. "Come here."

But she shook her head and left the room, and I thought about how my parents never called each other by their names but by their relationship to each other.

"Go find her," my father said, but I stayed.

"Daddy," I said. "You're going to be okay. I'm going to go away for a little while, but I'll be back soon. Maybe you'll be better by then."

"Where are you going?" he asked. "Shopping?" His eyes were so large in his face.

"I have to go back to Chicago to handle some stuff for my dissertation. But Hannah will be here."

My father frowned. He didn't speak. He'd gotten so thin so quickly, and looked different lying in his bed than he had even five days ago. He could get better just as quickly, I told myself. This was how miracles worked: first they took you to the edge. Then they pulled you back.

I took a deep breath. "If you want me to stay, Daddy," I said, "I can stay. I'll do whatever you tell me to do."

"No," he said, waving his hand vaguely in front of him. "Go."

I let out the breath I'd been holding. I didn't know whether I was disappointed or relieved. "I'm only going away for a little while," I said.

"Yes," he said, but he frowned and didn't say anything else.

"It's for you," I said, and my eyes filled with tears. I really meant it. "I want to get this done for you."

He didn't respond. "I want to get up," he said. "Help me."

I pulled him up as gently as I could, and then we sat on the bed together. He took my hand in his dry, hot one. They were so thin, the veins as large as ever. He swayed, and I leaned against him to keep him steady.

My mother came back into the room. My father blinked up at the clock. "What time are you leaving?" he asked.

"In half an hour."

He nodded. He squinted at the clock again, as if it was difficult for him to figure out the time.

When I stood up to leave, my father shook my hand, which he had been holding. His legs dangled on the bed.

"Tell her to stay," my mother said. She began to cry again.

My father looked at her wonderingly, and did not answer. He turned back to me and smiled. His lips were so dry they pulled on his teeth.

"Be good," he said. He made his voice strong for me. "Work hard."

"I will," I said. I felt his arms go around me, and I held on to his arms. I was suddenly terribly frightened, that this could be it.

He kissed my head, my hand, and then he pulled me down and kissed me all over my face. His lips were dry and scratchy. I couldn't remember the last time my father had kissed me. I must have been a child. I wanted to cry. I wanted to stay. I wanted to run away as fast as I could.

"Daddy," I said, "will you always love me?"

My father let go of me and nodded. "Yes," he said. He smiled.

When I stood and walked to the door, he smiled again and waved. He smiled and smiled. How he shone. Only my father had the power to smile this way, as if everything in the world were perfect, as if he was welcoming me home. Oh God, let me never forget his face.

20.

On the bus to the airport I sat next to a man in a suit who avoided eye contact and spread his newspaper out on his lap and read. I flinched away when the paper touched my knee. I watched everything go by, the tall buildings, the stoplights, and the people on the street. I wanted the bus to go faster, faster. When I got to the airport and finally checked in and went through the long security line and had my passport stamped I walked fast. But when I finally strapped myself into my seat and felt the lift under my gut as we took off, I felt a tremendous sense of dread, as if I would never come back, and as if everyone around me knew what I had done.

I arrived at my apartment in Chicago bleary-eyed and stumbling. I'd arranged to stay at the place of some anthropology graduate student I'd found online, and after I retrieved her key from under her mat I spent several minutes jiggling the doorknob before it would open. She had left in a hurry: the shades were drawn closed, and papers and clothes were strewn about the floor.

I opened the curtains and looked around. There were dishes in the sink, a bra draped over a chair, socks crumpled beneath the desk.

In her bedroom, the blankets and sheets were mussed up, the pillows scattered. I gathered everything into a pile: her jeans in the bedroom and living room, her bra, her socks, her sheets, and put them in the hamper. I was exhausted and jet-lagged, but I walked to the laundromat and sat with my chin propped up on my hand and waited. When I returned, I made the bed and folded the laundry. I straightened her papers and washed her dishes, and felt satisfied, cleaning up this other person's mess, fixing up this other person's home.

The next day I met my advisor. He looked at me as if he'd forgotten what I looked like, and then he reached out and gave me a hug.

"Welcome back," he said, his fingers pressing into my back. I was surprised and touched by the gesture. Then he closed his office door, and took my notebook, and I tried to explain the results I'd achieved so far. I waited while he looked over my work.

"Ah yes," he said, holding up his hand and leafing through the pages. He read for a while. "I'll be frank," he said after some time, closing my notebook and looking up at me. "You have real talent. You're an original thinker. I've had my eye on you."

I swallowed. My mouth was dry.

"Listen," he said. "I understand where you've been and why, and yes, your family is important. But you know how hard it is to get back into the swing of things: you can't expect to neglect your work and then find it waiting for you."

"I know."

"You have momentum now," he said. "It's best to strike while the iron is hot."

I thought of my aunt telling my father when we were children that he needed to think of his career first. I thought of the tumor in his brain, how it had changed the chemistry and made him seize, how it had slowed him down. "Of course."

"So you have to stay focused," he said. "How long will you be here?"

"Two weeks," I said. "And then I'll come back next semester."

He nodded approvingly. "I want you to go to the secretary and get your paperwork under way, and to make a schedule to complete your requirements in time. And then I want to see you every day this week."

"Absolutely," I said. "Whatever it takes."

As I was leaving, he reached out and hugged me again. "It's good to have you back," he said before letting me go.

"Thanks," I said, a little awkwardly. He'd never hugged me before, and I wondered as I pulled away if it was my progress on my thesis or sympathy for my father's situation that had brought on this sudden affection.

The next day I tried to work, but I thought of my parents all day long. I thought of my father saying, "This is great!" when he read my notebook, and then I remembered him falling, and the way he smiled at me when I left, and our neglected garden in the countryside. I thought of my mother and Hannah and our individual lives, and how I did not know what was going to happen, and how whatever it was, I was not prepared.

When I called them that night, my father said he was doing better. He sounded cheerful on the phone, but when he talked, his words were slurred. He didn't stay on for long. I hadn't told anyone in Chicago that I was coming back, and I didn't want to talk to anyone about my life when there was nothing good going on.

So I called no one else. I sat in my empty apartment and Googled miracles instead.

One woman had been given three months to live and went on a ski vacation and returned with no detectable cancer. One man had been cured of his terminal illness after eating only grapes for a whole month. One guy had laughed away a tumor at a comedy show. A woman's dead dog had come to her in her dream and licked her breast: the next day her cancer was gone. Miracles, Wikipedia said, were interruptions of the laws of nature that could only be explained by divine intervention.

My mother had told me a story when I was growing up about a man who had been sentenced to death for some reason I never remembered. Just before the day of the execution, a monk came to see the doomed man. He told him if he said the Buddha's name ten thousand times between then and the time of the execution, the man would be spared. So the man chanted the Buddha's name ten thousand times, and everything the monk said came to pass. I remembered this, and tried to chant in my mind, all the time. I tried to pray. *Let my father be well, Buddha, let my father be well. Whoever can hear my thoughts, let my father be well.*

For the next week, I met with my advisor nearly every day. He told me about what my classmates had been working on, and tipped me off to several new papers he thought I should read. He was encouraging, and kind, and I found myself relaxing and opening up in response to his enthusiasm. I told myself I'd made the right decision, that I was doing the right thing. I sent my family glowing updates about everything I was accomplishing: I wanted them to know. I wanted my father to know I was doing well.

One evening I went to my advisor's house for a meeting, and when I arrived he was wearing an apron. I would never have imagined that he owned an apron. "Come in." He smiled. He led me into his dining room. "Sit down," he said. "Make yourself at home."

There were unlit candles on the table. The silverware had been laid out. There were place mats.

I eased my bag off my back. "I'm sorry, did you have other plans?" I asked. "Should I come another time?"

"Oh, I thought we'd eat together tonight," my advisor said. "You've been working so hard, and I know it's been a difficult time for you. I thought maybe you deserved a break."

I was immediately grateful. I hadn't shared a meal with anyone since returning to the States. I followed him into the kitchen, and set out the water in the glasses he gave me. I helped him toss the salad and take out the pasta.

"Thank you for doing this," I said.

He shrugged. "It's been just me in this house now," he said. "I thought of my own daughter going through something like this, God forbid." He reached out and patted my shoulder. "I know I've been driving you pretty hard, but I wanted you to know that I understand."

I looked down and nodded, surprised and touched. "Thank you," I said.

Then he lit the candles on the table, and while they flickered at each other, he poured us each a glass of wine. He raised his glass, but didn't say anything, so I was quiet, too. We touched glasses and drank. We began to eat. When I looked up, he was looking at me and smiling.

"Janie," he said, "it's been good to have you here."

"Thanks," I said. "It's been a relief to be here, and to get back to work."

He leaned forward, carefully reaching around the candle and the plates and putting his hand on my hand. He did this very slowly. His hand on mine was very light. "I'm not talking about work," he said.

I looked at his face, at the way his wrinkles pulled down the sides of his eyes. I looked down. "I thought we were going to talk about the next part of my proof," I said. I pulled my hand away.

My advisor shook his head. "Not tonight."

"That's what I'm here for though," I said. "Not that dinner isn't very nice."

"I just wanted to say that I've sensed a change between us lately," he said. "You've been more open to me. You smile more." He smiled as he said this. "You're a beautiful young woman, Janie." He leaned forward, and took my hand again.

I pulled away, and put both my hands in my lap. "You're my advisor," I said.

"We're two adults."

I shook my head. "No," I said.

"I think our minds are compatible," he said, leaning forward, his hand inching closer. I pushed my chair back so that I was out of reach. He sighed, and leaned back.

I fiddled with my silverware. After a pause, I said, "I was hoping to show you something I figured out last night."

"That's fine." He didn't say more. He shoved a forkful of pasta into his mouth. I watched him chew, I watched him swallow, and I sat there and waited for him to be done.

"Let me see the thing," he said when he was finally finished with his meal.

I went to my backpack and fetched my work, and handed it to him. "These are the new sketches," I said.

He nodded at me curtly, and got up to go to the next room, where he sat down in an overstuffed armchair.

"I'll clean up," I said, following him in and standing awkwardly between rooms.

"Go ahead," he said curtly.

So I went back to the dining room and blew out the candles. I took the dishes into the kitchen and washed them. I looked at the mess of food everywhere in his beautiful house, and wondered how long it had taken him to prepare our meal. Instead of gratitude or guilt, I felt anger. How long had he planned this?

I crossed the rooms to where he sat, leaning over my notebook. A dripping plate was still in my hand. "Listen," I said. "I need you to tell me if there's something there."

He looked up. "Yes, of course there is. But as you know, you also need to bring better results than you've been getting. What you have won't necessarily be enough."

"What?" I looked down. I'd been so excited by his enthusiasm this past week. "My dissertation topic was your suggestion. I've been making progress, and you know it," I said, my voice rising. "You've done nothing but encourage me."

He held up his hands, and smiled. "What can I say?" he said. "It's my job to tell you these things honestly."

"I came all the way from Korea because you said I should come."

"It's hard to tell sometimes when you sense promise if that potential will be fulfilled."

"You seemed able to tell yesterday," I said. I thought of how far I'd traveled to be here, and the silence on the other end of the phone when I called my parents these days. "You seemed to know two weeks ago when you told me to come."

"Janie, come on," my advisor said. "Let's both be grown-ups here."

"Grown-ups?" I said. "Give me my notebook."

"You're overreacting." He was laughing now.

"No," I said, lifting his plate over my head. "This would be over-reacting." I dropped the plate. It shattered on impact. "I want my notebook, please."

"Settle down," he said, and now he was irritated. "There's really no need to be so agitated." He stood up and sighed. "There's no problem here." His voice was so smooth that I realized suddenly he had done this before. "Janie," he said, stepping around the shards of plate and coming toward me, arms outstretched, my notebook in hand. "You need to learn to loosen up. There's no need for property damage."

"Stop it," I said, as he came closer. I stepped backward onto a piece of plate. Pain shot up the ball of my foot. "Shit," I said. Blood seeped through my sock.

"Careful now." His hand was gripping my shoulder.

I shook him off and snatched my notebook away. "You're a good advisor, okay?" I said. "So don't be gross."

"What?"

"I mean it, just don't be gross." I was so tired suddenly, and my foot was bleeding, and I realized I didn't care. I didn't want to fight with him. I limped back, surveyed the mess on his floor. "You're standing right on the line," I said. "But you haven't crossed it. I'm asking you not to so that I can continue to work with you."

He stepped back, too, then. "All right," he said, suddenly brisk and businesslike. "I was just joking with you. I was trying to be fatherly. Since I know you've been having a rough time."

"Did you just say 'fatherly'?" I said. I pushed my throbbing foot into the ground to feel the concreteness of the pain. "Are you seri-ous? You're a dad," I said. "Jesus Christ." I stomped my foot on the ground. I'd left one responsibility to chase another, but I'd chosen wrong. I had been a coward. Everything that mattered, everyone who cared about me, was elsewhere.

I limped home that evening, each step shooting a stabbing pulse up my foot. I washed it and wrapped it in gauze before bed, and slept in the next day until noon. When I woke, I watched a romantic comedy from the DVDs in the apartment. I was all alone here, I realized: I didn't have any close friends to speak of after my absence.

I called my airline and changed my flight to leave the next day. I called my parents and told my mother I was coming back.

"Good," she said, but she sounded distracted. "It's about time."

"Is everything okay?" I asked.

"We're just busy," she said. Her voice was impatient; it sounded on the edge of panic. "I'll call your uncle and let him know when to pick you up. What time are you arriving?" She took the details and hung up quickly. I sat in the empty apartment and looked at the walls.

From my bed, I Googled the address of my father's hospital. On satellite, it took up several city blocks. I hit zoom. I hit zoom again. I was so close I could see the ripple of light off its windows, a flock of birds gathered on the roof.

If there was a God, I wondered, what did he see? This wide expanse of roof, the birds scuttling on the top? All concrete and glass surfaces. The manicured lawn and the garden to the side, a miniature fountain blowing its wisp of water up in a tiny arc. Was this what he saw? Or did he know that somewhere, on the seventeenth floor, my father lay in a bed with rails, growing smaller. Would he know about something like that?

21.

When I returned to Korea, I'd only been gone for a little over a week. But it had already been too long. My father had had another seizure, and on the day I returned, he could no longer get up or speak. The doctors said he might not talk again. His eyes were enormous. "Hi, Daddy," I said. He smiled then, and it was still his smile. He squeezed my hand. I pressed my fear down: there was no time for it, no room.

That evening, we took turns eating the dinner that was delivered to our door. My father no longer ate on his own, but was hooked up to an IV that fed something into him the color and consistency of glue. I sat in the chair next to my father's bed and looked at him. He looked at me. A couple times, I thought he tried to speak, but his mouth opened and closed, he swallowed, and nothing came out. I gave him water, and he drank it with both hands, but I had to hold the glass steady with mine. His mouth worked. When he was finished, he pointed to a book on the lamp stand next to his bed. It was *The Little Prince.*

"Do you want me to read it?" I asked.

He nodded.

"Where'd you get it?" I asked.

"I bought it from the bookstore in the basement," Hannah said from her corner. "It was my favorite book when I was a kid. Dad used to read it to me."

"Yeah, he used to read it to both of us," I said.

My father patted the bed next to him. I looked over my shoulder at my mother and Hannah. "Does he want me to get into bed with him?" I asked.

"Ask him," Hannah said.

"Do you want me to get into bed?" I said.

He smiled. I lowered the safety rail between us. I climbed halfway into the narrow hospital bed, still sitting up. It had been so long since I had been in bed with him. When was the last time? I wondered. How old had I been? Seven? Eight?

I opened the book. My father's body was so light beside mine: there was hardly any warmth coming from his arm. The cloth of his hospital gown was very flimsy. Everything about him seemed as if it could float away, even the fine hairs that were left on his head. Only his eyes were large and burning, as if everything about my father was diminishing, everything nonessential falling away.

I opened the book and began. I read the introduction to Leon Werth when he was a little boy. I read the part that made fun of grown-ups, and then I showed my father the drawings of the boa constrictor that had eaten an elephant. I remembered as I read that my father had wanted to be a cartoonist when he was a boy. How he still said if he could have done anything, that is what he'd have done.

I kept reading. We had taken weeks to finish this book when I was a child, but it went so much faster without his laughter interrupting us. As I read, my mother came and sat in the chair next to me. Hannah lay down on the cot. They had told me my father could not sleep at night anymore, so they took turns sitting next to him, and slept whenever they could. Hannah turned over so she had her back to us. I read on.

I read about the lamplighter, the tippler, and the conceited man. I looked at my father, who nodded and did not wish me to stop. Next to us, my mother dozed. I was struck by how sweet it was to read to my father. I could not explain it, but I felt how precious this was, this painful reversal.

I got to the story of the fox, of the water that saves the pilot, of the prince's meeting with the snake.

"Everything that is essential is invisible to the eye." I could not go on.

I looked at my father and could not read any more. My mother stirred. "Go on," she said.

My father nodded. He looked like a child, I thought, with his large, hopeful eyes. Still, I couldn't continue. I knew what happened next. I did not want to read about the falling prince, or the narrator's uncertainty about whether the sheep he had drawn would eat the prince's rose. I did not want to read about the stars that either laughed or cried. I shut the book.

My father rested his paper-light hand on my knee. I kissed his cheek. His skin was dry and thin, not like skin at all. I crawled out of his bed. I put the rail back up.

"I'll read the rest later," I said.

I pulled out the extra cot, began to lie down on it, and changed my mind. My mother was leaning forward, her hand on my father's shoulder, murmuring.

"Actually, I'll stay up," I said. "You should sleep."

"We can take turns," my mother said.

"It's okay," I said. "With the time difference, I'm not tired."

"Okay." She nodded, leaning forward and kissing my father's head, releasing his shoulder slowly. "Rub his legs," she said. "And make sure you change his position every couple hours. It's important."

"Sure," I said. "I will."

"Turn off the lights around one a.m.," she said. "He won't like it, but it's good for him to try to get some sleep as well."

Then she lay on the cot I had pulled out, and pulling up the thin blanket at the foot of it, fell asleep immediately, under the glare of the fluorescent light.

I was grateful for the time alone with my father, and I thought how strange it was to be already used to his not being able to speak. It felt simple enough, familiar almost, to be sitting next to him, rubbing his legs and arms.

After one a.m., when the lights in the hallway were dimmed, the shadows around us pressed in and grew longer, and I could barely see the outlines of things. I could understand why my father did not like the lights to go out. As I sat rubbing his legs, the sound of weeping filled the hallway from the other rooms. Gathering strength, the sound seemed to enter our room and press in from all directions. It wasn't spooky, though; it was too urgent for that. I tried not to listen. I tried to distract my father.

"I might have messed up my thesis," I whispered, kneading my father's feet and legs. "I really wanted to finish," I said. "For you."

My father put his hand on my arm and rubbed it while I rubbed his leg. It made me feel better.

"I haven't given up," I said. "I'm going to try."

I thought he smiled. My heart rose. Sitting there in the dark, rubbing his legs, I realized that we had come to Korea not only to save him, but failing that, to make his death somehow beautiful.

We had wanted all the visitors, the green mountains, and the hot, white sun—to sit here beside him and face the painful, vibrant beauty of his ravaged body. Perhaps in some way I had always been waiting for the gift of this fierce and desperate love.

In the days that followed, I finished reading *The Little Prince*. I started over from the beginning. The doctor came in and announced the time had passed to drain my father's swollen stomach. My father was sprouting tubes everywhere, a tube to drain his pee, the tube that fed the thing that looked like wood glue into his body, a tube that pumped in something that looked like water. His body, which had been so light when I first arrived, got heavier and heavier, swelling up, weighed down by whatever was going in, and refusing to come out.

"Pee," we told him every day. "Poop! It's good for you." But he hardly ever did.

My family slept so little that it was hard to keep track of the time. Visitors continued to come. I was humbled by how patient they were, how willing they were to sit and smile, and how most of them did not look away from my father when he grimaced in pain, but leaned forward and took his hand.

My uncle came to see us every day, bearing food packed in little glass containers from my grandmother for us to eat. He exchanged these for the empty containers from the previous day, for my grandmother to wash and fill again. She made soup for us, and lunch boxes, and for my father she made drinks that might give him strength and packed them in little thermoses, though they tasted so bad my father frowned and would not open his mouth after the first draft.

Each day my uncle passed on anxious messages from my grandmother. She wanted to visit, but each day my mother sent back the same message: do not come. She told my uncle that my father would be better soon, and that my grandmother could come then. I wondered what my uncle actually told my grandmother when he returned home to her: if he repeated what my mother said, or if he told her what he saw for himself.

For the most part, we didn't talk to each other, my mother, Hannah, or I. We hovered around my father like anxious moths: we fluttered past each other, and spoke only to work out schedules and meals. We set everything aside except for him.

One bright day we took him outside in a wheelchair, and he blinked, pale in the sun, watching the butterflies in the garden. He looked transparent in the daylight. It frightened me, and at the same time, it was beautiful to see, so much light it hurt to look, and all the blankets we'd packed around him the only solid thing.

My aunt visited twice a week. She came alone, and fluctuated between talking in a loud and hearty voice and suddenly breaking down in tears. She wept right in front of him, while he stared. If she cried too long, he blinked and turned his head away. His cousin came more often, always reminding us that he and my father had been like brothers. If my aunt was also in the room when he visited, she stiffened and seemed just about to contradict him, but then she would clamp down her lips tight over her teeth and shake her head a little to herself—enough so the rest of us noticed, but subtle enough that we wouldn't be encouraged to ask what was wrong.

It was as if the two of them, Komo and Big Cousin, were competing for my father's attention. As if we all were. I wished he could enjoy it. Growing up, he'd always been the younger one, the one who wanted approval from them. His illness had reversed that.

Even with us, my father, who had felt overlooked in his household of women, was suddenly the focus of everything. Hannah and I had left school behind, had left America, our lives. And my mother had left her home, her friends, her job—it was not her first time following my father where he needed to go. I found myself growing resentful when my aunt monopolized the chair next to his bed, or when Hannah whispered something in his ear that made him laugh his painful laugh.

I prickled most when my aunt sat murmuring to my father of their childhood. She told him stories from when they were very young. It was as if she was trying to exclude us by taking him back to a time before we existed.

"There is still time," she said to my mother one day. "Call a minister. There is still hope for him. God works miracles."

"He doesn't want it," my mother said calmly. "I asked him already. He said"—and here my mother's voice twisted a little with pride—"he said he doesn't wish to go to heaven if I won't be there. He'd prefer to be with me wherever I am."

"What?" My aunt turned to my father. "How could he dare say such a thing?" She turned back to us, and threw herself down on her knees. "I am begging you," she cried, on the floor. "I am on my knees."

I stared at her. Was she serious?

Hannah stepped back. "Jesus Christ," she said.

From the ground, my aunt cried, "I knew it would be like this when he married you. God is punishing him for turning his back. Now, God is turning his back."

Unexpectedly, Hannah laughed. My aunt looked up at her, startled out of her tears. Hannah drew herself up and said in a low voice, "And yet there is no hiding place in the wide world where troubles may not find you, and there has never lived a man who was able to say more than you can say, that you do not know when sorrow will visit your house." She pointed at my aunt. "So be sincere with yourself, fix your eyes upon Job; even though he terrifies you, it is not this he wishes, if you yourself do not wish it."

There was a moment of silence. I half-gasped, half-laughed, but my aunt was scrambling up, her face red—from her tears or outrage, I could not tell. Before she could speak, my mother stepped forward, placing herself between my aunt and Hannah. "Hang on," she said, holding out her hand to my red-faced aunt. She turned to Hannah. "What was that?" she asked, a smile working on her face.

"Kierkegaard," Hannah said.

"How dare you," my aunt said, advancing.

This was a *circus*, I thought.

And then my mother turned to my aunt. She gave her a soothing look, and touched her arm. "I was just thinking it would be nice if you sang to him," she said.

Every day since my father had come to the hospital, my aunt had wanted to sing the songs their mother used to sing to him. Christian songs. Religious songs. And every day my father had glanced at my mother and nervously shaken his head.

We were all taken aback by my mother's offer, and sensing this was a concession not to come again, my aunt abandoned Hannah and took her place by my father's side. My father gazed blankly up at her. She put her hands on the rails of his bed and took a breath.

She began to sing in a low, quiet voice. The hymn she had chosen was beautiful and solemn, and though I resented her for trying, even now, to impose her past upon him, to wedge it between him and us, as she sang I saw how much she loved him, and how she had been beautiful to him, when they were the only two people who cared for each other in the world.

Her voice trembled. It was a sad, lonely song she chose to sing, the song of an old woman, and as I listened I realized she was older than their mother or father had ever lived to be. Then, as she was singing, my father spoke. He spoke. And then he tried to speak again, for the first time in weeks, and what he said was, "Wife," looking past my aunt's shoulder, reaching out one hand, "Wife."

My mother went to him instantly, sidling around my aunt, who did not move aside. My father took my mother's hand and started to laugh.

"Did you like my song?" my aunt said, excitedly. She looked at my mother, and Hannah, at me. "It was my song that got him to speak, isn't that so?"

But my father wasn't looking at her. He held my mother's hands and said, "Don't let go."

"I won't," my mother said. "I'm here."

My father was laughing: it was so out of place, a thread of giddy laughter as if it had been stopped up all these weeks and was bubbling out of him. I had never heard him laugh quite like this before, and his voice was thin and rough, but he said laughing, again and again, "Don't let go," and my mother, infected, surprised, began to laugh, too, and said that she would not, she never would.

We were thrilled. We were even kind to my aunt. "Maybe it was the singing," we said. That morning was filled with joy.

When the doctor came we were practically dancing. We crowded around him. "He's talking again," we said.

"Yes," the doctor said.

"Isn't it good news?" we asked, and the doctor looked at us in surprise.

"It doesn't change anything," he replied. He looked at the chart in his hand. He looked at my father. He stuck out his hand, in front of my father's face. He waved it. "Grab my hand," he ordered.

My father smiled at us, but didn't seem to hear the doctor.

"But he talked," my aunt said. "Isn't that an improvement?"

"He's losing his mental faculties. It's a chemical thing. I've explained it already," he said.

Stricken, my aunt walked to a corner of the room and began to weep quietly. Hannah watched her with faint disgust, then leaned over my father's bed and put her hand gently in front of my father. "Shake," Hannah whispered into my father's ear. My father looked at her, and seemed to focus. He grabbed her hand. Hannah looked at the doctor triumphantly, but he shook his head.

"Sorry, but no," he said.

My mother stepped forward. "You," she said. She sounded impatient, irritated. It was a voice she used on me when I'd done something stupid. It was a voice she used on someone who had something to learn. "Who among us here won't die?" she asked. She pointed at him, and he flinched. "You?"

The doctor shut his folder filled with all those papers, records, and measurements. "There is nothing more I can do," he said.

"You have made that clear," my mother said. "But listen well: all of us are dying. And you are, too. You will die one day. You can be sure of that. So for now, right here, you can make him comfortable. You can be kind." Her voice rose. "There is no reason to be proud that there is nothing you can do for him. It does not put you above us. One day you will be here, too."

I was aghast. But my father watched all this, and then he opened his mouth, and laughed.

22.

A few weeks later, nothing had changed. Each day the doctor said the end was approaching. Each day my father persisted. I told my mother that it was time for us to take my father out of the hospital. He had always said he didn't want to die in a hospital, and I thought moving him was one last thing we could do for him, the one thing that might give him hope.

"We need to take him somewhere else," I said.

My mother looked up at me from her place on the cot as if something had lifted from her shoulders, as if she had been waiting for this moment. She nodded.

"Let's take him to his family home," I said.

"How?" my mother asked. "The ride is too long." She had grown vague in the last few days in a way that frightened me.

"We can figure something out," Hannah said. "I think we should go, too."

So when my father's cousin came to visit later in the afternoon, I said, "We want to move him."

"But they can take better care of him here," Big Cousin said.

I looked around the small room, with the caged bed and the antiseptic smell. The light was always the same; the sounds were always the same. I couldn't bear for him to be here another week. There was no beauty here.

"He wanted to go to his family home," I said.

Big Cousin glanced down at my father, who was sleeping, for once.

I paused. "He said you were like brothers."

Big Cousin looked at me. "Really?" He looked at my father, yellowing against the crisp white sheets, the remaining tufts of hair so fine on his head. "Did he really say that?"

I nodded.

He sighed then, as if a burden had been lifted. "Well, I'll arrange it," he said. He started making plans. He said he'd get his other cousins to go and get the house ready. He'd rent a van and arrange for my father to be moved.

My mother thanked and thanked him.

He shrugged. "We grew up together," he said.

He waited a while until my father woke. Then he was by his side, ready to tell him the news. My father smiled as he always did to see his cousin, and nodded, but did not seem to really understand.

"Home," his cousin said. "We're taking you home!" When my father smiled vaguely, he continued. "And I want you to know that it will be all right for you to be buried there as well," he said. "I've been meaning to tell you that."

My father frowned.

"Not now," I said from my corner. "Don't talk about that now."

"Your father asked me himself for this favor." Big Cousin sounded injured. "When he first arrived. I wanted to put his mind at ease."

"Oh," I said. When I first arrived, my father had told me he wanted to be cremated and taken to America, not buried. Now I understood: my father had always wanted to be buried in their family plot, but it had taken this long for his cousin to respond to his request. My father had told us he wanted to be cremated so that we wouldn't worry if that's what ended up happening. He hadn't wanted us to know he'd asked for this favor, for us to blame his cousin if he didn't come through.

"Did you hear me?" Big Cousin said, talking loudly into my father's face. "I will do this for you."

My father did not try to respond either way. Instead, he looked unhappy and frightened.

That night it was my turn to stay up with my father. I was exhausted, but he was anxious, and did not want me to fall asleep. He shifted in his bed and made soft noises, waving a hand in front of my face whenever I started to doze.

After a few hours of this, I leaned forward over the rail of the bed and took my father's hand. "Daddy," I said. I thought of him asking his cousin months ago if he could be buried near his childhood home. Why had he never hinted of such things to me? "You have to live," I said. I could not stand the look on his face when his cousin mentioned the burial site, or the thought that he was discouraged.

My father blinked. "Why?" he asked.

The question hurt me. I squeezed his hand. "I haven't had children yet," I said. He had wanted me to have children by now. "You have to teach them math. How else will they learn it properly?"

My father smiled but did not answer. He squeezed my hand, and looked away.

I didn't know how to say what I really meant: that imagining his death felt like a betrayal. That I would have given him my lungs, my liver, my stomach. I would have given him back everything he'd given me. He couldn't die yet. I hadn't done anything to make him proud.

We both drifted off for a while, but he woke a couple of hours later, and called for me. When I leaned forward, he said, "The ground will be hard."

I turned on the lamp by his bed. "What are you talking about?"

In the dim lamplight, my father's eyes were large and liquid, devouring the room. "We buried her too shallow," he said. "She wasn't deep enough."

Damn his cousin, I thought, for mentioning the grave.

"I told you it was too shallow," my father said.

My throat clamped up. "It's all right," I said. I swallowed. I took his hands in mine and rubbed them. They were so dry, like they could flake away between my own. I took some lotion and began to work it into his skin.

"When the floods came," he said, "I worried."

I didn't know what he was talking about, and in some ways, didn't care. The important thing now was to soothe him. "But it was fine," I said.

"No, no," he said. "Sometimes I saw her," he said, "floating down the stream."

I wanted to wake my mother. Was this hallucination or memory? "That's just a dream," I said. "She's fine. She's where you left her."

"Why?" he asked. "Why did she die?"

"Who?" Who could he possibly be talking about?

"I don't know," my father said. His voice was high and panicky. "Why did she die?"

He was gripping my hands.

"It's okay," I said. I tried to sound like my mother: calm, reassuring. "She's all right, Daddy," I said. "I promise. It's all right." I patted his hand. "Should we chant the Buddha's name?" I asked. "Would you like me to do that?"

My father nodded.

And so I began, keeping my voice low and calm. I was soothed by the sound, by the feel of my own voice coming quiet and steady out of my body. Had this been what my mother's voice had sounded like when I was young and sick, and she laid her hands on me and prayed? I chanted for what felt like a long time. I was tired, and it was dark, and I did not want to wake anyone else. I wanted to sleep, like this, to fall asleep chanting with my hand clasped in my father's.

But he had other ideas. He squeezed my hand whenever I started to doze off, jerking me awake. When I got so tired that even this stopped working, he called out. He croaked out the Buddha's name in his pitiful, unused voice—and it was a strange sound, the sound high in his throat—like the call of a bird. I straightened up at once and began again. My father chanted with me the first few times to keep me going, and then his voice faded away and he was still and satisfied. "Kwansenbosal," we said again and again. "Namuamitabul Kwansenbosal."

I knew he wanted me to stay awake with him, to keep this vigil through the dark. I had heard somewhere that most people die at dawn, just before sunrise, and every day I thought if we could get past the sunrise, we would be safe. As I chanted away the dark hours, I prayed that he wouldn't get worse. I had stopped asking for his recovery. I didn't want to ask for too much.

Halfway through the night, when I was almost unable to continue chanting, Hannah woke up. Her voice, calm and assured, joined mine. We carried the chant together. We did this all night long, and the longer it went on, the more I was filled with an ebullient kind of hope that rose inside my chest and lifted my spirits. Finally, when the sun was just reaching its fingers of light through the window, the three of us fell asleep.

The drive the next day to the house my father had grown up in took five hours. My father rode strapped into the back of a van in his bed, my mother beside him. Hannah and I rode in a separate car with Big Cousin, and along the way he told us stories and pointed to landmarks, and I watched Hannah smile and laugh.

When we finally arrived, the estate was as beautiful as my father had always said. The sky was blue, and the air had a chill in it. I felt as if everything could change right here. It had been so long since we'd been outside, since we'd been in the mountains. I looked around at a place I'd heard only the briefest of stories about. There was the courtyard, the persimmon tree with its orange fruit flaming in the sky. There was the apple orchard, a flock of birds circling overhead. Here was the place where my father had grown up. Until now it had existed entirely in my imagination, and I was surprised by a sense of recognition, a feeling in my bones that I had come home.

But the sense of wonder that came with this feeling was replaced by regret as soon as I saw my father. His face was frozen in pain, and my mother's face was panicked.

"Everything rattled in the back of the van," she said, horror etched in her face. "His bed, the rails, and the IV bags and the pole on his bed. All of it shook every time we took a turn. Even the restraints." It had been hard for her to give him water with a steady hand. "We shouldn't have come," she said, wringing her hands. "We should have turned back."

"I'm sorry," I said. This had been my idea, my fault.

My father's cousins were lowering his bed onto the ground, and they accidentally jolted him as they put it down. My father's mouth opened wide, as if he would scream, but he didn't make a sound, his face just frozen like that.

"Careful!" my mother cried, jumping forward. "Be careful."

And then there was my father. Everything in his body was tense, stiff, suffering. He did not lift his head. He did not look up. His arms were flat against his bed, his back arched, his eyes rolled back and unfocused, his mouth open like a fish.

My mother stood next to his bed, running her hand up and down his unresponsive arm. She followed as his cousins wheeled him into the house, calling, "We're home!" in cheerful voices, as if this could undo the suffering none of us could bear to acknowledge.

After they had gotten him settled in his room, Big Cousin turned to Hannah and me. "Let me show you the grounds," he said.

My father was still lying there stiff and unmoving, but my mother nodded at us to go, and so we followed willingly, hoping that when we returned, my father would look a little less horrible.

Outdoors, Big Cousin showed Hannah and me how to pick the persimmons. They were impossibly high, at least four times as high as we were tall, and there was a long wooden pole with a small basket on the end that you balanced up and then underneath each persimmon. You gave a quick twist, and then you lowered the pole and the basket, upright to keep the persimmon from falling out, all the way down. They were gorgeously dark and heavy in the hand. They were so ripe that they burst at the touch and then there was the sweetness of them, a deep persimmon taste. I wondered how my father had satisfied himself with the small hard stubborn ones we'd bought at the Asian market each year, leaving them in the garage for days at a time to ripen to a flavor that was just the faintest echo of what they tasted like here.

"Let me show you the apples, too," my father's cousin said, and we walked past barrels of them to the orchard. They were enormous: both my mother and my father had always been able to break apples in half with their hands. In the orchard, the apples were dark flashes showing through the leaves.

All around us, between the neatly kept fruit trees and the mountains, was a ring of trees. The property was surrounded by them. The leaves on the outer trees had turned color, and from inside the orchard walls they looked strange and bold. I looked at Hannah. When we were children, we had chased leaves as they fell, losing all sense of balance as we looked up, the sky fixed, the branches rushing past.

This was where he had come from, my father who had planted trees in a circle around our house in Michigan, and pulled up all of those raspberry bushes one by one. I looked around me, standing in a ring within a ring, and I turned to the path that led out of the orchard. For a brief moment, I imagined that the path that led out of this orchard and to the road that took us to Seoul could show me the whole trajectory of his life.

"Can we bring him an apple?" I asked Big Cousin. "And a persimmon? Just to show him?"

"Yes of course," he said. He seemed more relaxed now. More himself. I wished my father had been the one to show us this place, these things, but I felt as if something about him had still been revealed to me. Of who he'd been and what he'd tried to make for us, everywhere else we had lived.

When we went inside, my father was lying in his bed, his body still frozen in that frightening rigidity. I showed him the persimmon and apple we had brought from outdoors, but he stared blankly at the ceiling. When he flicked his eyes in my direction, they rested on me only for a second before he flicked them back up.

The nurse we'd hired arrived, and said the ride had been too hard on him. His second cousins had also come, and were gathered around him, weeping and exclaiming at him, calling his name, telling stories of his youth. They had brought out an old book of photographs, and were pointing to the ones with my father in them. He was the youngest of the entire clan, the baby. I stood over the shoulders of these strangers, my relatives, and peered at these pictures I had never seen.

He had been a very thin and serious boy, his back ramrod straight, and he gazed straight at the camera, his hands on his hips or in his pockets. He was never smiling: even at his youngest, he was drawing himself up as tall as he could stand next to his sister, both of them sober with the same dark-eyed gaze. In all the pictures we had of him after we were born, he was always smiling. That was how I thought of him. But in these pictures, his arms crossed in front of his chest, the mountains behind him, his mouth was a straight horizontal line across his face, his eyes assessing.

"And this is him the year before he left," Big Cousin said.

There he was in the orchard I had just stood in, surrounded by two rings of trees. He was looking past the camera, his hands in his pockets, looking as if he had already left this place, the barest hint of a smile upon his lips. I wanted this picture very badly—but could not bring myself to ask for it. I would not have been able to explain what it meant to me—this image of my father so young and determined, ready to meet the future, not knowing what it held, or everything that would happen next.

Even after all his relatives left, my father remained motionless. I had never seen him so still. My mother leaned over his bed and murmured. He lay there, eyes half open, unfocused. She pulled up a chair.

"So we are finally here," she said. She looked up at Hannah and me. "We never came to this house, but he brought me out here to this part of the country once." She smiled. "To show me where he was from."

That year, my mother had already received three proposals of marriage and rejected them all. She had told herself that when the time came, she would shoot my father's down as well. She hadn't forgiven him for forgetting who had saved him at the demonstration. For never knowing. The thought of retribution filled her with glee. Let that teach him. This was the reason, she told herself, that she allowed him to woo her.

One day, he took her to his hometown. He did not show her the house he'd grown up in, but took her walking in the mountains, and together they visited the nearby lake. On their way back to the car, they passed a rice paddy, and on a whim he threw off his shoes and asked if she wanted to walk through it. So she threw off her shoes and stepped in. Together they waded through the water. The sunlight skimmed off the surface of the water like stones, and the frogs cleared a path for them as they walked through the stalks of rice that grazed their skin. Close up, the clear shallow water that shimmered like glass from a distance was cloudy with perforated depths. The rice was planted in rows, and between the rows were furrows that formed a pattern, as though a large honeycomb had been buried under a layer of dirt, which had then been immersed in water. Shoots of green rice plants stood upright with straight, steady backs, waving stiffly in unison to greet the wind.

Beneath the water the shoots reached down and gripped the loose soil there very tightly. My father told my mother that when he was a child, he had curled his toes into the mud and stood up very straight, pretending to be one of the slender green stalks. But more fun than that had been to look for fighting fish. The fish lived in the little bowls separated by rice plants, and they circled around and around in their tiny enclosed homes, coming up to take gasps of breath. Sometimes they would follow his finger when he trailed it along the surface of the water. When it rained and they were washed into the same tiny bowl, they puffed out their cheeks mightily and charged, fins streaming. They fought to the death.

My father led my mother through the paddies, the hem of her skirt trailing in the water. She felt the weight of it pulling down on her, grounding her in the earth. She could take root here, she thought, stepping carefully between the rows of rice plants. And then my father stopped and went suddenly still. He let go of her hand and reached into a tiny foaming fray of water. He lifted up a fish that was clamped in the jaws of another fish. They were both blue, with purple fins, and they looked identical, as if a single fish had reached up and caught its reflection by the fin. The dangling fish would not let go, and when my father shook the slippery bodies, a fin tore off in a long strip before the hanging fish plopped back into the water with a dull splash. The shredded fin floated along the surface of the water and caught on my mother's ankle like a strand of ribbon. She cried out and lifted her foot, the dead skin of the fish dangling—and then so quickly she hardly noticed the movement, my father knelt down and plucked the fin from her skin and cast it from them.

My mother said she would never forget that. While it was happening, his hand was on her back. And the water from his wet hand seeped through her shirt. It wasn't the wetness she felt through the cloth that made her stand up straighter, but the warmth of his skin. She shivered. She asked him how fast a fish heart beats. She could feel her own heart speeding up.

He told her then of the time he had found a fish with its mouth puffed gently out in bubbles, tender with the baby fry it carried within its cheeks. He had caught it in a jar and watched it for hours, hoping to be there at the moment when the fish were released. He wondered if it was because in the beginning of their lives the fish had to share a home in the mouth of their mother that they fought so fiercely once they had made their escape. He watched all day, but the fry never emerged, and in the evening he dipped the fish back out. He described watching the fish with her cheeks puffed out, waiting for her to release her cargo, and my mother forgot everything except his cheeks, blowing out to show her what it had looked like. She forgot everything but that and his hand on her back.

And then a moment later, she found her hand in his, the insistent warmth of it pressing into hers. So this was how it could start then: the touch of a hand against a hand. How lightly he held it, how loose. The gentleness of that touch was almost more than she could bear. It made her weak just to remember.

They walked back through the paddy and back to the place where they had left their shoes. As he pulled her onto dry land, he asked her to marry him. She was silent, feeling her hand in his hand. Everything important, it seemed, was held there between them. She did not say yes or no, but she let him keep her hand in his.

Every day in the house we had brought him back to, my father lay with his face frozen in pain, and every day my mother sat by my father's bed and told stories I had never heard before. She spoke of their life together, of her childhood, of their love, as if the stories could bring him back to us. Hannah and I sat on the other side of the bed from her and listened.

Remember when you took me to the pond? my mother said. Remember when we kissed in the pagoda under the rain? The first time my father came to her house, my mother said, he brought her cheese. He stood in front of their door with the cheese cradled in one palm, and then he offered it to my grandmother, holding it out with both hands. When my grandmother took it, he stiffened up and stood a little taller, as if he had brought something of great worth. It was wrapped carefully in soft waxy paper, and my grandmother looked at it in her open hand.

"It's cheese," he said, and stepped into their living room.

My mother had laughed out loud. How grand he thought he was, with his gift of cheese! How proudly he stood, like a gamecock. It offended her, to see him standing there as if he were the man of the house. She had already held him up as he stumbled, she had already watched him sleep. Now she wanted to show him how unimpressed she was. She tried to hold her head in such a way as to communicate her scorn.

But my grandmother had already been won over. My mother snorted when my grandmother thanked him so warmly for the cheese, as if he had brought them a bar of gold, as if it was indeed the treasure he meant it to be.

Later, my mother said, she found out that my father had spent hours at the specialty store trying to pick out that cheese. He had never had any before, himself: it was too extravagant. The cheese he brought her was the first cheese he'd ever tasted: he'd gone to the market and looked at dozens of varieties in their rinds. He was baffled by them: hard and soft, yellow, white, orange, speckled blue. He called the clerk over and asked which was best, but the clerk had never been able to afford such luxuries himself. Together they looked, hefting each specimen in their hands, one at a time. Finally, he permitted himself to buy the smallest one of the most expensive kind.

When he finally had his first taste he found he did not like it, and he wondered if he had chosen poorly. When he returned home, he told my aunt, who broke down and cried a little, because he had never bought her anything so fine.

It hurt my mother afterward to think of his sharp pride at having brought something so small. It pained her to think of how she'd laughed at him, and to remember the look her mother had given her that had stopped the laugh in her throat. After they were married, after they moved to the U.S., he would watch her cut slices of cheese with a knife and eat them piece by piece. But still, the ludicrousness of it pained her, how precious a thing he thought he had brought to her. When she remembered his pride, she could still see it there in his face, like a light.

. . .

While my mother told these stories, my father's relatives came to visit every day. They stood over my father's bed while he lay rigid and unmoving, and my mother's voice strung story to story together. They frightened me with their intense, collective watching. They shook their heads, murmured, touched everything in the room tentatively—including us. My father's friend Mr. Lee drove five hours to see my father, and then wouldn't come in the room but stood outside the door, wiping his eyes.

My uncle came; my grandmother did not. She'd been furious when we drove out to the countryside without telling her, and my uncle hinted that she was not doing well herself, but we did not inquire for more details. He said she wanted to come, and I thought that we should let her, but my mother was firm.

"Jeehyun," she said, when I protested. "She's not well either, and I can't take care of her or deal with her coming every day and worrying. Maybe later, but right now I just can't do it." So we put off everything outside my father's room for later; we would be able to deal with everything after we had seen this through.

"Right before we moved to America," my mother said to Hannah and me one day, "I went to the DMZ. Perhaps you remember, I stayed away one night and didn't come home. Your father was so angry at me."

"I remember," Hannah said. "You didn't tell anyone. We didn't know where you were."

"You were so young then," my mother said. She sounded surprised.

"I had bad dreams about it for years," Hannah said.

"Me too," I interjected. "Dad called the police."

"Yes, he did," my mother said. She sounded embarrassed.

"So what was it like?" I asked.

"And why did you go there?" Hannah added.

"I don't know," my mother said. "It seemed—when we left Korea it seemed irrevocable, like we were leaving forever." She was quiet. "I can't explain it."

But I knew the reason. She had gone because of her sister who had been kidnapped. She had followed her as far as she could. I wondered why my mother didn't tell Hannah the story, now.

"I had never dreamed of leaving Korea," my mother said. "By the time I met your father I was tired of the military government, of curfews and school closings and the tear gas. In some ways, I was ready to leave. But I had dreamed of that place, that border. I had to go.

"So I went. I bought a ticket and didn't tell your father. I meant to return the same day, but then I got there, and looked across the DMZ, and there were so many soldiers, just boys, you understand, dressed up in uniform. And it didn't look like anything but a field with an ugly wire fence and boys standing too still around it, and I thought, Is this all?

"And I couldn't leave. I looked at the mountains that stretched into the north and into China. I wondered if somewhere out there, maybe there was a woman I once knew sitting in one of the Diamond Mountains, maybe singing a song to her child. And I thought if I left Korea I would never have a chance to see her again."

"Who was she?" Hannah asked.

My mother smiled. "Someone from another life," she said. "Someone I knew when I was a little girl."

"And what happened next?" Hannah asked. "Why didn't you come home?"

"I skipped my train back." My mother looked down at her hands. "I slept in a house that belonged to people I didn't know. I gave them money for a bed."

She looked at my father, who no longer looked like my father, and then she reached out and touched his face, which stayed frozen in that terrifying expression of pain under her hand. "How could I do such a thing?" she said to him. "How did I ever think I could leave you?"

So she had almost left us. I heard Hannah exhale slowly, and I looked over at her. She nodded.

My mother continued. When she heard the first explosion, she did not sit up, but lay in the dark in her unfamiliar bed, staring at the ceiling. The second time, the stand near her bed rocked back and forth, and she got up and put on her clothes. It was past curfew, but my mother put on her shoes.

She wondered vaguely as she prowled through the dark hall to the front door if the soldiers would arrest her if they saw her outside; she wondered if the war had come. She should be running away, she knew, or hiding. But the thought of that empty field pulled at her. She wanted to see if there were soldiers running across it, the lines of guards dissipating into scattered men.

No one stopped her from leaving the house; it was silent throughout, as if they were used to the explosions, to the sound of her padding through the hallways, walking out in the middle of the night.

My mother walked a mile to the DMZ, shuffling in the dark. She wondered what my father would say if he could see her. How she would explain.

And then she saw them.

Behind the soldiers, behind the fence, was a group of deer

running in the moonlight. Their throats glowed pale and milky, their undercoats gleaming luminous against their darker fur.

My mother had never seen anything as graceful as those deer, their spindle legs gliding weightlessly beneath them. Her breath caught. It was like ballet, my mother said. It was like flight. She watched the deer skim over land no human foot had ventured to cross in twenty years.

The thought came to her suddenly, with the shock of revelation: *All boundaries are imagined.*

She could not see into the dark of the other side.

When the first deer exploded, it was into a deafening light. Afterward, the darkness thickened with smoke, and though my mother squinted, she could see nothing but the ghostly forms of the deer veering silently away from the sound. My mother stood and watched them through the line of soldiers, framed by the cold glint of the wire fence. She shivered, she thought, *We are doomed.*

She turned to walk back to the house she was staying in. Ahead of her, the moon drifted down and hung like a lantern from a nearby tree branch. She looked up: beyond the low-hanging moon, the night was deep and constant. My mother watched the stars divide and divide again: beautiful and impossibly remote. They shattered the sky.

23.

My father's stillness seemed interminable. The nurse wandered in and changed his IV bags, she took his pulse and blood pressure; she went back to her room shaking her head. My mother ran out of stories. When this happened, she sang. He had always loved her voice. Every day Hannah and I wandered around the house and the property; we took turns making rice and fixing the most basic meals. Our clothes began to hang off our bodies as if we, too, were wasting away. Meals were just sustenance; we ate only enough to keep going. My relatives brought food, and everything piled up in the kitchen. But my mother did not leave the room in which my father lay. And she did not stop singing. She had stopped sleeping, and it seemed that every corner of each day was filled with the sound of my mother's voice, as if she was casting a spell: even when she was resting, she sang to my father, softly, under her breath.

And then it began to snow. It was too early, weeks early, though the year's harvest had mostly been gathered. The snow that came down was light and melted instantly on the ground. Such large white snowflakes! And my mother sang on, as if she had called it down upon us.

My father, who lay in his bed expressionless, not seeming to really see anything, even when we massaged his body, or put lotion on his dry skin, or moved his limbs, seemed somehow to sense the falling snow. He had not stirred for anything, not even noticing when the nurse gave him a new shot, or changed his needles. He had not even turned his head to my mother's voice, but the snow, falling silently outside, seemed to waken him from his stupor. He began to stir. His eyes moved, searching, and for a few seconds fixed on us.

"Did you see that?" I asked.

"Maybe he's starting to recover from his trip here," I said.

Hannah went outside, and in front of the window she gathered enough snow to make a tiny snowman. She put him on a plate and brought him in. "See?" She showed my father.

She took the snowman back outside and arranged him on the windowsill. She made three more, each smaller than the last. A little family of snowmen, looking in on us. I touched my father's hand. How slow it all was, I thought. There was enough time for the snow falling on the roof, for my mother's stories. There was time enough for all of it.

That day my father began to take water when we gave it to him. He began to look at us. Encouraged, I offered him some persimmon in a spoon: he opened his mouth. The persimmon was so ripe that the skin caved away and the soft inside just fell into the spoon. It slipped smoothly in.

He swallowed. He blinked. He blinked again. His voice sounded strong when he spoke. "That's good!" he said.

"He just talked!" I said, looking to see if anyone had heard.

My mother and Hannah rushed over, calling out to him, excited. They stroked his arms and said hello. He didn't speak again, but let them take turns feeding him spoonfuls of the persimmon. We should have given him one mouthful each, and stopped, but it had been weeks since he had eaten anything, so long since he had responded to anything, that we got carried away. It seemed miraculous. We let him eat the persimmon until he closed his mouth and turned away.

In the long list of many mistakes, this is the one I regret most. Because after that, my father did not speak again, but several hours later he began to moan.

"What's wrong?" I asked, leaning forward and rubbing his arm. My mother and Hannah came to his side, just in time to see him shit himself. This was the first time he'd moved his bowels in weeks, since we'd put him on the IVs back at the hospital. We'd waited for him to do so, encouraged him. We'd known it was bad when he'd stopped, just as it'd been bad when he stopped peeing on his own, and had to have a catheter put in.

But this was worse. This was not what we'd been hoping for. Now my father grimaced and writhed, holding on to the rail of the hospital bed, and each time he shuddered he shit black water and a horrid, putrid smell filled the air. We turned him over each time, the nurse rushing over to help my mother slip the soiled sheets out from under him while Hannah and I spread clean new sheets beneath him. He cried out each time we moved him; he held out his hand, begging us to stop.

By nightfall of that long, horrible day, my father's breath was rattling. We had run out of clean sheets, and we went back and forth from the laundry room to the bedroom, an endless exchange of linen, except that now my father had to lie in his fouled bed until we came back, yanking his poor body back and forth as we cleaned it up.

Here's a secret. You think there are limits, you think it can't get worse, there's just dead and that's it, but there's worse. There's your father's mouth, open, but he can't speak, and instead he makes sounds no person should make. There's the sore you discover on his back the size of your fist, and you don't know how long it's been there or how you missed it this whole time he's been lying there, arched and stiff, looking at you, everything in his face begging for help.

Then lesion after lesion breaks open on his legs, and when he runs out of pants, the black watery shit has ruined them all, you sit beside your father who is naked for the first time in front of you, a tube running out of his swollen, misshapen penis, and tubes running into his stick-like bruised arms, and you rub aloe into the open wounds of this man whom you have loved your entire life. And here's the thing: you are the one who has brought him here. You are the one who forced him to be bumped and jostled in a van for five hours while he struggled to breathe through whatever's been filling his lungs; you are the one who gave him that first spoonful of sweet persimmon; and it is you who have forced on him again and again the foolish, impossible weight of your wanting.

The price you pay now is his open mouth, which is screaming and not screaming, the price is the gurgle in his throat, the tendons in his neck stretching and aching, and yes, yes, for the first time you wish for his death because you finally know you have been asking too much, and that neither of you can bear it.

24.

The next morning my father's spasms had quieted. He had emptied himself out, and the world was covered with pure, white snow. It was so beautiful from the window that the previous night seemed like it could have been a joke. Hannah's family of snowmen had been blanketed so they were no longer recognizable, just four white lumps. My father was lying in his bed, utterly motionless, his face etched with the pain of the previous day. But now there was a relief to his stillness, and I was grateful he had not died in the night.

The three of us sat exhausted by my father's side. His breath still rattled. It came shallower and shallower. It snowed all that day. It held our little house in its shifting embrace, and the world was blanketed in a hush, the only sound the grate of my father's breath.

My mother called our relatives, one by one. I didn't want her to: I wanted it to be just us with my father huddled under the snow. But of course they came. Car after car pulled into our driveway, and my relatives entered the room and walked up to my father and touched him. My grandmother came, too, and she put her face close to my father's and called his name. Then she pulled away and looked at my mother, and then me, and then Hannah. We had not seen her in weeks, and she looked smaller than she had before. I wondered if it was true that she'd been unwell, but we did not say anything to each other. We just looked. I felt as if we were enacting some ritual. She did not blink. Then she slipped to the back of the room, and waited there.

As for everyone else, I did not take notice of them, did not raise my eyes from my father's face, but I did not like to see all the hands come and brush over his body lightly, as if something was already gone and he belonged to everyone else now. As if they were taking something of him away with them by their touch. I leaned forward and chanted the name of the Buddha into my father's ear, very low, so that if he was listening, only he could hear.

When my aunt walked in, the room was already crowded with my father's relatives, but as she entered, a silence fell. Hannah was standing between her and my father, and my aunt pushed her aside with her hand as she came. Her head and coat were covered in a thin layer of snow. She had brought the cold with her from outside.

"Jeehyun," my mother hissed from across my father's body. I got up reluctantly and crossed the room.

"Komo," I said. "Let me take your coat."

But my aunt turned away from me. She took my sister's face in her hands, and looked hard into her eyes. She seemed ready to say something terrible. I reached out for her arm and pulled on her sleeve, my hand melting the snow where I touched. "Komo," I said. "Let her go, and I'll put your coat away."

My aunt shook her head. And then she burst into angry sobs.

From around me I felt the murmur of my relatives as they closed in around us, anxious to touch my aunt and reassure her.

Then in the hallway a door opened; Keith and his father came into the room, brushing snow from themselves.

My father's breath rattled from the corner like a wind trying to escape, and when I turned my head to look at him, Hannah broke free of my aunt's grip and the circle that had gathered around us, and ran out of the house and into the snow in her slippers, without her shoes or her coat. There were too many people around us, and I was suddenly overwhelmed. I stepped forward—I should have gone after her, but I just watched her through the snow on the window as she ran from the house with her head down, clumsy and flailing.

I knew I should go after her, but I looked at my father breathing so laboriously in his bed and could not leave him. She had not returned an hour later when my father's breath became harsh and slow. "Wait," I kept telling him, "wait."

At the exact moment he took his last breath—a harsh, grating sound like the juicer we had used to grind his carrots every morning in the house we'd rented by the river what seemed like years ago—my mother moaned, and the noise seemed to come from beneath the floor. She fell into the chair next to him, and was still.

"I love you," I said into his ear. And then, because Hannah wasn't there, I said it again for her so he would know she had said it, too. "I love you," I said. That was hers.

There was a moment of motionlessness, of quiet, and my uncle put his arm around Keith. I was astonished by the jealousy that suddenly overtook me with the realization that I no longer had a father, and that Keith did. I turned back to my father and gripped his hand in mine. It was still soft, and I could arrange his fingers around mine, but my mother said harshly, "Open his hand. Don't let it go stiff like that or it will set like a claw." Horrified, I let go and smoothed it open.

"We should chant," my mother said, so I lowered my head and chanted with her. We took no more notice of those around us, who moved back and forth in eddies, touching my father and then moving away. I felt that I was floating and my hand smoothing my father's hand was the only thing keeping me down. I held it open and tried to keep it soft for when Hannah returned.

There were so many different death-related ceremonies in Korea. At first there was the three-day wake, for which my father's body was driven back to Seoul. Then came the funeral, for which my father's body would be driven again, back to the countryside. Then there would be the 49th day ceremony, and the 100th day ceremony. And every year there would be Chuseok, and his birthday, and New Year's, and the anniversary of his death.

What I remember of my father's wake: A bright light. The clean smell of chrysanthemums and white light so clear it pierced the solidity of things. We bowed to everyone in our white dresses; my grandmother sat pale and silent at a table, my uncle tapping his feet next to her. I tried to talk to her, but when I approached, she reached out her hand and fixed my hair, and told me to talk to the other guests. She looked away from me, and she did not go to my mother or Hannah.

I asked if she was angry with me, and she shook her head, her eyes filling with tears. "No," she said. "But tell your mother she must come to me later, when this is all over. But this is not the time for it, my dear."

So I went and greeted my father's cousin, who was counting the flowers. There were so many flowers, but there was no one to pour the wine.

"Let Keith do it," Big Cousin said. "It should be a boy." The oldest son was supposed to pour the wine and offer the first prostrations to my father's shrine, which was waiting, laden with fruit and rice, and presided over by a photo of him taken several years ago.

"Really, it's the son's job," Big Cousin said. He was commandeering all the arrangements. I'd been surprised when he stepped in, but he was the head of the family. This was his responsibility. Earlier, when the other relatives arrived, he had suddenly raised his handkerchief and pressed his hand hard to his eyes, flexing his wrist. This man had loved my father, I realized, actually loved him.

"Yes," my aunt said. "More's the pity that he never had one."

"My father didn't care," Hannah said, defiantly. "He told me he was glad he had us instead. And that he was always glad of it, and would never have traded us in for anyone else."

"When did he say that?" my mother gasped. As if she was the one who had felt unwanted all these years.

"A couple months ago." Hannah shrugged. "When we first got to the hospital."

Why had he never said that to me? I wondered. I stepped forward. "I'll do it," I said. "I'll pour the wine." I thought they would protest, but Big Cousin, my aunt, and the rest of my relatives stepped aside, and nodded, just like that.

I glanced at Hannah, and then at my mother, who was crying, covering her mouth. Nobody moved to comfort her, and I also stood where I was. Yes, I thought. I would play the part of the son.

. . .

Afterward, my mother, Hannah, and I took a break in the little room given to immediate family for privacy: right outside the room were all our guests, including my aunt and Keith. I thought we had handled things pretty well, and said so.

Hannah shrugged dismissively. "I don't want Komo or Keith at the funeral," she said.

My mother looked taken aback. "She's his sister," she said. "It's not a matter of invitation."

"Then I won't go," Hannah said. She was sitting on the little sofa, her hands tucked inside the sleeves of her white dress. I recognized the stubborn tilt of her chin.

She had come in two hours after my father had died, her feet cut and bleeding, shivering and cold. She'd waited until the cars had left the driveway, she'd waited for everyone to go away. She must have known then that he was dead, even before she saw him.

I wondered if this was revenge for that. "You'll ruin things," I said.

"If they come, I won't," she said.

I looked to my mother, but she didn't respond. She was just quiet, looking at Hannah thoughtfully.

I said, "You can't do that."

Hannah pinched her lips together and didn't respond. I looked at her and at my mother, who had also become markedly quiet, and I wondered how they had both learned this particular trick of being silent while everything else fell down around them.

"Don't you care what it will look like?" I said. "Don't you know what people will say?"

"So what?"

"It's his funeral," I said. "This is the last thing we can do for him."

"That's not what this is really about. It's just another chance for a performance by the perfect daughter."

"Did you really just say that?" I asked. "Is that what you think?"

She shrugged.

"Only someone as self-centered and narcissistic as you could come up with something like that. At the end of the day, everything has to be all about you."

"Fuck you," Hannah said.

"The truth hurts."

"Stop it," my mother said, coming between us. "Stop." Someone knocked at the door, and my mother turned to it. "Go away," she cried, and cast herself onto the sofa, sobbing. We ignored her.

I said, "You always get what you want in the end, no matter who it hurts."

Hannah gasped, "What?"

"You've always done what you wanted to do," I said. "You never have to think about anyone else. You never have to be responsible. I'm sorry that I couldn't protect you from everything. But, Hannah, I didn't even know about Gabe. And I was twelve years old."

"That's not what this is about."

Someone rattled at the door again. I looked at it. Outside that door were all our guests, and I wondered how much they could hear. I didn't care. "You got to have everything," I said. "Whatever you wanted, and I was the one who had to keep you safe."

The unfairness of it rose up and choked me. I had always been the dutiful one, the one who tried to always be the missing daughter, the missing son, the one who had to try to fill the missing pieces and keep our family together. "You always got to be the one who was loved," I said.

"What are you talking about?" Hannah gasped. "What the fuck are you talking about?"

"I'm sorry," I said. "And I love you. But I can't be in charge of every-thing. I'm tired." I knelt in front of her then without meaning to; my legs gave way beneath me. For three days I had bowed over and over to all our guests, and now, exhausted, I could no longer stand.

When I touched her she melted down onto her knees, and she clasped her arms around my neck. I tried to push her away, to tell her that the weight was too much. Her tears ran down my neck, and I trembled at the feeling of them, unless it was her body trembling in my arms. Her fingers laced together as she cried, and my knees were sore against the grounds as I held her awkwardly.

"Hold on," I said. I was afraid we would topple. But she had let herself go limp, and awkwardly, unsteadily, I held her.

The next day, my mother rode with my father's body for the five hours back to the country, and Hannah and I rode with my uncle. My grandmother did not come. We were wearing the same white dresses we'd worn for the last four days. Hannah was quiet and subdued. It seemed wrong to think of anything like the future while my father was being buried. There would be time for that, I told myself. Time and time, and only today for this.

When we parked at the house, I looked at the courtyard cov-ered with snow. The ghost of our old footprints remained. Han-nah's snowmen had blended into a single lump on the windowsill. Up where he was to be buried, the sun shone. A clearing had been made around his gravesite, and from it we could look out into the valley.

It was a good place, with a beautiful view, but I was worried that the grave looked too shallow. It was only a few feet into the ground, maybe chest deep. I asked Big Cousin if it was okay. He said it would be fine because it'd be covered with a mound, but I wasn't sure. I stared at the gap in the ground. The dirt to the side was mixed with rocks and snow. My grandmother had said the dead rise with the rain. My father had dreamed of a woman who floated down a river, her hair covering her face.

I felt a hand on my arm. "After this," my aunt said into my ear, her clawlike fingers grasping my elbow, "every death will call you back to this one." I tried to pull away from her, but she continued. "Every great sorrow will lead you back to this."

I wrenched my arm free. I turned my back on her and looked up at the sun, which was still shining as bright as I had ever seen it.

After the ceremony, after the first shovelful of dirt had been thrown on the coffin, during which time I looked neither at my mother nor at Hannah but fixedly at the ground, my aunt threw herself onto the snow and screamed.

"Not again," I muttered. Her husband knelt forward and tried to pull her up.

Keith stood above her and looked around uncomfortably. He caught my eye. We had not spoken since the day he came to my father's wake, when he muttered his awkward condolences. I thought of the day he came to our house and we walked around the pond, how comfortable we had been and how friendly, until he saw the snake in the pond. I felt as if I owed him something, a word, a reassurance. He was my cousin. But it was too much, and I blinked and looked down and made my face utterly blank.

When my aunt finally rose, she began to wail, going from person to person, pressing their hands again and again. "He was my only brother," she said. "He was all I had."

I was ashamed of her, making a scene like this, although I'd also been told that the women of the family *ought* to make a scene. It was expected. But neither my mother nor Hannah nor I had.

"We had only each other," my aunt continued. "How could he die before me?" she said. She stopped in front of me. "How could he?"

I was aware of everyone watching us. I was angry with her for pulling me into this performance, the pageantry of it.

"I never loved anyone as much," she said. "This was my sin. This was why God took my son."

Her husband stepped forward. "Don't say such things," he said, but his voice sounded so much older than the deep, commanding voice I remembered from childhood.

My aunt was finally silent. I met Keith's eyes. He looked away. I wondered if my aunt had ever said that before, if she'd been waiting to say that all these years.

She clutched the white sleeve of my dress and looked at me. Her eyes, I realized then, were just like my father's eyes. "I carried him," she said, tugging my sleeve, her voice desperate. Her hand on my sleeve was the briefest of weights. "I carry him still."

In the days following my father's funeral, my mother and Hannah and I packed up our things. We washed and folded all the sheets, clean and sweet-smelling again, everything foul washed away. I tried to work on my dissertation. It seemed suddenly important to take it up again. "I'll dedicate this to you," I'd said to him, in his grave.

While I was working, I heard a clatter in the bathroom. When I went to see what had happened, I had to look over Hannah's shoulder. She had gotten there first. My mother was sitting on the floor: perhaps she had fallen, and there were pills still spiraling around her and she was trying to gather them up. My father's pills, I realized. The painkillers he had not taken.

"What's going on?" I asked.

"It doesn't matter," Hannah said, turning a white, frightened face to me. "Just help me clean it up." She knelt down by my mother. "We don't need these anymore," she said, very gently opening her fist and taking the pills from her palm.

My mother's hands shook. I helped her up while Hannah swept the floor with her hands. I told my mother she ought to go to bed. "Take a little rest," I said, and she shuffled away from us, her hand on the wall for balance.

I turned to Hannah. "What happened?" I asked.

She sighed. "Let it go," she said.

So I did. I left her there to clean up the mess by herself.

Here's a story about a place I've never been to called Nak Wha Am: The Cliff of One Thousand Falling Flowers. It's a real place, a true story from hundreds of years ago, when Korea was still three kingdoms. The kingdoms were always warring, fighting to be one. When the Silla Kingdom defeated Paek Jae, the maidens of the castle rushed out the gates. Their white-slippered feet pounded as desperately as their tightly bound hearts. Their legs rustled through and through their petticoats, so delicate that it seemed with every step that their waists might break.

They giggled breathlessly under their hanboks, holding hands, each pulling each farther and faster. Their lips pressed tightly together to hold in the ecstasy of their sudden escape. Together they flew, in all their bright colors, streaming toward the inevitable cliff: leaping like deer. Their stride broke, almost at the edge.

And then in a rush they strained against their clothes, against their own bodies, and broke free into flight. They burst into the air as silently as the beating of wings, like so many scattered leaves: each falling maiden with her skirts blossoming through the rush of air, opening like a fan as she flew toward the ocean below. Together they fell like a downpour of brightly colored rain, each petal suspended in air before drifting down to the crashing of the sea.

My whole life I had always belonged to my family, and there had been a comfort in the belonging. I'd always thought Hannah and I were irrevocably entangled: the connection always between us no matter how far she went. I had spent my whole life afraid that I would be bound to her, responsible. I had been afraid my family would never let me go.

A few years after we moved to Michigan, my family had taken a trip to Chicago and we went to the museums there. Our favorite of them all was the Adler Planetarium. We went to the star show. We'd loved the stars ever since my father first read us *The Little Prince*, and Hannah asked the guy who ran the presentation about wormholes. I asked about infinity.

He had asked how old we were and told us to wait until after the show. So we waited around while all the other families asked their questions and then got up and left.

He had eyed us warily. "Real scientists don't ask those kinds of questions."

"Yes they do, we have books about them," Hannah had retorted, referring to our Child Genius picture book series at home. "Have you written any books on science?" His answer had been unsatisfactory, and she immediately lost interest in his expertise. "Well then," she said.

My father told his acquaintances about that for years, even though both Hannah and I had given up on wormholes and the Child Genius series very soon afterward. This must have made my father sad, as it had made him sad when we stopped being excited by family vacations, when we stopped being open about our interests, and left home and pursued lives of our own. It was just regular growing up, of course, the kind everyone does—but it still hurt him, I know, like the memory I have of the time he dropped me off at the train station when I was going back to Chicago. I could see him through the window of the train, but he couldn't see me through the tinted glass.

I waved, trying to get his attention as he walked up and down the platform trying to figure out where I was sitting. From up in the train, he looked so small. If he'd seen me, he would have smiled and waved, but he didn't know I could see him, and the sadness on his face was exposed to me then. He looked lost. He stood there on the platform a long time, even after my train started pulling away, still trying to catch a glimpse of me waving back.

25.

Hannah and I bought our tickets to leave Korea about two weeks after my father's funeral. She was scheduled to leave a day before me. We were leaving my mother to do the 49th day ceremony, the 100th day ceremony, New Year's in Korea—we were leaving her to do it all alone.

"I can't stay longer," Hannah said, and I told my mother I couldn't either. I told myself I needed to get back to my own life, though I wasn't sure what that meant. I knew that it was cowardly to leave her in Korea alone, now that my father was gone.

"You must take care of your mother," my grandmother told us. "You're all she has left now."

"She has you, too," I said, but there was a new constraint between them, as if grief had made them strange to each other. They were careful and polite together, but my grandmother would pull me aside whenever she could and overwhelm me with questions about my mother's spirits.

We did not know when my mother would leave my father's

cousin's house, but we knew she'd live with my grandmother for the four months she had to remain. We didn't know where she'd go next. We did not ask; we did not fuss, but bought our tickets one after another, and then left each other carefully alone.

The night before Hannah was scheduled to leave, I dreamed of fireflies. They hung suspended in the air, thick as leaves, beyond counting. The air was hazy with their light. Their bodies were stifling. Their wings beat against my mouth like tiny pulses, tiny beating hearts. There were so many of them I could hardly breathe.

I awoke to darkness and quiet. I could hear Hannah breathing in the other room. I turned over and looked at my clock. It was four-thirty a.m. I knew it was no use trying to get back to sleep, but there was nothing else to do. I knew, though, that I could not lie here, waiting for the day to come and usher Hannah away.

My own mind was strangely blank. It seemed the darkness of the countryside had embraced it, covered it up somehow, and this blankness was a relief. I sat up and dressed in the dark, as quickly as I could. I tiptoed past my mother's room, and past Hannah's. I opened the front door. It had snowed again in the night, and I could barely make out the driveway in the dark as I stepped out into the cold.

I walked toward the hulking forms of the mountains, toward the hiking path. I could hardly see the road, but it was lined in trees, looming shadows, and I stepped between them. My lungs hurt. I thought of all those North Koreans, starving in their huts. I had heard they ate their children. Did anyone really believe that? The snow crunched under my boots. I tripped on a log. I told myself that my father had walked these paths as a child.

Somewhere, my mother had also been living, walking similar

paths. I could see now that all the lives I'd mapped out for us intersected here. My father was in the ground. Beneath the dirt, his face was stuffed with cotton. I kept walking. *If I could walk to the end of the earth,* I thought, *I might survive this.* I was aware of my legs beneath me, going on.

The dark was pulling back, and as I walked I could feel the fog lifting like a breath. My mother and Hannah were sleeping in their rooms, breathing in, breathing out. I wished I could believe in something. Heaven. A place. In these woods my father had grown up in, it seemed I could be in any wood, in any country in the world.

The sky lightened as I walked, finally, up the steep path that had just been cleared. I could make out the dim outline of footprints in the thin snow, and I wondered whose they were. Hannah's? My mother's? For a moment, it seemed they could even be the ghost prints of my father's own feet.

Then I was there: in the clearing, and standing over his mound at the center was my sister. How had she come to be here? I had been so sure she was asleep. She turned to me and smiled, and there was such an unreality to her in the dim light I could almost imagine she was a vision, anyone but my real and breathing sister. I felt a momentary fear. And then she spoke.

"God, you startled me," she said, and stepped to the side a little, so there was a place for me to come beside her, and I did. So the footprints had been hers.

I faced the valley, which spread out before us. Everything white. Everything covered with a layer of snow that looked, in the dark, like ash. We had stood here two weeks ago, my mother and Hannah and I, each in our white dresses. Now my sister and I stood in front of my father's grave together.

"What do you think happens when somebody dies?" she said. "Do you believe in heaven?"

"No," I said. "No heaven."

"Me neither."

I looked at her. I thought of the year she'd lived away from us, of all the things we didn't know about each other. "All I ever wanted was for everyone to be okay," I said.

She tilted her head, a funny smile on her face. "But that's impossible," she said. She started to laugh.

"I know."

After a while, she said, "I think that life is only okay because we die. I mean, because things end."

"That's grim."

She smiled again. "Do you want to know what I think happens when you die?"

"Sure."

"I think you kind of just fade away, your body, your consciousness, all of it. No heaven, no reincarnation. You just dissipate a little more every year, but slowly. Slow enough so that you're still around a little bit while everyone you love is alive, but fast enough that you're gone by the time no one needs you anymore."

"Sounds nice enough," I said. I didn't ask if she felt like she still needed my father.

"Do you think that's possible?"

I shrugged. "Why not?" I said.

"It can't be that you just die, and that's it, can it?" she asked. "You can't just become nothing like that, can you?"

"I don't know," I said. It was so cold, and my throat hurt. Everything ached. "Hey, can we not talk for a while?"

She nodded. So we stood there, looking out at the valley, not talking.

In college I'd taken a class on knot theory, and learned that sometimes a knot is impossible to unravel without cutting it apart. Sometimes it can't be undone. For my whole life my family had been so tightly bound that we had stifled each other just trying to breathe, just trying to go our own ways. I had worried I would never get free. And now, Hannah and I would board our separate flights and cross the world and leave my mother behind.

When we were children, my parents told us a folktale about two frog children who never obeyed their mother, but always did the opposite of what she said. When it was time for her to die, she called them to her, and told them to bury her in the ocean. She thought she could trick them into burying her close to them, but when she died they repented for how badly they had treated her, and fulfilled her final wish. They wept as they watched the water take her away. There was no grave to visit each year. They could not offer her food. This is why frogs always cry in regret, "Gegul, Gegul."

What I had thought of when my parents told this story was not of disobedience but of the shocking expanse of the ocean. How far away it could fling a body, how deep. And I had thought of my parents, and what a loss it had been to them to leave their country, and their parents, and the graves of their parents, the ocean always between them. And now I would leave my father here.

"I don't want to leave," he'd said, the last day in our house, the sun across his face. I'd said nothing in response, unable in that moment to speak.

. . .

They say the earth is always moving underneath us, always shifting, but that the change happens so slowly that we are unaware. They say that, too, about gravity, the earth's spinning, its circling the sun. When the movements are vast enough, we cannot sense them.

I had assumed my father would prefer to be buried here, that his land had called him home. But now I wondered if he wouldn't have wished to be taken with us instead. The thought of leaving him behind filled me with grief.

I wanted to lie on the mound, to lay my body over his body and press my cheek into the snow. But it would be improper, I knew. So instead I sat on the hard ground next to him, feeling the cold creep up my body through the earth. Hannah sat beside me. I could feel the warmth of her body reaching through the cold ground, and filling the air between us. We did not touch, but I could feel the rise and fall of her breath.

Past the village and the house my father had grown up in and died in, where our mother slept now, past all the fields around it, past everything we could see, a soft pink glow had started to collect above the horizon, far in the distance, on the other side of the world. I watched it spread. It intensified in color until it was a deep, deep pink.

"Look," I said.

How quickly it rose. How quickly it filled the sky with light.

ACKNOWLEDGMENTS

I would like to give thanks . . .

First and always, to my mother, Sejin Chung, and father, Moon Jung Chung, for their courageous example and unwavering love and support. To Heesoo Chung, the best of brothers: the stories we told each other were the first stories I ever told. Also to the Chung and Park clans, especially my grandmother.

To my beloved teachers Richard Stern and Alane Rollings, Dan McCall, Stephanie Vaughn, Helena Viramontes, Alison Lurie, Maureen McCoy, Michael Koch, and Lamar Herrin. Great thanks to my champions Alexander Chee, Michelle Herman, Meakin Armstrong, Patrick Ryan, Tommy Pico, Roy Pérez, Michael Lowenthal, Martin Moran, and Jan Freeman. So much gratitude to Benjamin Warner, Michael Simons, Brian Clarke, Lyrae Van Clief-Stefanon, Pilar Gómez-Ibáñez, and Helen Oyeyemi, with special thanks to this book's fairy godmothers: Lauren Alleyne, Autumn Watts, and Rita Zoey Chin. Thanks also to my students, from whom I have learned so much.

These places made a home for me while I wrote this book: the MacDowell Colony, the Corporation of Yaddo, the Camargo Foundation, SFAI, Hedgebrook, and the Jentel Artists Residency. Thanks also to the Constance Saltonstall Foundation and the Ludwig Vogelstein Foundation for financial support and much-needed shots of courage.

Thanks to Elaine Wacuka Hurt, a stranger who rescued the manuscript I left on a bench in the Dupont Metro Station. Love to Jenny Tsai and the memory of Cindy Tsai. Also to Jennifer Lin, Kimberly Tsau, and Sarah Johnstone for their friendship and faith. Gratitude to the American Studies Department at the University of Leipzig, especially Anne Koenen and Sebastian Herrmann. And to the late Frank Meinzenbach, who is truly missed. Thanks also to Tomiko Jones for the most beautiful book trailer.

Finally, endless gratitude and extra sweetness to the incomparable Maria Massie, who said this would be fun, and made it so, and to Megan Lynch, my brilliant and thoughtful editor in whose hands this book came true.